LEADER OF BATTLES

By David Pilling

Copyright David Pilling 2015

More Books by David Pilling
Soldier of Fortune (I): The Wolf Cub
Folville's Law (I): Invasion
Leader of Battles (I): Ambrosius
Leader of Battles (II): Artorius
Leader of Battles (III): Gwenhwyfar
The White Hawk (I): Revenge
The White Hawk (II): Loyalty
The White Hawk (III): Sacrifice
Caesar's Sword (I): The Red Death
Caesar's Sword (II): Siege of Rome
Caesar's Sword (III): Flame of the West
Robin Hood (I)
Robin Hood (II): The Wrath of God
Robin Hood (III): The Hooded Man
Robin Hood (IV): The King's Pardon
Nowhere Was There Peace
The Half-Hanged Man
The Best Weapon (with Martin Bolton)
Sorrow (with Martin Bolton)

Follow David at his blogs at:
www.pillingswritingcorner.blogspot.co.uk

http://www.boltonandpilling.com

Or contact him direct at:
Davidpilling56@hotmail.com

INDEX OF PLACE NAMES

Amorica - Brittany
Anatolia - term for much of modern-day Turkey
Caerleon - Caerleon, near Newport, Wales
Celliwig - Callington, south-east Cornwall
Cotyaeum - Kütahya, western Turkey
Dumnonia - Devon and part of Somerset
Ergyng - part of Herefordshire & Monmouthshire
Isauria - a region inside Anatolia
Isca Dumnoniorum - Exeter
Kernow - Cornwall
Phrygia Epictetus - north-west Turkey
Rheged - north-west England
Viroconium - Wroxeter
Ystrad Clud - Strathclyde

GLOSSARY

Bretwalda - Saxon term for High King or Over-King
Ceorl - A free-born Saxon peasant
Gesith - Companions or followers of Saxon kings
Spatha - Type of Roman cavalry sword
Túath - Old Irish word, meaning both 'people' and 'nation'

1.

Kernow, 491 AD

"Run home to your mother, boy," growled Morholt, "or I'll cut off your balls and send them to her as a present."

"My mother is dead," replied his enemy.

Morholt spat on the ground between them. Known as Morholt the Reaver, he was a famous Hibernian pirate, squat, muscular and red-haired. He wore no armour, after the fashion of his people, and had doffed his crimson plaid and woollen tunic.

Barefoot, clad only in loose breeches, he carried a light wooden shield called a targe, and a long sword. His pale shoulders and chest bore thickly woven patterns of tattoos and old battle-scars. Two javelins were thrust into the ground beside him.

The two warriors were alone on a rocky, misted island off the south-west tip of Kernow. They had sailed here to settle an age-old dispute by single combat.

A light drizzle fell, and draped the island in a grey shroud. The mainland lay several miles to the north-east, lost behind the gauze of mist and rain.

His opponent looked absurdly young, little more than a boy. Fair, pale and slender, pretty as a girl.

He was not fooled. A good judge of warriors, he had noticed the lad's agile gait, the deceptive strength in his graceful slender limbs.

For protection the youth wore a thin leather cap in place of a helm, and a light deerskin tunic. Like Morholt, he went barefoot, and shunned the weight of mail.

"Tell me your name and lineage," rasped Morholt, "so I may boast of your death in the mead-hall."

"I am Drystan," said the youth, "son of King Marcus. I am here to defend his honour and deny you tribute."

Morholt furrowed his heavy brows. "Liar. Marcus has

no son."

"A bastard son. One of several. My mother was a kitchen slave."

"Your father saw fit to send one of his by-blows against me? A deliberate insult. When you are dead, I shall double the yearly tribute."

Drystan's smile was angelic. "Perhaps you shall die. Are you done with your boasts now?"

By way of reply, Morholt wrenched one of his javelins free of the turf and hurled it at Drystan's head.

Drystan ducked behind his shield - a timber oval with an iron rim, much larger and heavier than Morholt's targe - and braced his feet wide as the javelin stuck harmlessly into the wood.

He also had two light throwing spears, stuck into the ground. He seized one and cast it at Morholt.

The Scotti warrior dived aside, almost choking on the curse that sprang to his lips. Drystan's spear flew like an arrow. The tip was leaf-shaped, and one edge sliced off the lobe of Morholt's right ear. Pain and anger flared inside his head. The hot blood-gush flowed down the side of his neck.

Morholt rolled as he landed on the springy grass. Honed battle-instincts saved him as his eye caught the flight of a second spear. There was no time to dodge, so he caught it on his targe. Sharp iron pierced the flimsy leather covering and into the back of his hand. The shaft broke off at the head and left the tip buried in his flesh.

He gasped in agony. Drystan charged. The glint of his sword lit up the grey dawn.

Morholt thrust aside the pain of his wounded hand and cut savagely at Drystan's head. His blade had a keen edge. Twelve skulls it had split in single combat, twelve fools who dared to test their prowess against Morholt the Reaver, Morholt the Ravager, the red right hand, the scourge of Kernow, most dreaded of the pirate captains of Hibernia.

Morholt's sword whistled through empty air. His breath

hissed in frustration. Drystan ducked, spun away, and attacked again.

Their whorled blades clashed and ground together, both men equally matched, both probing for a gap in the other's defence.

Morholt grinned wolfishly. There was faery blood in his veins, or so he believed, and he grew stronger with the rising of the sun. At its zenith, he possessed the strength of five ordinary men. Beyond noon, his power slowly ebbed back to normal.

Every one of his twelve single combats had been fought at dawn. Not one of his opponents lasted until mid-morning.

"You've fallen into a trap, boy," he mocked during a brief lull in the fight, "I asked King Marcus if I could fight his champion at dawn. He accepted, and thus condemned you to death."

"Watch the sun," he added, "watch it rise. I will not tire. You are young, but even the strength of youth cannot outlast me."

Morholt's boast had little obvious effect. For his tender age, Drystan was self-possessed, and showed no sign of fear.

No sweat, thought Morholt, *he has yet to break sweat. Meantime I bleed. My left hand is numb. My heart beats too fast.*

The fight swiftly resumed. Morholt found himself driven backwards, guarding desperately against a storm of blows. Drystan's blade whirled before his eyes, a white flame, blinding and relentless.

Morholt began to despair. *Where is my strength? Have the spirits of old deserted me? My blood is on the grass. I tire - I tire!*

The morning sun was hidden behind the sea-mist. Too late, he realised his blunder. If the mist failed to lift, if the orb of the sun was not clearly visible, then the magic could not work. Morholt would remain an ordinary man, wounded and afraid, locked in a death-duel against a much younger opponent forged of steel and muscle and whipcord.

Drystan was merciless. He hacked at Morholt's wounded hand, forcing him to use the targe in defence. Thin leather and fragile wood proved little defence against hard-forged steel.

One savage blow cleaved the targe in two. The bottom half fell away, and Morholt was left with a scrap of timber stuck fast into the back of his hand by Drystan's spear.

I bleed!

The swords clanged, locked for a moment, parted. Morholt was too slow to avoid a cut at his naked chest. More blood welled from a deep slash over his breastbone.

Fear, the cold stranger that Morholt had seldom known in his life, seized him in a death-grip. He panicked, and unleashed a wild overhead swing. The youth turned it with contemptuous ease, gripped Morholt's wrist with his free hand, drew back his sword, and stabbed.

The tip of the blade punctured skin, flesh and muscle, drove deep into the pirate's guts. Morholt gasped soundlessly as shrieking, white-hot pain flooded his entire being. Frozen where he stood, impaled on Drystan's sword, he could only stand and watch his bright blood soak into the ground.

"Look at me," said Drystan.

There was calm authority in his voice, a maturity and assurance beyond his years. Morholt obeyed, and stared into the eyes of his killer: large, soft brown eyes, such as any maiden might fall in love with.

"I shall present your head to my father. Your body shall be returned to your men, who may take it back to Hibernia for burial. Kernow shall pay no tribute this year, or for many years to come."

Drystan's voice became a whisper. His beardless face dimmed as the world fell into shadow. Morholt was blind, and heard nothing save the sluggish pumping of his heart.

He fell, and knew little of his landing. The last thing he saw on earth was a pair of brown eyes, looking down at him with a mixture of triumph and pity.

2.

Artorius was at meat in Caerleon, his chief court, when word reached him of war in the north.

The weary messenger, a youth named Eri, knelt before the High King's chair and gasped out his tidings. "The whole of Rheged is disturbed, lord king," he said, "three battles have been fought already, and the dead litter the ground like autumn leaves. Fire and sword sweep the land, the hall of Llwyfenydd is burned, and all her folk scattered or slain. All on account of a woman."

Artorius glanced at his wife Gwenhwyfar, seated to his left, and said nothing.

"It happened thus," Eri went on, "Gwythyr, a prince of Rheged, was at feud with his neighbour, Lludd. Lludd desired peace, and invited Gwythyr to feast at his hall. Gwythyr came, and there beheld Lludd's daughter, Creiddylad."

The king sighed. "And Creiddylad is very beautiful," he murmured, "Gwythyr saw her and, enflamed with drink and passion, fell in love with her on the spot."

Eri glanced up in surprise. "It is an old ruse," Artorius said with a smile, "Lludd baited a trap with his daughter. Gwythyr fell into it. Continue."

The other man did so. "Gwythyr demanded Creiddylad as the price of peace. Lludd agreed, and Gwythyr took the girl away with him that same night. He declared he would deflower her before the sun rose, and make her his wife in the morning."

"They follow different customs in the North," remarked Cei, to a guffaw of laughter from the mead-benches.

The Round Hall of Caerleon was thronged with

Companions, famed warriors of the Island of the Mighty, veterans who had never tasted defeat. They sat at the Round Table, each man in his red cloak, their bodies decked with ornaments of red gold, eyes bright as any jewel as they listened to the messenger's account.

"Creiddylad is indeed very beautiful," said Eri, "and another man desired her. His name is Gwyn, a prince from beyond the Wall with Pictish blood in his veins. He had already asked to marry Lludd's daughter, but Lludd refused, not wishing to wed a woman of his house to one of barbarian blood."

"Gwyn heard of the marriage of Gwythyr and Creiddylad, and swore to take the girl by force. He gathered his war-band and swooped on Gwythyr's hall at Llwyfenydd like a hawk upon a dove. The hall and stockade were burned, and many warriors and servants slain or captured, though Gwythyr himself escaped the slaughter with his bride."

"He swore revenge, summoned his kinsmen to arms and marched against Gwyn. The conflict has spread across Rheged like a plague. Every prince and lord must choose sides, or risk destruction."

Eri paused for breath. All eyes looked to the High King. A breathless silence fell over the vast, shadowy hall.

Artorius tapped his fingers on the arm of his chair and gazed into the leaping flames of the hearth.

He had expected trouble in Rheged, sooner or later. Its king had recently died, leaving two young sons. Neither were old enough to rule, so Artorius had placed a steward in charge of the kingdom until they came of age.

"What of the steward?" he asked, "what has he done to quell this feud?"

"Little and nothing," replied Eri, "in fairness, his hands are tied. His warriors are all men of Rheged, and deserted him to join the rival war-bands. He sent me to beg you, lord king, for military aid."

Artorius cursed silently. His forces were already stretched. If he led an army into Rheged, it would mean leaving a garrison to keep the peace. He had scarce enough men to guard the territories under his direct control without adding another.

"You said three battles have been fought," he said, "who was the victor?"

"None, lord king," replied Eri, "three times the warbands fought, and three times neither held the field at the end of the fighting. Gwyn and Gwythyr are well-matched. Save..."

Eri lowered his head. His skin was pale, and coloured easily. Artorius frowned when he saw the lad flush.

"Well?" he snapped, "save what? Spit it out, boy."

"I...I have said Gwyn has Pictish blood," stammered Eri, "he has also inherited the savagery of his forebears. Among the captives he took was a warrior named Nwython, and Nwython's son Cyledyr."

"Gwyn wished the captives to kneel before him, and call him lord. Cyledyr refused. He set Gwyn at defiance, laughed at him, and spat in his face. In revenge Gwyn cut out Nwython's heart and forced Cyledyr to eat it. Cyledyr went mad with the horror of it, and was released to wander alone in the wild, witless and raving."

This met with a sharp intake of breath from Gwenhwyfar. Otherwise the hall remained silent. Artorius looked at the stern faces of his Companions. They were all hardened fighting men, even the youths. There was little left in the world that could shock them.

Every man looked grim. If Eri spoke true, then this Gwyn had sealed his own fate. The half-Pict prince from beyond the Wall was a mad wolf, and mad wolves had to be hunted down.

One face among the Companions glistened with tears. This was Llwch Llemineawg, one of Artorius' most trusted captains. Llwch was a survivor from the old days, long before Artorius took up the kingship. He had fought in the battles against the Saxons, and in Hibernia, and helped to defeat the Twrch Trwyth. He was one of the tiny handful of men Artorius trusted with his life.

Artorius had never seen Llwch weep. It made him afraid. One of the pillars of his throne had suddenly cracked.

"Lord king," said Llwch, his voice heavy with grief, "I am a man of Rheged. Nwython was my cousin. This feud is now mine. I beg the right to leave Caerleon and go north to seek revenge."

Artorius reacted quickly. "You shall go north," he said, "along with myself and two hundred Companions. These crimes cannot go unpunished."

The rafters shook to a chorus of cheers and war-yells. There was an edge to the noise that disturbed Artorius. Ten years of relative peace had bred resentment and boredom among his warriors. They were fighting men, with no other talent or purpose, and needed to fight. Now they had the chance.

A chance to die, Artorius thought sadly, *to know the pain of blue-tipped spears, and rest forever in the ground. Is that the only peace that will satisfy them?*

He looked to Gwenhwyfar. Her face was cold and pensive, and she would not meet his eye. There was little comfort for him there. Artorius was a man stripped of comforts, alone on a rocky shore. One day, he knew, the tide would engulf him.

The dragon banner went north, through the Kingdoms of Gwent, Ergyng and Powys to the borders of Rheged. Artorius felt a touch of pride when he beheld the quiet villages and farms, the crops of golden wheat and barley ripening in the midsummer sun. Herds of livestock, cattle and sheep and goats, grazed in the fields turned over to pasture, and fled in brute panic when the Companions thundered past.

This was a land at peace. Once, the smoke of burning homesteads would have blackened the skies in every direction. Now the only smoke rose from the hearths of cottages or the roof of an occasional hill-fort: the draughty timber stronghold of some local ruler, oath-sworn to keep the peace and enforce the laws of the High King.

After a lifetime of struggle, Artorius had succeeded in taming Britannia - or at least, those portions of the island he controlled. To the east, beyond the borders of Powys, the Saxons and their kin held sway. Artorius had long since given up the dream of one day marching east and driving the Germanic invaders back into the sea. They were already too well-entrenched, their infant kingdoms guarded by many hosts of warriors. Every year more of them made the perilous journey across the grey northern seas.

They came, not as brutal conquerors hungry for blood and plunder, but as farmers and settlers. Every farmstead they built, every stake and fence-post they drove into British soil, was another nail in the coffin of a free and independent Britannia. Not since the coming of the legions had the native people enjoyed the right to govern the whole of their own island.

Despite his fiery speeches, Artorius knew in his heart that such freedom would never come again. At best, the Britons could hope to live in peace with the invaders, and in time merge their bloodlines. It was not unknown for Saxon warriors to take British wives or concubines: their Bretwalda, Cerdic, was himself a halfbreed.

Artorius gathered another fifty mounted spearmen on his way north. Thirty were men of the war-band of Caradog Freichfras, the aged King of Gwent and his closest ally among the sub-kings of Britannia. Twenty were given - grudgingly - by King Gwrgan of Ergyng. Artorius knew Gwrgan secretly hated him, and chafed under his strict laws.

He also knew the King of Ergyng was plotting with other disgruntled men. They longed for a return to the days of blood-feuds and cattle raids, with no High King set over them to curb their excesses.

I should cut off his head, thought Artorius as he shared a platter of roast beef with Gwrgan in the latter's hall, *and mount it over the gate at Caerleon as a warning to his fellow conspirators. Vortigern would have done so.*

He exchanged false smiles with his host. *I am not Vortigern. I will not play the tyrant, and wake up one morning to find my hall on fire, and the people chanting for my blood.*

After three days the Companion arrived at the edge of war-torn Rheged. It was like riding into the past, before Artorius drove back the Saxons and won a decade of peace. The land was bare and desolate, the fields untended, the peasants fled, slaughtered or taken as slaves. Their homes bore the marks of fire - roofless, charred, silent as the grave.

Artorius was almost overcome by rage. "This is the work of native-born ravagers," he snarled as the Companions rode past yet another wrecked village, "men who should turn their spears against our enemies in the east. Instead they prefer to squabble among themselves, like angry children, and destroy all they swore to defend."

"Rheged suffers for lack of a king," said Bedwyr, "you cannot wait for the sons of old King Meirchion to grow. Once you have put an end to this war, choose a man to rule the kingdom. A strong man in place of a mere steward. Someone you can trust to keep these petty warlords at heel."

Artorius glanced at Bedwyr: gloomy, haggard, one-handed Bedwyr, known these days as the Witch-Slayer after his ruthless execution of Morgana, the Seer of Britannia. Artorius' old sword-brother was haunted by demons, and made for utterly joyless company, but could be relied on for sound advice.

"If I was to disinherit the sons of Meirchion," said the king, "and set up some other man as King of Rheged, what would I do with the boys? Once they reached manhood, they would gather spears and try to take back their inheritance by force. Must I spend my old age at war with ambitious young princelings?"

Bedwyr gave a narrow shrug. "Perhaps they should not reach manhood. Kill the little turds, and have done. Smother them in their beds."

Artorius shivered. "I am not yet at the stage of murdering children for the sake of peace."

"You sow dragon's teeth, Artorius," Bedwyr replied with one of his cynical smiles, "and shall reap a bitter harvest."

3.

Rheged

Battle was joined in a broad valley flanked by rugged hills. The bare hillsides echoed to the screams and shouts of the men in the valley, while purple clouds rolled above and a storm threatened in the distance.

Artorius urged Llamrei, his glossy black mare, onto a ridge overlooking the valley from the south.

As Eri had said, the hosts of Gwyn and Gwythyr were well-matched. Two solid lines of shields heaved and shoved at each other near the middle of the valley floor. A thousand men, perhaps. Artorius could see the banners wave, the gleam of spears and axes, and hear the oaths, shouts, curses, shrieks and pleas for mercy - the old, familiar din of battle.

"Leave them to fight it out," said Bedwyr, "once all is over, ride down to the valley and pick out the survivors. With luck, Gwyn and Gwythyr will not survive. Save you the trouble of hanging them."

"I want Gwyn alive," snarled Llwch, "I want to draw out his heart on my spear, and watch the light in his eyes fail."

"What bloody men you are," Artorius said, more harshly than he intended, "have the years of peace made you so hungry for blood? We are here to stop a war, not prolong it."

He had brought Bedwyr and Llwch as his captains. Cei remained behind at Caerleon, to govern as steward in his absence, and Gwalchmei to command the city garrison. These four men were his pillars, his chief supports, upon which his power and confidence rested.

"I am here to avenge my kin," said Llwch, "the blood-price demands it."

There was genuine anger in his voice, and the skin of his narrow, dark-skinned face was taut with passion. Llwch had never set Artorius at defiance before. Once again the High King felt unbalanced, as though the ground shifted under his feet.

I grow old, he thought, *and frightened of my friends.*

"Enough talk," he said abruptly, "I shall lead my company forward. Bedwyr, you have the left flank, Llwch, the right. Skirt the edges of the valley and wait for my signal. The men below should stop fighting once they see the dragon banner. If not..."

"If not," said Bedwyr, "they will pay in blood for their disobedience."

Artorius glanced at him in irritation. He expected Bedwyr to help him curb Llwch's desire for vengeance. Instead he seemed set on encouraging it.

"They must be taught a sharp lesson," he said, "sharp and brief. I want as little bloodshed as possible. Order your men to use the butts of their spears and the flats of their swords. Strike if necessary, but there is to be no wanton slaughter. Remember, we are here as watchmen, to restore peace and order."

Neither of his captains looked convinced. Llwch didn't seem to hear. Instead he gazed down at the battle in the valley, long fingers curled tight around the hilt of his sword.

Artorius shook off his doubts and drew Caledfwlch. He had not wielded the sword in anger for many years, and felt almost giddy with nerves and excitement, a raw recruit, as he raised it high to catch the sun.

"Forward," he cried. His trumpeter, Cilydd, sounded the note to advance.

Llamrei picked up speed as his company cantered down the steep rise to the valley floor. Artorius was reminded of Mount Badon, his greatest victory, and the cavalry charges he led that day against the shields of the Saxon host.

Badon was twelve years gone. He longed for the simplicity of that time, the straightforward fight for survival against foreign invaders. The battle between civilised, Christian men on the one hand, and barbarous pagans on the other. Now the so-called civilised men had turned on each other.

The fight raged on before him. Some of the men in the rear ranks heard the thunder of hoofs. They broke away, cast down their weapons and fled towards the hills. Artorius ignored them. He had given Bedwyr and Llwch strict orders to round up any fugitives.

Cilydd's trumpet rang back and forth across the valley as the Companions approached the battlefield. Artorius kept his men at a steady canter, giving the fighters plenty of time to see the dragon banner.

The fight raged on, shield-wall pressed against shield-wall. The men locked in combat either failed to hear Cilydd's trumpet, or paid no heed to it. Their chiefs goaded them on, spear to bloody spear, sword to sword.

Artorius ground his teeth. As he feared, the battle would have to be ended by force. He looked left and right, and saw the companies of red cloaks drawn up on the flanks of the valley. Llwch and Bedwyr waited for his summons.

"Now," he said, with a nod to Cilydd, who paused to moisten his lips and take several deep breaths. Then he flung up his head and blew the note to charge.

Llamrei reacted instinctively to the signal, and surged into a gallop. Artorius fought to rein in his own instincts, the wild battle-fury that overcame him at such moments, the red mist of the born warrior.

These men are my subjects, not my enemies, he reminded himself, *my countrymen, my brothers. I am here to chastise, not to kill.*

Another thought welled up from the pit of his soul. *They are traitors. I gave them the chance to obey me. They threw it back in my face. They must be punished! No-one defies my will!*

The conflict still raged inside his head as Llamrei carried him into the flank of the contending armies. Now men saw him, the giant figure of the High King in his golden mail and dragon helm and cloak of rich imperial purple. They scattered from his path like frightened sheep. Shields and spears fell onto the trampled grass.

Artorius dragged back on his reins and wrestled Llamrei to a halt. "Mercy, lord king," cried the nearest warrior, his eyes brimful of terror. He was one of the poorer sort, and wore no helmet or ring-mail.

Artorius lashed out with the the flat of his blade. It caught the man on the side of the head and knocked him, sprawling, into a shallow pool. In their wisdom, Gwyn and Gwythyr had chosen to fight on a wide patch of boggy ground. As a result every warrior was smeared with blood and filth.

The iron discipline of the Companions had not fallen to rust over the years. The red-cloaked horsemen moved among the ranks of warriors, ordering a few stubborn souls to lay down their arms. Here and there a scuffle broke out, rapidly quelled as the nearest Companions beat the troublemakers senseless with the butts of their spears.

"On your knees," shouted Artorius, "every one of you! On your knees before the High King!"

His voice carried like a bull-horn to the edges of the valley. As one, those warriors of Rheged still on their feet sank down to kneel in the mud.

Silence fell, broken only by the groans of dying men and the howl of the wind across the surrounding dales.

This was a bleak land, a place of mists and rains, dark forests and bare hillsides. It reminded Artorius of the far North, the tribal lands of the Votadini where he was born. A terrible sense of longing crept over him, even as he slid Caledfwlch back into its sheath and looked over the battlefield.

"Where are your chiefs?" he demanded, "where are Gwyn and Gwythyr? Bring them before me, dead or alive."

They still lived. Both men stepped from the ranks of their hearth-guards, and advanced boldly to kneel before Llamrei. Neither looked at the other.

"Well?" said Artorius, "which of you fools is which? Name yourselves!"

The rivals might have been brothers. Both were slender, with sandy-coloured hair and clipped beards. Unlike most of their followers, they wore long shirts of ring-mail, spattered with blood, helms with dangling cheek-pieces, and carried swords.

Both looked no older than twenty. *I am forty-one*, Artorius thought glumly, *twice their age...they must see me as a relic of the past, as I once saw Ambrosius.*

"I am Gwythyr, lord king," said one of the princes, "I welcome your presence in Rheged. Doubtless you have come to arrest this villain who invaded my lands, set fire to my hall, and slew my folk."

Gwyn said nothing. Artorius could not tell if the man was afraid or indifferent. His startling blue eyes were unreadable as they met the High King's searching gaze.

A fresh rumble of hoofs sounded across the field. Artorius looked up, and raised his hand to greet the arrival of Llwch and Bedwyr.

Llwch urged his horse through the host of kneeling men. "Which of these two chiefs is my enemy?" he demanded, "which of them tormented and dishonoured my kin?"

"Me, I suspect," replied Gwyn with cheerful smile, "I am Gwyn son of Nudd of Ystrad Clud. Who might you be?"

Llwch threw down his spear and reached for his sword. "Llwch Llemineawg," he growled, "come to avenge the heart's blood of Nwython, my cousin, and the madness of his son."

Gwyn gave a chuckle. "Ah yes, Nwython. Joy it was to me to cut out his heart, and feed the still-warm flesh to his fool of a son. Much laughter among my warriors as Cyledyr choked down that tender morsel."

Naked steel blazed as Llwch drew his sword. He slid from his horse and moved towards Gwyn with murder in his eyes.

Artorius rode forward to place himself between the two men. "There has been enough death here," he snapped, "Llwch, put away your sword."

For a long moment he thought the other man might disobey. What then? Discipline was harsh among the Companions, and applied to officers as well as ordinary troopers. The penalty for refusal to obey orders was summary execution.

Don't force my hand, Artorius pleaded silently, *I will do it. You know I will.*

Llwch looked away. The tension in the air eased a little as he rammed his sword back into its scabbard. His lean, sunburned features were twisted with rage and frustration, and flushed even darker when Gwyn uttered a soft laugh.

"You keep your hounds on a tight leash, Artorius," he said with another grin, "I commend your wisdom. Otherwise I might have had to draw this one's teeth."

Artorius glanced briefly at the warriors of Rheged. Scores of rough, bearded faces, spattered with blood and dirt, gazed back at him. Some five hundred spears, maybe the largest war-band any northern prince could put in the field.

To slay Gwyn as the man deserved would not put an

end to the blood-feud. Artorius was himself a man of the old North, Y Hen Ogledd. He knew the customs of northmen. Gwyn's followers would vow a fresh oath to avenge the blood of their chief. Before he knew it Artorius would have a full-scale rebellion to deal with.

Llwch, and probably Bedwyr, would advise him to strangle the threat at birth by executing Gwyn and every one of his men. They were his prisoners, and could offer little resistance against the Companions.

Artorius made a great effort to prevent himself from being cruel. A warlike man himself, who had lived his entire life by the sword, it was hard for him to take the path less well-trodden. To strive for mercy and justice over wanton bloodshed.

"Men have died," he said, "mead-halls have been burned, homes and farmsteads destroyed. All for the sake of a woman. I care not how beautiful the lady Creiddylad may be. No woman, no matter how wealthy or desirable, how sweet of face or rich in land and cattle, is worth the destruction of an entire kingdom, and the deaths of so many good men."

He glared at the two young chieftains who knelt before him. "How the Saxons will laugh at us. Cerdic has spent the last ten years gathering a new host, to replace the warriors we slaughtered at Mount Badon. He must wonder why he makes the effort. He only needs to wait for the Britons to destroy each other."

Gwythyr bowed his head in shame, but Gwyn's expression remained indifferent. His careless manner, even when faced with death, reminded Artorius of Gwrgi Wyllt, the madman who sacked Eboracum and put the entire population to the sword.

Artorius took a deep breath. "This is my judgement," he declared, "I will take the lady Creiddylad back to Caerleon, where she will live as one of the ladies of the court. The feud shall be settled by single combat between the principals, Gwyn and Gwythyr. No-one else will suffer for their wounded pride."

Llwch started forward. "Lord king..." he protested.

Artorius raised a hand to silence him.

"No-one else," he repeated firmly, "I decree this single combat shall take place on the first morning of every May at Caerleon, and continue until sundown. If both survive the first trial, it shall be repeated the following May, and so on, until one of you is dead. The eventual victor shall win the right to marry Creiddylad."

Gasps and oaths rippled across the field as the nearest men of Rheged heard this, and passed the word to their comrades.

Bedwyr grunted with approval. Artorius knew he would appreciate the subtlety of the judgement. It was now July, and many months would pass before Gwyn and Gwythyr could settle their dispute in single combat. In that time they would be obliged not to make war on each other, which in turn allowed war-ravaged Rheged a chance to heal.

"I refuse to accept this judgement," said Gwyn.

Artorius pointed Caledfwlch at him. "Accept it," said the High King, "or I will unleash all my power on Ystrad Clud. Can you fight the Companions? Can you fight the combined war-hosts of the Kings of Britannia? I think not. The fate of Vortigern shall be yours. You and all your kin, your warriors and your servants, shall burn inside your houses. I will burn you all. There will be nothing left of your people save blackened gables and charred bones."

Now, at last, there was a flicker of uncertainty on Gwyn's smooth features. He blinked, and a nerve twitched at the corner of his mouth. His lips worked, but no words came forth.

Artorius nodded. He had broken this little chieftain to his will. Harsh judgement, backed up by the threat of force. The same method he had used, time and again, to keep the Britons in some semblance of order. It was the curse of his people - his curse and his burden - that they could not be brought to respect the rule of law for its own sake.

He took Gwyn's silence for acceptance. To make certain, Artorius took a number of hostages, including five of the chieftain's closest kin. These men would be held in tight but honourable captivity at Caerleon, and suffer the death of traitors if their lord broke his oath to keep the peace in Rheged.

Artorius' satisfaction at a task well done was marred by the behaviour of Llwch. His old comrade said little during the journey south, and shunned the company of Artorius, even when invited to share a meal in the High King's pavilion.

I have made an enemy of him, thought Artorius as he sat alone one night. He had left Bedwyr as steward of Rheged, with eighty Companions to help enforce his authority. The stewardship was only temporary, until Artorius could send some other man: he needed Bedwyr at court, as a trusted advisor and one of his dwindling band of friends.

Bedwyr had won back the High King's trust by slaying Morgana, daughter of Ambrosius and Artorius' foster-sister. The High King had loved her once, until Bedwyr returned to Caerleon with clear proof that Morgana was responsible for the death of Medraut, Artorius' youngest son: Bedwyr brought back Medraut's bloodstained jerkin, the same one he had worn before he went missing, so many years ago.

According to Bedwyr, Morgana had boasted of her crime before she died. Artorius' grief at her treachery was almost as exquisite as his pain at the loss of Medraut. When Bedwyr placed her severed head before the throne, Artorius had spat on it, and ordered it to be burned. The stained jerkin was cast onto the same fire. For his efforts, Bedwyr was allowed to resume his place among the Companions.

Yes, Bedwyr was a true friend. Llwch, on the other hand, could no longer be trusted.

He is a northman to his roots, thought Artorius, *and*

northmen have stiff necks. He had every right to demand vengeance on Gwyn. I denied him that right.

The king stretched his long body and took another long swallow of heated wine. *Perhaps I should allow time for his blood to cool. I have known Llwch Llemineawg for twenty years. Rode with him, fought with him, bled with him. He is almost as proud and stubborn as Cei, but a good man at heart. Loyal.*

His thoughts took a darker turn. *Loyal, yes. Loyal to his kin. One of his cousins was foully murdered, and another has run mad. Their fate will nag at him. He will blame me. Over time, that blame may turn to resentment. Hatred.*

Outside the wind howled across the darkened moor, and rain pattered against the canvas. The Companions had pitched camp for the night just inside the northern border of Gwent, on a patch of barren heath surrounded by forest. Artorius felt relatively safe here, a day's ride from Caerleon, yet had still ringed the camp with sentries and a shallow ditch. Even deep inside friendly territory, it paid to be cautious.

Old comradeship only counts for so much. I cannot afford to nurture treason at court. Llwch must be watched. Closely.

Artorius sighed. This was his greatest fear when they placed the crown on his head. To be alone, and resented, and forced to suspect his friends.

This is the fate of all kings. God help me.

4.

Caer Y Brenin, Kernow

King Marcus gnawed a knuckle. Outside the people were

cheering. The cheers were not for him, and he hated and feared the noise. It was the sound of death.

'Drystan! Drystan! Hail Drystan!'

He thought of a certain day, nine summers gone, when the people had cheered his name. That was after he murdered his elder brother, Bouduin, and stole Bouduin's crown.

Marcus could still feel the impact of his dagger as it slid home. Hear the gasp, and see the whites of his brother's eyes as they rolled back in their sockets.

Everyone knew Bouduin had been murdered. Few cared. Those of the old king's bodyguards who protested were quickly silenced. Forever. Still the people had cheered, and sang, and wished blessings and good fortune upon his successor.

Marcus bared his teeth in the gloom of the mead-hall. The people would cheer a bladder on a stick, if it meant they continued to enjoy good harvests, and were kept safe from pirates.

"Lord king."

The rough voice of Carrow, the captain of his guard, broke through the darkness in the king's mind.

Darkness, and the glint of a bloodied dagger, and the fall of a body upon the stair...

"Lord king," Carrow repeated, "it is time. Your son waits outside."

Marcus gripped the arms of his chair, rose a little, then sat back again. "Is he unharmed?" he asked with a passable show of concern.

Carrow hitched up his belt. His ring-mail glimmered in the shadows. At night, the hall was lit up by torches and the blaze of a great fire in the central hearth. Now it was dark and cool, and the only light slanted in from narrow windows. Marcus might have ordered a fire lit, but the twilight atmosphere suited his mood.

"Yes, lord," replied the captain, "he took not a scratch

in the fight against Morholt. He carries the pirate's head in a bag, and has placed it on the threshold in your honour."

Marcus hated the undisguised joy and admiration in the other man's voice. Drystan was a hero now. He, not Marcus, would be hailed as the saviour of Kernow.

"Lord," Carrow added, "the people are waiting for you to greet their champion. You must be seen."

The king steeled himself. He would need all of his considerable willpower to muster a smile, appear pleased before his subjects, and receive Drystan with a smiling countenance.

He rose, swayed a little - he was suddenly light-headed - stepped down from the dais, and walked the length of his hall to the entrance.

It seemed a long walk. His shadow flickered in and out of the narrow bars of light thrown across the earthen floor. Somewhere a fly buzzed. Marcus wished it to hell and damnation.

The double doors stood ajar. Carrow flung them wide open. A wave of noise and light rolled into the hall.

Marcus stood exposed. He almost cringed, and suppressed a desire to throw his cloak over his face.

A great throng of people were packed inside the inner stockade of his fortress. The stockade was circular, while the outer rampart was in the shape of an oval. Usually none save the king's servants were allowed inside the heart of the fortress, where Marcus held court inside his mead-hall, but today was different. Today saw the return of a hero.

The din of the crowd redoubled when they saw their king. They - slaves, freedmen, farmers, courtiers, priests, scribes, beggars and herdsmen - roared his name with gusto.

"Marcus! All hail the King! Marcus!"

The king smiled weakly and raised a hand in greeting. They sang his praises. His nostrils flared at their stink.

Marcus was flanked by two rows of green-cloaked spearmen. The walkway of the stockade was crammed with archers. At the first sign of trouble, the bowmen had orders to shoot into the crowd. The spearmen would close up around the king, and shepherd him back into the safety of the hall. Marcus distrusted his subjects almost as much as he despised them.

He looked down at his son. The throng had parted to form an avenue for Drystan, from the timber gatehouse of the stockade to the doors of the mead-hall. He stood, young and slender and brave, at the foot of the lowest step before the entrance. His spear and shield were laid in a neat pile on the ground, and a bag placed on top of them.

The leather covering of the bag was peeled down to reveal the severed head of Morholt the Reaver.

Morholt's dead eyes stared up glassily at the king. His bright red beard was rank with dried blood. The dead man's tongue dangled limply from his twisted mouth.

Drystan flung up his arms. The noise of the mob instantly died away. "My noble father," he cried, "I have slain the enemy of our people, and lay his head before you in tribute. Morholt is dead. No longer shall his pirates threaten our shores. No more shall we pay tribute to the men of Hibernia, or live in fear of their longships. They have sailed home, taking the headless carcase of their chieftain with them. It is their turn to mourn the dead and taste the bitter shame of defeat. Their turn to grieve over the burial mound, chant laments for the fallen, wonder when his like shall come again."

The young man's voice, high and pure, rang out like a trumpet. Fresh cheers burst from the throats of the people clustered around him.

My noble father, Marcus thought furiously, *he had to remind the people of our kinship. That he is no mere warrior, but the son of a king. Clever. This bastard of mine is a subtle creature.*

He cleared his throat and waited patiently for the acclaim to die down. "Fair son," he said, raising his voice so all could hear, "you have proved yourself a worthy child of my blood. The slaying of Morholt was a noble deed, one that has rid our kingdom of a great and merciless enemy. Despite your tender years, I knew you would prevail."

In reality, Marcus had been faced with little choice but to send Drystan, young and untried as he was, to fight Morholt. None of his more seasoned warriors, aware of the Hibernian chieftain's terrifying reputation, would agree to do it. Nothing Marcus said, his threats or pleas or curses, could overcome their fear of him.

For nine years, ever since Marcus murdered and deposed his brother, Morholt had ravaged the coasts of Kernow. His pirates were seasoned in battle, and destroyed every war-band Marcus sent against them. In the end, the king had resorted to buying the pirates off with yearly tributes of grain, cattle, weapons and other goods.

Predictably, the tributes increased every year. No longer able or willing to pay, and threatened with rebellion if he failed to deal with the pirate curse, Marcus had sent a challenge to Morholt to single combat. Each side could pick a champion. If the champion of Kernow prevailed, the pirates would quit the land and never return. If Morholt's champion had the victory, then the tributes would continue.

The king had long studied the character of his enemy, and knew he was too proud and arrogant to refuse, or to choose anyone save himself as champion.

There was a flaw in his plan. Marcus had not bargained on almost all of his warriors, even the most experienced and battle-hardened spearmen, proving too cowardly to face Morholt in combat. The dreadful prospect of having to fight the pirate himself was only averted when Drystan knelt before his father's chair one night and offered to save Kernow's honour.

Now, against all odds, Drystan had returned in triumph. The tall, golden-haired youth stood waiting for his reward, and the eyes of the crowd were fixed on Marcus.

The king could only do what was expected of him. "Tonight you shall sit in the place of honour," Marcus declared, "and let the Almighty Father be thanked for your courage and prowess. Kernow suffered a long harrowing by Morholt, but God saw fit to lend strength to your sword-arm. Enter my hall, my son, and be welcome."

That night there was a feast in Drystan's honour, and the hall was filled with music and light and laughter. The king's bard, unbidden by Marcus, composed verses to celebrate the young hero's victory over Morholt:

"The people of Hibernia,
Will have little cause to welcome,
The return of Morholt,
They lost him on the spear-ground,
Foredoomed, cut down,
Their women in shock,
Overcome by grief,
How could Morholt,
The reaver, the sea-rover, the bloody right hand,
Hope to prevail over Drystan?
The pride of Kernow,
The bright sword of the dawn,
He laid low the great warrior,
The glutton sword,
Prize of king's halls,
Was a tool of God's resolve,
In the hand of Drystan,
The great days of Morholt are ended,
He lies, headless, blood-plastered,
His body borne away,
Over the sea-lanes,
Back to Hibernia,
His warrior troop,
Shall bear his body home..."

The poem was greeted with shouts of approval from the men crowded onto the mead-benches, and the thunder of knives and fists on the board. Marcus hitched his lips into a smile, and glanced sidelong at Drystan, seated at his right hand in the chair of honour.

His son's mood was difficult to gauge. Drystan greeted the poem with a nod to the bard, but otherwise showed no emotion. Another man might have gloried in the moment, wallowed in the acclaim. Not Drystan. He seemed aloof somehow, serene above the noise and bustle and laughter of the hall-throng.

Marcus studied him a moment. The boy had glamour, no doubt of that. His shoulder-length hair, parted in the middle, was thick and shone like burnished gold. The colour of ripe wheat. Gold rings and arm-bands - gifts from Marcus, appropriate to a hero - adorned his fingers and upper arms. His pale complexion offset the gold, along with the tunic of red wool he had donned for the feast.

He also wore a belt of silver rings, another gift, fastened with a buckle forged in the shape of a stag. Save for his eating knife, Drystan was unarmed.

"Where is the sword I gave you?" Marcus asked in a tone of mild reproof, "you should be proud to wear the blade that struck off Morholt's head."

Drystan turned to look at his father.

There is little of me in this face, thought the king. Drystan's soft brown eyes, rosebud mouth and aquiline nose were all gifts from his mother, a kitchen slave Marcus had not even thought of for many years.

"I did not wish to boast," said Drystan, "besides, the sword is not mine. Only one of true noble blood, or a favoured member of a king's retinue, has the right to carry a sword."

Marcus despised this show of humility. Drystan was forcing him into a corner, to promote him from a mere bastard, just another spearman, to the ranks of the hearth-guard.

Once again, Marcus was left with little choice. He could sense the air of expectation in the hall.

"The sword was a gift," he said, though the words stuck in his throat, "treat it as such."

A ripple of applause echoed in the smoke-blackened rafters. Drystan smiled - he had a beautiful smile - while his father inwardly raged.

In the early hours of the dawn, long after the feast was over, Marcus stalked the outer ramparts of his fortress. Pale light stole over the land to the east and cast a dim glow over the hills and forests of Kernow.

To the south, a short ride away, the land sloped down to the sea. Marcus had spent his entire life within sight and sound of the grey waves, the cry of gulls, and the crash of breakers upon splintered cliffs.

Caer Y Brenin was the chief stronghold in Kernow, a sub-kingdom of Dumnonia. From here, this remote earth and timber fortress perched high above the sea, Marcus had ruled with an iron hand for nine years. He taxed his people heavily, collected all power into his own hands, and stamped down hard on the slightest hint of protest or rebellion.

He rested his elbows on the rough timber stockade and stared out to sea. The cold of the dawn knifed through his fur-lined woollen cloak. Marcus welcomed the cold. It cleared his head of the taint of mead, and pushed back the waves of fear and exhaustion.

How best to deal with Drystan? He could almost smell the boy's ambition. The slaying of Morholt was merely a stepping-stone.

Marcus blamed himself. *How could I be so blind not to see it? Next, Drystan will demand to be named as my heir. I have no reason to deny him.*

The king was thirty-five, and had yet to father any legitimate sons. True, he had fathered a number of bastards, scattered about Kernow - seven he was certain of - but most were no-marks, with no talent or desire for kingship. One had even taken holy orders and become a monk.

Only Drystan showed any promise. Only Drystan did he fear. If Marcus made the boy his heir, how long before he met the same fate as Bouduin, and felt the sharp kiss of steel in his back one dark night? He was still in the prime of life, and might live for many years yet. Drystan, if he had anything of his father in him, would not be content to wait.

Marcus calculated the odds of his own survival. Unless he acted, he would probably be dead inside six months. The life of any king was precarious. As soon as he let the advantage slip, he may as well cut his own throat.

It was suddenly vital he married again. His first wife had died the previous winter, worn out by a life of misery, loneliness and failed pregnancies. If Marcus took another wife, he was young enough to father a son and watch the boy grow to manhood. A legitimate heir of his blood (or several) would foil the ambitions of illegitimate upstarts like Drystan.

There remained the problem of what to do with Drystan in the meantime. Simply having the boy murdered was out of the question. Suspicion would immediately fall upon Marcus. The people would call him kinslayer, and demand his blood in vengeance for the death of the young hero.

His supple, knife-sharp mind fought with the problem. Then, as bright morning sunlight flooded over the fields, Marcus struck upon a way of solving all his difficulties at once.

5.

Hibernia

Morholt's followers raised a mound for their dead chief on a headland overlooking the sea. In ancient heathen fashion, his body was housed inside the barrow, buried alongside torques and jewels and weapons, and sundry other precious goods he had won in life.

"Let the ground keep these treasures now," declared one of his warriors when the barrow was closed, "and keep his dear body safe from carrion-eaters and evil spirits."

Afterwards twelve warriors, Morholt's closest companions, rode slowly around the mound, chanting his death-song. They mourned his loss as a man and a chieftain, praised his courage and noble exploits, his victories in single combat, churches he had plundered, enemies he had slain or enslaved, the boatloads of treasure he had carried home across the seas.

Esyllt watched the ceremony from a respectable distance, guarded by ten of her father's spearmen. It was a shamelessly heathen ritual, an echo of the far-off days before the first Christian missionaries came to Hibernia, and ought to have horrified any decent Christian princess.

"Have you seen enough of this pagan farce, child?" muttered Ronan, one of her father's priests, "it is vile, and blasts my sight. Your father should outlaw such things. They are not good for Christian folk to look upon."

Esyllt ignored him. She hugged her cloak tighter against the wind sweeping in from the sea. The dreary song of Morholt's warriors mingled with the cries of gulls.

The ritual fascinated her. It was a glimpse into a forgotten world, one the priests did their best to pretend had never existed. Morholt had earned their displeasure by stubbornly refusing to give up his lifelong worship of pagan gods. He cared little for the friendship of priests, and laughed to scorn their curses and threats of hellfire.

Esyllt secretly admired his courage. Morholt had been her uncle, younger brother to her father, Niall, King of the Uí Liatháin in south-west Hibernia. Niall was a devout Christian - priest-ridden, his brother had called him - and disapproved of Morholt's insistence on clinging to the old gods.

Niall often spoke of forcing his brother to accept baptism, but never acted on it. Esyllt always suspected her gentle, mild-mannered father was afraid of his warlike brother. Certainly he did nothing to restrain Morholt's bloody raids on the coasts of Britannia, even though Niall feared it would incur the wrath of Artorius, the dreaded High King of the Britons. Artorius had already waged one war on Hibernia, against the kingdoms of Osraige and Laigin to the north, and left them in ruins.

Esyllt was fascinated by the tales of Artorius and his invincible cavalry, the Companions. Just turned fourteen, she was fascinated by many things. The only child of King Niall was blessed (or cursed) with an enquiring mind, and an intellect stifled by the restrictions placed on her freedom.

Beside her Ronan shifted impatiently, hopping from foot to sandalled foot. Niall had appointed him as Esyllt's teacher and moral guardian. Dependent on her mood, she found him amusing or tedious company. He was still quite young, in his mid-twenties, and concealed his obvious desire for her behind an irritable manner.

She wouldn't dream of trying to corrupt him. Ronan was not to her taste. Tall and stringy, born with a hideously deformed right ear that made him half-deaf, his long nose, thin features and overgrown tonsure put her in mind of an ugly bird.

"Enough, enough," he said, placing a clammy hand on her forearm, "I cannot witness any more of this heathen rite. It shall be dark soon. We must return before nightfall."

Esyllt could not deny the sense in that. Outside of his ringfort, her father's kingdom was a dangerous and lawless place, assailed by pirates and enemy war-bands. Esyllt went nowhere without an armed escort. Otherwise she was liable to be abducted and carried away into a neighbouring kingdom, to be held for ransom or forcibly married off to some prince or other. Worse, she might be taken by bandits who would think nothing of raping and murdering a woman of royal blood, and dumping her body in the marshlands.

The riders slowly jogged back towards the ringfort, following the rough dirt tracks through the damp meadows and forests that formed much of Niall's kingdom.

It was late summer, melding into autumn, and heat shimmered in the air. Flies buzzed around their ponies, clustered around the eyes and nostrils of the luckless beasts. Esyllt used a whisk to swat the insects from her pony's head while she talked to her maidservant, Golwg.

She and Golwg were the same age. Strangers often found it difficult to tell them apart. Both were slender and willowy, with long blonde hair, grey eyes and sweet, heart-shaped faces. They might have been twins, save Esyllt was of royal blood and Golwg a mere slave: a bright slave, however, witty and cheerful. Esyllt valued her, as she might value a favourite hawk or wolfhound.

One of Esyllt's favourite pastimes was to play off Ronan and Golwg against each other. She thought twice as fast as the pair of them, and they never seemed to notice her deceptions.

"Remind me, Ronan," she asked innocently as the riders picked their way through a wood, "why has my father betrothed me to one of his chief enemies?"

Ronan wiped a cloth over his streaming eyes. He was a mass of allergies, and suffered in the summer heat.

"We have been over this several times before," he replied crossly, "really, child, you should pay more attention."

As ever, he melted under the warmth of her sweet smile. "Oh, very well. King Marcus of Kernow was an enemy of your uncle, Morholt, not your father. Naturally, as Morholt's kinsman, Niall inherited the feud. He has no desire to prolong it, and only wishes for peace with Kernow."

He paused to blow his nose. The obscene noise echoed through the woods and startled the ponies. Esyllt exchanged looks with Golwg, and barely stifled the giggle that rose in her throat.

"Thus," Ronan went on, oblivious to the black looks of the spearmen whose ponies he had disturbed, "when King Marcus sent an envoy to your father's court, offering peace in exchange for your hand in marriage, King Niall was glad to accept."

Esyllt winked at Golwg. "Ronan hopes my father will allow him to accompany me to Kernow. He hopes to impress King Marcus with his piety, and be given a monastery to rule over, rich robes to wear, and a mitre of pure gold to carry."

Golwg's shrill laughter pierced the gloomy silence of the woods. "He will end his days as a bishop!" she cried, "and shall be carried to Heaven after his death by a host of cherubim."

"Look!" she added, pointing at the priest, "I think I can see his angel wings already."

Ronan flushed. "I hope for no such thing," he protested, "and you do wrong to mock a man of God."

He wagged a finger at Esyllt. "Tread lightly, my lady. Your father has forbidden me to chastise you with the rod, but he said nothing of your slave."

Golwg clasped her hands. "He proposes to beat me!" she exclaimed, "would you strip me, holy father, and make me kneel on the cold flagstones of your church? See, my lady - see how these impure thoughts excite him!"

The priest had gone red. Fuming, he urged his pony forward and refused to speak for the remainder of the journey.

Esyllt pitied him. "We went too far," she said to Golwg, "it must be hard for him, a young man, chained to Christ."

She leaned in close to whisper in the other woman's ear. "I have never understood why priests are not allowed to take wives, like other men. They look so miserable all the time. Surely that is the cause?"

Golwg sniggered. "That is blasphemous," she replied in a low voice, "Ronan will appeal to the Pope, and have us both excommunicated."

They reached King Niall's stronghold shortly after dark, the last stage of their journey lit by hanging lanterns the king had ordered to be erected on either side of the rough track leading to his fort.

The fort was built on the crown of a hill, surrounded by deep forest. Two earthen banks with timber ramparts formed the outer defences, while the third and highest rampart was made of stone. The king, his warriors and slaves had their dwellings inside the stone circle. Their horses and livestock were housed in byres on the lower part of the slope, guarded by the earth and timber fortifications.

As was her custom when she returned home, Esyllt chanted an ancient rhyme under her breath:

"What is the due of a king who is always in residence at the head of his túath? Seven score feet of perfect feet are the measure of his stockade on every side. Seven feet are the thickness of its earthwork, and twelve feet its depth. It is then that he is a king, when ramparts of vassalage surround him. What is the rampart of vassalage? Twelve feet are the breadth of its opening and its depth and its measure towards the stockade. Thirty feet are its measure outwardly."

Niall's ringfort, the home of a king, was built according to these measurements. She had learned the rhyme from her father, who instructed his daughter never to forget her birth and lineage, and to always bear in mind the honour of her family.

In her secret heart, Esyllt cared little for her ancestors, a dull lot of savage warlords and bloody-handed murderers so far as she could tell, or for family honour. She was fond of her parents, who had always been kind to her. Too kind, according to Ronan. He claimed they had spoiled and indulged her most shamefully, spared the rod when they should have plied it, and altogether ruined their only child.

"What you need is a strong husband," he was fond of saying, "an older man, who will cleanse you of the sin of pride, and remind you of the proper humility and obedience of your sex."

Esyllt thought he was wrong. She came from a proud and wilful race, and could only act true to her nature. Her future husband, this King Marcus, would have his hands full trying to cleanse her.

A horn sounded on the rampart above, and the gates were dragged inward to admit the princess and her escort.

6.

"What a sty," said Goron, "I can smell the pigs from here. Do the Scotti sleep with their swine, do you think?"

Drystan grinned. Goron was his closest friend, spear-brother since childhood, and always spoke his mind.

"Learn to control the viper that serves you for a tongue," he said, "and pretend to know what courtesy is, at least while we are guests at King Niall's court. This is his chief palace and stronghold."

Goron snorted. The two young men of Kernow sat their horses on a stony ridge, with a good view of Niall's ringfort to the west. Behind them, waiting patiently on the lower ground, were the thirty mounted warriors King Marcus had sent to escort his son to Hibernia.

"*Palace*," sneered Goron, "a fortified byre for cattle. I expect beasts are allowed to wander in the king's hall. The floor will be rank with dung and piss."

"My father's palace at Caer Y Brenin is no larger," Drystan said mildly. It was one of Goron's traits that he regarded Kernow as the centre of the civilised world, its people as the most valiant and beautiful, its meanest farmstead greater than the palace of the High King himself.

"Don't mention Caer Y Brenin in the same breath," Goron replied, "how I long to get off this island. It stinks.

The people are ugly and ignorant. I can scarcely believe King Marcus wants to marry one of them. Why would a lion seek union with a pig?"

Drystan put a finger to his lips. "Hush, my friend. The Scotti are both proud and quarrelsome. If any of your insults reached their ears, we should have another war on our hands. Remember, this is a peaceful mission. My father's envoy said the girl is beautiful. Like a May morning, were his words."

"The envoy is a fool," Goron retorted, "and must have been drunk when he saw Princess Esyllt. I hear the mead the Scotti brew is even thicker than their wits."

"You forget, or pretend to forget," said Drystan, "the Uí Liatháin were once Britons. They were driven out of Gwynedd by Cunedda and his sons, back in the days of Ambrosius, and founded a new kingdom in this part of Hibernia."

Goron shrugged. "Some lying bard or scribe told you that. They are barbarians, like all the people on this benighted isle."

Drystan gave up and turned his horse to canter back down the slope. He understood Goron's animosity towards the Scotti and Hibernia, even if he didn't share it. King Niall's people had been at war with Kernow for decades, and often held the advantage. It offended Goron's pride, and the pride of many warriors of Kernow, to know they had lost so many battles to a race they regarded as barely civilised.

They were fools, Drystan thought, ignorant and lacking in vision. Hibernia was the cradle of Christianity in the West. A great many holy saints and missionaries had come from these shores to reinforce the truth of Christ in Britannia, now half-conquered by pagans.

Raised as a mere warrior, a lowly spearman in his father's war-band, Drystan was illiterate. Despite his lack of education, he had done his best to pick up information wherever he could find it - from priests, hermits, wise women, ancient lore and histories recited by the court bards at Caer Y Brenin. He was intelligent enough to know that men of learning had a power of their own. An educated man who could also fight was a formidable prospect indeed. Drystan strove to turn himself into such a man. Then the world - and its legs - would be open to him.

The warriors of Kernow were received with great ceremony by King Niall, who seemed determined to both impress them and win their friendship. Drystan was shocked to see the prematurely aged man before him. Niall wore his kingship heavily, and his silken hair and beard were white as snow. His eyes were bloodshot under bony brows, his face grey and wrinkled, like an old sack.

For all that, there was strength in the king's body still, and his fingers were strong as they gripped Drystan's shoulders.

"Son of King Marcus," said Niall in a husky voice, "I am honoured by your presence. You are the champion who slew my brother."

Drystan tensed. He had been perturbed when King Marcus sent him to Kernow, to fetch back the king's new bride. Surely Niall would exact revenge for his brother's death?

"I loved my brother," sighed Niall, "but he followed his own course, shunned Christ, and ended as he had lived. By the sword. It was inevitable. I bear you no ill-will, Drystan son of Marcus. Bid your warriors sit, drink deep, and eat their fill of the good things set before them."

Relieved, Drystan gestured at his followers to take their places at the benches, alongside Niall's warriors and courtiers. Goron and a few others scowled when they found themselves seated between men they still regarded as enemies, but held their tongues.

Niall's hall was smaller than the one at Caer Y Brenin, and circular, like a glorified roundhouse. The trusses of the thatched roof were supported by timber columns, and the upper parts of the columns decorated by a curling, flowery runic script Drystan didn't recognise.

The floor was bare earth, but clean, and strewn with fresh rushes and sweet-smelling herbs. There were no beasts in the hall, save a couple of old wolfhounds stretched out next to the fire. Drystan caught Goron's eye and grinned wryly at him. Evidently the Scotti were not so barbaric after all.

"You may have heard tales of my daughter's beauty," said Niall, shortly after the feast began, "rest assured they are all true."

Drystan sat in the place of honour, between Niall and his queen, a small, brown-haired woman who smiled much and said little. She had passed the golden mead-cup among Drystan's warriors, as was her duty, and afterwards seemed content to sit and listen.

Looking at the royal couple, plain and tired as they were, Drystan found it hard to imagine they had produced an attractive daughter. He suspected the girl was really a shrew, short and pudding-faced like her mother, her meagre beauty enhanced by layers of cosmetic and the lies of her father's bards.

"If she lives up to the stories," he replied, gnawing at a hot peppered chop, "my father shall be well pleased, and peace shall reign between our peoples for many years to come."

Niall took the hint. He signalled at his steward, who ducked his head and vanished through the doorway. Drystan plucked another chop from the heaped platter before him. He chewed on it thoughtfully and listened to Niall's bard pluck a gentle melody from his harp.

The noise and chatter died away. The harp was stilled. In later days, when Drystan recalled the moment he first beheld Esyllt, it seemed to him a strange enchantment fell over the crowded hall.

A girl stepped through the doorway. Out of darkness, into light. She was fair - like a May morning, as the besotted envoy had said - and more than fair. Her gown was light blue, her mantle grey, and her brow adorned by a slender band of red gold.

"My daughter, the Princess Esyllt," murmured Niall, quite unnecessarily.

Drystan didn't hear him. The girl had entered the hall with a confident step that belied her years. She stood still, a smile on her red lips as she basked in the attention of so many warriors.

The smile died a little when she met Drystan's gaze. Her eyes were grey, like her mantle, and reminded him of the sea. The rushing in his head was the crashing of waves on the cliffs of Kernow. He thought to stand, but dared not, in case his legs gave way.

A wave of melancholy engulfed him. Drystan's mother had the Sight, and he had inherited a little of her talent. His ingrained foresight told him that Esyllt would be his only love on earth. His only love, and his doom. Their union was inescapable, woven by the fates long before they were born, and would lead to nothing but sadness.

Sadness, and war, and broken kingdoms.

7.

Isauria

Dusk, when crimson light flooded across the barren hills and plains, was Medraut's favourite time of day. Unlike his comrades, who yawned and grumbled and wished they were back in camp, he would cheerfully have spent the night in the open, alone among the desolation.

To the east, rugged foothills dominated the landscape. The highest peaks of the mountains beyond were wreathed in purple clouds, and the shadow of night seemed to creep down from the high passes to envelop the lowlands. The foothills marked the border of Isauria, the wild mountain kingdom in the south-east of Anatolia.

Medraut's troop were on their way back from patrol, to the fortified camp that lay some six miles to the west. The troop was made up of thirty men, twenty-nine Goths and one Briton. They were foederati, so-called barbarians in the service of the Eastern Empire.

One of the Goths emptied the last few drops from his leather flask onto his tongue. "I'm parched," he growled, stuffing the empty flask into his belt, "be a good comrade, someone, and lend me your flask."

He looked meaningfully at Medraut, who was the nearest. The Goth was a fearsome sight, short-tempered and hugely strong, capable of hurling a javelin clean through a man's body. His blue eyes gazed down fiercely at the dark little Briton.

Medraut was not intimidated. "Patience, Euric," he said mildly, "we'll be back at camp within the hour. Then you can swill and quaff to your heart's content, and doubtless wake up tomorrow with a sore head, just in time to go out on patrol again."

He wagged a finger at the other man. "You drink too much, my friend. Fill your flask with water instead of ale, and you won't get so thirsty. It might help to take the edge off your temper."

Euric's massive hands curled into fists. His nostrils flared. For a moment he resembled the angry red boar painted on his shield. Medraut looked straight ahead and refused to meet his glare.

The Goth uttered a harsh bray of laughter. "You're probably right, midget," he said, "I do pour too much of the bad stuff down my throat. It does me no good, yet what else is there to do? Ride around in circles and chase ghosts. No wonder I drink more than I should."

Medraut gave a thin smile. He knew Euric would back down. The Goths might insult him on occasion, treat him like a halfwit, but they wouldn't push their luck too far. They had seen him fight.

"Agreed," said another man, "this hellish heat is enough to drive any sensible man to the ale-pot. Why in God's name has the Emperor sent us to this hellish desert? The Isaurians won't come down from their hills to fight, and we can't go up there to look for them. Strange kind of war, if you ask me."

There were some murmurs of assent. The men spoke in low voices, so their officer, Wulfila, wouldn't overhear them. He rode well to the front, ten paces ahead of his men. The red light of the dying sun reflected off his hauberk of scale mail, and the silver pommel of his sword. His head, covered by a crested helmet with cheek-pieces, swung constantly from side to side. Wulfila was clearly nervous, mindful of ambush.

Medraut also wore a shirt of mail, though the rest of his comrades had to make do with leather tunics. He had grown used to their jealous glances. None would dare to try and rob him.

The mail, and his exceptionally fine long-bladed sword, were his own gear rather than standard army issue. They were gifts from Clovis, King of the Franks, presented to Medraut as a reward for good service.

The Frankish court, where he had grown to manhood, was half a world away. Britannia, the native land he abandoned when young, even further. Medraut, child of one king and favourite of another, had abandoned his heritage and chosen to wander the world as a mercenary, a common sword-for-hire.

After years of campaigning and rootless wandering in Frankia, Germania and Italy, he had fallen in among the Goths, and joined a contingent of foederati. A gift for languages helped him settle in among the Germanic warriors, who eventually accepted the quiet, dark-haired foreigner as one of their own.

Ten years of military service had honed his instincts to a keen edge. "We are being tracked," he said, "I suggest we ride on swiftly, or turn to face our hunters."

His warning fell on deaf ears. "Anastasius is an old woman," grunted Euric, "how old is he, anyway? Sixty? Seventy? He won't last long. The empire needs a young man on the imperial throne. A proper soldier.

Anastasius was the new Emperor of the East. He had recently succeeded Zeno, a native of Isauria. During his reign Zeno had promoted many of his countrymen into high office, but since his death Anastasius had stripped the Isaurians of rank and expelled them from Constantinople, the imperial capital.

The Isaurians resented this rough treatment, and a number of them had returned to the desolate wilds of their homeland, where they were suspected of plotting rebellion. Hence the presence of increased numbers of imperial troops on the Isaurian frontier, most of them foederati.

"Watch your tongue, Euric," said Wulfila, who had finally overheard some of the conversation, "else I might be obliged to cut it out. To speak ill of the Emperor is a serious crime. I will overlook it, this time."

Medraut winced. To threaten Euric, especially out here, where Wulfila had no means of enforcing his authority, was a mistake. The famed discipline of the Roman legions was long gone, and sensible officers were deaf and blind to the excesses of their men.

"Overlook it, will you?" hissed Euric, "that's generous of you, sir. Very generous. Or maybe I can't take that risk."

He placed his big hand on his sword. His comrades looked at Euric in alarm - they would all be implicated if he drew steel on a superior officer - and Medraut quietly brought his horse to a halt. If a fight broke out, he didn't intend to be caught in the middle of it.

His instincts still nagged at him. While Euric and Wulfila faced each other, he twisted to study the craggy rise of land behind them.

Shadows flitted among the boulders and scattered thorn bushes. The patrol had ventured a little way into the foothills, and the landscape to the east undulated in a series of barren curves. Further east, hidden somewhere among the mountains and valleys, was Isaura Vetus, the capital of Isauria. It was said to be a hilltop stronghold, more like the hill-forts of Medraut's homeland than a civilised town.

The patrol had been ordered to venture a little way into the hills, to show that Roman troops were not afraid to enter Isaurian territory. At first sight of the enemy, they were to withdraw. Armed clashes should be avoided until the Emperor had officially declared war on the rebellious province.

Medraut and his comrades hadn't glimpsed a single Isaurian. Even so, he was certain the Isaurians were watching them. The mountains offered endless hiding places and vantage points, especially to native-born people who knew them well. Medraut had fought alongside Isaurians before, and knew them for tough, resourceful hillmen, expert scouts and light infantry.

"Settle down, Euric," said Wulfila, "you've already said enough to earn a set of fresh stripes on your back. Don't make it worse."

Medraut heard the note of fear in his voice. The officer was very much alone, surrounded by men who might turn against him at any moment. His life hung in the balance.

He should have killed Euric by now, thought Medraut, *Euric is the threat. Remove him, and the others will fall into line.*

"Listen to him, Euric," said another of the Goths, "see sense, man. You'll get us all hanged."

"Craven," spat Euric. He ripped out his sword.

"I'm going to kill you, you little turd," he sneered at Wulfila, "and leave your body for the wolves. We'll tell the centurion you were killed in an ambush."

Wulfila uttered a nervous laugh. "Don't be so fucking stupid. Even the most halfwitted centurion wouldn't bel-"

He got no further. A slender black dart flew out of the shadows and hit him in the eye. Wulfila flung a hand up to his face, coughed, and toppled backwards off his horse. He landed heavily and rolled in the dust, tangled up in his cloak.

"Beware!" shouted Medraut, who had already wheeled his horse and slid down to take cover behind her.

The Goths scattered. A storm of darts and javelins and stones erupted from the dark. Medraut heard screams, a foul Germanic oath or two, and strange voices raised in anger.

Isaurians: he knew the accent, and could speak a little of their tongue. He pictured their slingers and javelin-men crouching among the rocks, lean and barefoot, clad only in light tunics or cloaks. They had probably tracked the patrol for miles, waiting for the right time to spring an ambush.

Medraut recalled a patch of wiry vegetation to his right. He seized his horse's reins in both hands and dragged her towards it, careful to keep her body between him and the enemy.

"Come out from your holes, you hill-rats, and face us!"

Euric's voice, thick with rage. Medraut glimpsed his giant form bound towards the rocks, battle-axe in hand. A stone rebounded off his helmet, two darts skipped past his feet, another stuck into his round shield.

Medraut's horse whickered and fought against him, almost tearing the reins from his hands as she tried to twist her head free. He abandoned her and leaped clumsily into the bushes. His mail protected him from the worst of the thorns, though they ripped through the wool of his braccae and scratched his legs.

He lay sprawled on his front, shield covering his head and upper body, gathering breath while the fight raged. Euric had broken into a war-chant, and his guttural voice mingled with the high voices of the Isaurians, the thump of metal on wood and the frightened neighs of horses.

Had the rest of the patrol fled? Unlikely. Gothic soldiers were not given to panic, and would never abandon a comrade. Or so they liked to boast.

Medraut crawled to the edge of the bushes and strained his eyes to see through the gloom. He saw Euric engaged with at least four other men. The hot-tempered Goth's axe caught the last rays of the sun as it swung down and chopped into the neck of an Isaurian hillman. Blood and filth spattered the barren ground as the blade cleaved his victim almost to the waist.

More shapes flickered among the scattered outcrops of loose rock. Medraut had no idea how many Isaurians there were. The rest of his comrades had fled into the night, all save Wulfila, who lay dead with a dart in his eyeball.

Medraut was blessed with sharp hearing. He overheard stealthy footsteps to his right, and realised the Isaurians must have seen him take cover.

He rose swiftly, ignoring the pain in his bleeding legs, and charged at the noise. A shape reared before him. He rammed his shield at it, and was rewarded by a stifled yelp as the iron shield-boss crunched against flesh and bone.

The shape dropped away. Medraut surged forward, stamped down hard on a man's stomach, stabbed with his sword as another silhouette sprang at him.

His blade lashed at empty air. He cried out as pain flared above his left eye. A spear had blunted itself against the iron rim of his helmet. Isaurian curses raged in his ears.

Medraut was too close for another thrust, so he punched with his sword-hilt. Another yell, and the crack of broken teeth. His opponent staggered away, hands pressed against the ruin of his mouth.

"Briton! Briton, to me! Help me, in God's name!"

Euric's voice. Medraut spun around and saw the Goth on his knees, shield raised to fend off a swarm of Isaurians. His sword was wrenched out of his hand, buried in a dead hillman's chest.

Medraut didn't hesitate: if Euric was slain, he would never fight his way out of this. He ran straight at the Isaurians, screaming to get their attention.

Three turned to meet him. They were barefoot, half-naked, armed with spears and long knives. The nearest hurled his spear, a deadly accurate throw that flew over the rim of Medraut's shield and slammed against his shoulder.

His mail saved him. The spear rebounded off the close-forged iron links. He lunged at the nearest man, cursed when his sword failed to make contact, parried a knife-thrust on his shield.

By now it was almost too dark to see. Medraut fought by instinct, parried a spear aimed at his legs, turned, cut, used the shield for attack and defence. Blows hammered against the timber. A knife flashed past his guard and opened a shallow cut on the back of his hand.

Medraut kept his head down, restrained the urge to lose himself in a battle-frenzy. If he threw caution aside, the lightly armed Isaurians would dance around him, cut him down like a mad bull.

*Patience....*the word turned over and over in his head, guarded him against fatal loss of control.

He had forgotten Euric. With a shout, the Goth dived at one of Medraut's attackers, seized his waist in an iron grip and dragged him to the ground. The Isaurian was barely half Euric's size and weight, and struggled in vain to escape as the huge warrior pinned him down.

Encouraged, Medraut aimed a savage cut at one of his remaining opponents. It knocked the man's knife from his hand. He sprang back, unarmed and defenceless. He looked to his comrade for aid, but the other Isaurian had seen enough and took to his heels, casting aside his spear.

Medraut was close enough to see the look of dismay on the last Isaurian's bronzed features. They twisted into a grimace of terror and pain when Medraut stepped forward and drove his sword deep into the man's heart.

He wrenched the sword free and nodded in satisfaction as the body crumpled to earth. A clean kill, with a parade-ground thrust even the harshest drillmaster might have admired.

"Euric," he said.

His comrade didn't respond. Euric had ripped off his helmet and was using it to beat the brains from the Isaurian he had dragged to the ground. He worked in furious silence, eyes bulging, spittle drooling from his clenched teeth.

He was clearly enjoying himself, so Medraut left him to it and took stock. The Isaurians had gone and left four of their number dead. Medraut's comrades had gone too. He and Euric were alone.

Not quite alone. A whinny sounded through the dark. He spied the bulky shape of his horse, trotting warily towards him.

Medraut was relieved to see her. With luck, Euric's horse would also be somewhere nearby.

"If you've quite finished," he said to Euric, once the other man's rage was spent, "we should return to camp."

Two hours later, Medraut stood outside the prefect's hut and listened calmly to Euric's description of events.

"These craven bastards abandoned us!" his comrade howled, jabbing his finger at the men who had fled the ambush, "ran away like a pack of frightened old women, and left me and the Briton to die!"

The other Goths looked nervous. They had been summoned from their beds by the prefect, who in turn had received conflicting reports from the centurion in charge of Medraut's company.

"These men told me that Medraut and Euric were dead, sir," said the centurion, "as well as their officer, Wulfila. Killed in an ambush earlier this evening."

The prefect, himself a Goth, stroked his greying beard. "I see. And then Medraut and Euric rode in, alive and whole.

Well, well."

He turned sharply on Medraut. "Does Euric speak the truth?" he demanded, "did your comrades flee, and leave you to die?"

Medraut felt the eyes of the Goths burn into him. Their fate depended on what he said next.

"Yes, sir," he replied, "every word is true."

The prefect chose to believe the testimony of Medraut and Euric, and confined their comrades to barracks. Come the dawn, they would be marched out in front of the rest of the company, and flogged as punishment for their cowardice.

"Discipline has gone to hell," remarked Euric, "in the old days, Roman soldiers were executed for showing cowardice in face of the enemy. I tell you, Briton, we abandon the old ways at our peril."

Medraut smiled mirthlessly. The two men sat around a small fire, eating a late supper of bread and beans.

The fire was an oasis of light in a sea of darkness. Other than the occasional neigh of a horse in the stables, or the low voices of sentries on the stockade, the camp was silent.

"You're a strange one," said Euric through a mouthful of bread, "you saved my life tonight, yet said nothing of it to the centurion."

Medraut, who had been staring into the west, stirred from his reverie. "I'm not the type to boast," he replied.

"Boasting be damned. You could have got a promotion out of it. You want to be an ordinary ranker all your life?"

Medraut shrugged. "I served as a junior cavalry officer under the Franks," he said indifferently, "and prefer the life of a common soldier. Promotion and high rank hold no special appeal for me."

"Why did you join the army, then?" asked Euric, "to fight and kill, nothing more?"

"No. I wanted to see something of the world. I wanted to serve in the greatest army in the world. I wanted to watch, and learn, and one day be good enough."

Euric raised a hairy eyebrow. "Good enough? For what?"

"Good enough to go home, raise an army, and kill my father."

Medraut's usually dull, neutral voice quivered with passion. His words were followed by a long silence, broken only by the sound of Euric's jaws finishing off the last of his meal.

"That's an evil ambition, lad," he said at last, brushing crumbs from his moustache, "God knows my father was no saint, but I never wished harm on the old goat."

Medraut smiled blandly at him.

"Did your father murder your mother?" he asked.

8.

Hibernia

Drystan bared his teeth in savage joy as the blade of his spear sank into the boar's hindquarters.

A squeal of agony echoed through the autumn woods. Snorting, blood mingled with the foam cascading down its tusks, the boar put its head down and charged at Drystan's pony.

Three broken-off spears were already stuck into the boar's hide, like the spines of a monstrous hedgehog. One of King Niall's young warriors lay nearby. He moaned in pain as blood pooled from deep slashes in his belly. Two wolfhounds sprawled about him, their backs broken.

Cornered by the huntsmen, the wounded boar had made a sudden charge from its den. His speed took the youth and his dogs by surprise. The beast had gored all three before Drystan could reach them.

He wheeled his pony aside, just in time. The boar missed by inches and skidded down a steep bank thickly carpeted with fallen leaves. It came to rest at the bottom, throwing up a great wave of loose soil as its hoofs scrabbled for purchase.

Drystan paused. Hunting horns sounded in the distance, along with the frenzied barking of wolfhounds. The rest of the hunt was near, but this was his kill. King Niall had staged the boar-hunt, both to gather fresh meat and provide entertainment for his guests from Kernow.

The boar shook itself and stood at bay, little red eyes glaring up at its enemy. Drystan carried no bow, and had run out of spears.

His fingers curled about the grip of his sword. Only a fool attacked a fully grown boar with a sword. Spears and arrows were the tools for the job. Keep the animal at a distance, away from his slashing tusks and brute strength.

On the other hand, this one was badly wounded. If left long enough, he would probably limp away somewhere to bleed to death.

"You deserve a better death," said Drystan, "an honourable death. You shall have it."

He slid off his pony's back and gave her a pat on the rump. She cantered away, nostrils flaring with the stink of the boar, eyes rolling with fear.

Drystan warily drew his sword. He half-expected the boar to launch another of its sudden charges, one last effort before pain and loss of blood robbed him of his strength.

"God help me..." he heard the wounded youth cry, "the pain...I am dying...help me...help me..."

Drystan chewed his lip. To venture down into that shallow gully was to seek death. It was madness. He had seen wounded boar kill even the most seasoned huntsmen in Kernow. Far better to wait for his companions to catch up. They could finish the brute off with a flight of arrows.

No-one would blame him for hanging back. He had already proved his courage by rescuing the youth. Why risk his life in such a pointless manner? A life of such promise, with a golden future only just opening up before him?

Esyllt's face seemed to hover before him. The sad grey

eyes, the mocking little smile. What would she say, if he failed to slay the boar? Would she say anything, or merely look disappointed, and shun his company?

He had only known her a short time, yet already come to fear her moods. The lash of her tongue. After barely a fortnight at her father's court - longer than he needed to stay - he was already her slave, and knew it.

Thus far, she didn't seem to share his belief in their entwined fate. At the hall-feast she had been merely polite. He noticed, however, how she followed him since, and liked to watch him spar against her father's warriors.

His friend Goron thought it shameful for a man of Kernow to lose his head and heart to a Hibernian princess. Drystan cared little. Only Esyllt mattered. He would win her praise or die.

"Esyllt!" he cried, and half-slid, half-ran down the bank.

The boar backed away, blood trickling down its flanks and hindquarters. It was unsteady, and its back legs shook as Drystan leaped.

He aimed to drive his sword down, through the nape of the boar's neck. It dodged aside. His blade slithered down its haunch and opened a fresh wound.

Drystan landed heavily. Before he could roll away the boar was on top of him. Its raw animal stench filled his throat, made him gag, his head swim. Blood and drool spattered his face. Little red eyes glared down at him, full of pain and malice, jaws gaped wide, exposing jagged yellow teeth.

Roaring wordlessly, Drystan reached up and seized the boar's tusks. If they ripped into him, he was dead.

Even in its weakened state, the beast was foully strong. Drystan's arms shook, muscles and tendons creaking, as he fought to keep its head upright. Hoofs like spears scrabbled at his tunic, gouged holes in the leather and ripped through his skin.

The ground shook under him. Cries of alarm sounded in

his ears, above the muffled grunts and growls of the boar.

"Get him out!" he recognised the voice of King Niall, "kill the boar, quickly, and get him out!"

Shadows fell over man and beast. The squat, muscular body pinning Drystan to the earth gave a shudder, and another, as more spears were driven into its flesh. The boar's dying squeals were torment to hear. Drystan gasped and twisted his head to the left, blinded by a torrent of hot blood.

The boar went into its death-spasm. It was rolled off Drystan by Niall's huntsmen, who helped Drystan to his feet and held him steady while he waited for his head to clear.

"Fool!" shouted Niall, "do you wish for death? If the animal had slain you, what should I have said to your father?"

He wrung his bony-knuckled hands. "It would have meant war. King Marcus is not a man to forgive the death of a servant, even if it was an accident."

Drystan shook off the men holding his arms and wiped the blood and dirt from his face. "I did it for the honour of your daughter, lord king," he panted, "and to save one of your young spearmen. The boy lies yonder, gashed in the stomach."

"Tonight, at the hall-feast," he added, "I would like the boar's tusks presented to Esyllt as a gift from me."

Niall looked at him uneasily. "It shall be as you say," he replied after a long pause.

The hunting party made its way back to the ringfort, with the body of the kill dangling from a pole and carried by four burly huntsmen. Drystan, whose wounds were slight, rode proudly beside King Niall, while the wounded youth was carried in the rear on a stretcher.

Drystan ignored the old king's silence. His thoughts were full of Esyllt. He pictured her delight when presented with the tusks. How she would look at him with new eyes, full of awe and admiration.

That night, Drystan insisted that Esyllt sit next to him at high table. He was aware of the rumours swirling around Niall's court, and the suspicious looks the king's warriors gave him.

Drystan ignored the danger. "Let the whole world come in arms," he whispered to Esyllt as they shared a platter of fresh-baked bread and soft white cheese, "and I would put them all to defiance. For you."

Esyllt avoided his gaze. "You are brazen tonight," she murmured, "are you not afraid? No, I can see you are not. Killing a pig has made you bold."

Their fair heads were close together, so none, not even her father, could hear what passed between them. A stranger might have mistaken them for brother and sister. Esyllt, the more cautious of the two, kept her eyes on her plate, while Drystan gazed at her with undisguised adoration.

"Did you not appreciate my gift?" he asked, "the boar's tusks. I faced the brute in single combat, all for your sake."

She grimaced. "Mine? I don't recall asking you to risk your life for my sake."

Drystan was dismayed by her lack of gratitude. "Do you harbour a grudge for the death of Morholt?" he asked, "I'm sorry if it caused you grief. He was a good fighter. Better he died by the sword, rather than wait for the slow disgrace of old age. Your father has forgiven me."

Esyllt chewed slowly on a morsel of cheese. "No," she said at last, "I don't bear a grudge. I liked my uncle, but the news of his death came as no surprise. He would never have made old bones, and had no wish to."

"Your father was very shrewd to send you against him," she added with a little smile, "I've watched you spar. You're quick. Quicker than any of my father's warriors. They are frightened of you. Otherwise..."

He frowned. "Otherwise what?"

"Otherwise they might have already spoken against you.

You stay too long, Drystan. You attend me too closely. I've heard your own warriors say as much. We must depart for Kernow."

Drystan sat back and exchanged a curt nod with King Niall, who looked hurriedly down at his plate. Drystan suspected his host's partial deafness was a sham, and that Niall could hear every word.

Thank God the old fool is a weakling, he thought, *another man would have torn my guts out by now.*

Drystan turned back to Esyllt. "You seem eager to wed my father," he said bitterly.

"I am betrothed to King Marcus," she replied, "our wedding will heal a rift between two kingdoms. It is only right I want to marry him."

She glanced at Drystan from under long lashes. "You seem to have little regard for your father."

"He was never a father to me," he replied grimly, "until I knelt before him and offered to fight Morholt, he didn't even acknowledge me as his own flesh and blood. He has bastards littered all over Kernow. I expect he can't even remember my mother's name. Just another slave he used and cast aside."

"He will use you as well, Esyllt. Treat you as a broodmare, and kill you with children. That's all he wants. Sons, and plenty of them. God help you if you fail. His last wife died of sheer neglect."

"I know," she said quietly, "it is the fate of many women, especially those of noble birth. Perhaps it will be mine as well."

The sadness in her voice lit a flame inside Drystan. "Lord king," he said, turning quickly to Niall, "I have spent too long at your court, enjoying the fruits of your generosity. I will sail for my homeland two days from now."

Niall looked both gratified and suspicious. "As you wish," he replied cautiously, "I should be sorry to lose my daughter, but on the other hand I gain an ally."

"My thanks, lord king," Drystan replied with a smile, "before I depart, I ask permission to hunt in your forests once more. The hunting in your realm is the best I have known."

The king raised his bushy eyebrows. "Another hunt? Have you not had your fill after today? That boar almost killed you. It is never wise to push one's good fortune too far, young man."

"I believe in the fates," retorted Drystan, "and it is not my fate to fall victim to a beast of the forest. If you prefer, I will take my followers into the woods. Yours can remain here. No blame will fall on you if I suffer an accident."

Niall backtracked, as Drystan knew he would. "Of course you may hunt," he said, "and my men shall go with you. It would be a slur on my hospitality otherwise."

The huntsmen rode out the next morning. Niall, who was taken ill in the night, didn't accompany them. Instead he sent ten warriors and four pairs of his best wolfhounds with their handlers.

On Drystan's request, he also sent Esyllt. She brought her companions, Golwg and Ronan, and two spearmen for an escort.

"Watch the hunt from a safe distance, my lady," said Drystan as they trotted through the sun-dappled woods.

"I'm not afraid of a little blood," she replied tartly. "the women of your country must be very pampered creatures. I have ridden out to hunt myself, many times, and am a fair shot with the bow."

He grinned, and restrained the urge to kiss her. Her eyes were full of mockery, as though daring him to do it.

Drystan had brought twelve of his own followers. These were the men he trusted most, personal friends he had grown up alongside at Caer Y Brenin. The rest were left behind at the ringfort.

It didn't take long for the dogs to pick up a scent. Their handlers struggled to keep up as the lean, hairy beasts crashed through the undergrowth, panting and straining at the leash.

The huntsmen spread out and followed at a canter. Once the dogs had flushed out the quarry - a fine stag, perhaps, or another boar - they would give chase.

"Stay to the rear," Drystan said to Esyllt, "I beg you."

"If you insist," she replied with bad grace, "but I resent being treated like a child. I hope your father is not so tender of me."

Drystan nodded at her spearmen. "Make sure your mistress keeps her distance," he said curtly.

With that, he wheeled his pony and rode back to the hunt. The other horsemen had galloped well ahead. For a short time he was alone in the forest.

He had a moment to take stock. His flesh prickled with sweat, and his breath came in short gasps. His heart beat too fast. Drystan could seldom recall being so nervous and excited, not even before the duel against Morholt.

Am I afraid? Perhaps. I must embrace the fear. Let it pass through me. Fear is good, if used as a weapon. It sharpens the wits.

He urged his pony into a gallop, careless of the obstacles in his path. She leaped a fallen tree and plunged through a shallow marsh. Low-hanging branches, like bundles of dead fingers, whipped at his face. Drystan ducked and guided her onto a wide heath.

The dogs were lost somewhere among the trees to the west. He could hear their frenzied barks, and the shouts of the handlers. It sounded as though they had flushed out their quarry.

Drystan's quarry was just ahead. King Niall's warriors were scattered about the heath, waiting for their prey to emerge.

The warriors of Kernow were drawn up in two groups behind them. Goron, in command of the larger group, twisted in the saddle and raised his spear to greet Drystan.

Now! The signal!

Drystan reined in, raised his hunting horn to his lips and blew a single high, pure note.

The echoes had scarcely died away before his men struck. Goron was the first to kill, hurling a spear into the back of the nearest Scotti warrior. His victim jerked in the saddle, screamed, and lurched sideways out of the saddle. He hit the ground and thrashed about like a dying fish, the spear firmly embedded in the middle of his spine. Goron drew his hatchet and galloped at another of the Scotti, face purple with battle-rage.

"Kernow!" he roared, "Kernow!"

The rest of Drystan's followers dispersed and set about the Scotti, each man choosing his target. Screams and curses erupted all over the heath as spears and axes bit deep. Taken unawares, a few of Niall's warriors stood their ground. Others wheeled their ponies and were chased into the woods.

Drystan had planned this treachery during the night, while King Niall and his household slept. His love for Esyllt, his aching desire to take her for himself, drove him to it. Goron, whose hatred for the Uí Liatháin equalled Drystan's passion, agreed to the cold-blooded murder of Niall's warriors, and the abduction of his daughter.

"Revenge," he growled when Drystan suggested the plan to him in the privacy of their quarters, "revenge at last, for the wounds these savages have inflicted on us over the years."

Drystan watched the slaughter for a moment, then turned and rode back the way he had come. He found Esyllt just as she and her escort reached the edge of the marsh.

"Drystan," she cried, "what's happening? Are we ambushed?"

Her obvious fear and distress made his heart turn over. "No ambush," he said gently, "but you must come with me. Bring your maid, and the priest if you wish. You two, dismount and lay down your weapons."

He spoke to her guards. Instead of obeying they rode forward to block his path.

"We will take Princess Esyllt back to her father," said one.

Metal hissed on leather as Drystan drew his sword. The massacre still raged behind him. He could hear Goron's voice raised in song. His friend always gloried in bloodshed.

"Do as I say," he ordered in a soft voice, "or die."

The nearest spearman charged. Drystan wrenched his pony to the left, ducked to avoid the jab of the spear, and stabbed at the other pony's head.

His blade cut open a deep gash on the beast's muzzle. She shrieked and bucked in agony, causing her rider to lose his grip on the reins. Drystan stabbed again. His sword plunged through the spearman's leather tunic, slid through flesh and muscle and punctured his heart.

Even as he dragged the sword free, the second of Esyllt's guards came at him. There was a scream - it came from Golwg - when spear and sword clashed.

The spear-thrust was aimed at Drystan's throat. He parried it in time to save himself, but the blade dug into his shoulder and drew blood. Drystan ground his teeth against the pain and hacked at the shaft. It broke under the weight of his keen sword-edge, leaving the owner holding a useless stump.

Drystan urged his pony forward and aimed a terrific cut at his opponent's face. The blade carved the man open from brow to chin and sliced through one of his eyes.

He howled and bent low over his pony's mane. His blood spattered the ground. The smell of it caused the animal to panic. She bolted and carried her wounded rider through the marsh into the trees.

"Now, my lady," panted Drystan as the sound of wild hoofbeats died away, "I have slain two good men for you."

Golwg threw herself in front of Esyllt. The sallow-faced

priest, Ronan, tumbled off his pony and stood between Drystan and the women, his arms spread wide.

"You will have to kill me too," he said, his voice quavering, "dare you slay a man of God, Drystan of Kernow? Your soul is already imperilled by this day's work."

Drystan's patience snapped. He trotted forward, kicked Ronan in the face and sent him flying backwards into a patch of reeds.

"Don't kill him!" cried Esyllt, "not the holy man! Please, let him be - let him be and I shall come with you."

Drystan took in a deep breath and sheathed his sword. Gradually, the frantic pulse of his heart slowed. The battle-fury lifted from his mind.

He opened his eyes again and smiled at Esyllt.

"As you wish, my love," he said.

9.

Caerleon

Gwenhwyfar sat her with her hands folded in her lap, and waited.

She and her husband were in the hall of the old Roman governor's palace at Caerleon. It usually served for an audience chamber, where Artorius received important guests.

Today, on a chill afternoon in early October, the hall was empty save for the royal couple and a half-witted slave boy sweeping the floor. The boy's mouth hung open as he swept dust and bits of food from the patterned tiles.

The queen watched him with mounting irritation. "Oh, in Christ's name," she snapped at last, "there's nothing left to sweep, boy. Do you mean to wear away the floor? Take your broom and clean out the kennels."

He stopped and looked mournfully at her. "Kennels were cleaned out this morning, Majesty," he mumbled.

Gwenhwyfar bared her teeth at him. "Then make useful yourself somewhere else! Go!"

He bowed hurriedly and scurried out, almost tripping over the broom in his haste. Dust motes fell from the rafters as the door slammed shut behind him.

"That was harsh," Artorius said after a moment, "Peredur tries his best."

He sounded distracted. For the past hour he had been fighting his way through a letter. Artorius disliked reading, and usually had a clerk read out his correspondence.

This letter was too important for the eyes of any common clerk. It came from Marcus, King of Kernow, and had been delivered by a messenger half-dead with fatigue. Gwenhwyfar, who hated secrets being kept from her, was desperate to know the content.

She glanced at her husband. He held the letter inches before his face, squinting as he slowly traced the letters with his index finger.

"Give it to me," she said irritably, "I'll read it for you in a trice."

Artorius ignored her. Sighing, she rested her head against the back of the chair and tried to relax.

The hall was pleasantly warm, thanks to the hypocaust. Outside was cold and grey, and she could hear the shrill cries of young warriors sparring on the drill-ground.

One of them was her son, Amhar. He was almost ten years old now, tall and fearsomely strong for his age, a worthy son to the victor of Mount Badon. Amhar already displayed the qualities of a natural leader, and most of the boys he sparred with looked up to him.

Only Gwenhwyfar and her husband knew that he was not Artorius' son. Amhar's real father was Diwrnach, the Scotti warlord known as the Twrch Trwyth. Ten years ago Diwrnach had captured and raped Gwenhwyfar, planting his bastard in her belly before Artorius could rescue her.

Diwrnach paid dearly for his crimes. His body was cut

to pieces and thrown into a river, while his oversized skull still decorated the wall of the Round Hall.

Gwenhwyfar tried to will away the memories. Even now, a decade on, they haunted her dreams. She was also terrified of the horrors that might befall if the truth of her son's parentage ever became widely known.

Artorius would be exposed as a cuckold. His enemies always probed for weakness, and such a revelation would turn him into a laughing-stock. His reputation, the chief pillar of his authority, would suffer a fatal blow. Gwenhwyfar, meanwhile, would be pilloried as a whore, even though she was the victim of rape. As for the boy...

She gave an involuntary shudder. Whatever the fate of his parents, Amhar's life would not be worth a straw. His only hope would lie in exile, or perhaps the church, where his father's enemies could not reach him.

Artorius' voice interrupted these gloomy thoughts. "Ambrosius insisted I learn to read," he grunted, resting the letter on his lap and wiping his eyes. "God knows why. A painful, wearisome and dull occupation, fit only for monks and clerks."

"Would you rather be illiterate?" snapped Gwenhwyfar, "the ability to read and write is what separates us from barbarians. From the beasts who would steal our land and make us slaves."

Artorius kneaded his brow. "Perhaps," he replied mildly, "though I am told Cerdic has taught himself letters. Clever man. He knows the power of words. What if he abandoned his old gods and chose to embrace Christ? Many of his followers would be forced to do the same, and then the Saxons will be fellow Christians rather than barbaric heathens. The Pope would have to acknowledge Cerdic as a Christian king. His people would become respectable in the eyes of the church. God help us."

"Cerdic is capable of it," he mused, "even if he didn't believe it. Anything to gain an advantage."

Gwenhwyfar looked at him in exasperation. Lately Artorius had developed a tendency to wander off the point and lose himself in idle speculation.

She thought the strain of kingship was beginning to tell. Her husband was barely forty-one, though he looked more like fifty. Few men lived beyond their fiftieth year, especially fighting men who carried as many old wounds as Artorius.

His weakness frightened her. Her security, the security of her son, and the kingdom in general, depended on him living a few more years. Neither of his true sons, by his dead concubine Ganhumara, were ready to assume power.

"The letter," she reminded him in a more gentle voice, "what does King Marcus have to tell us?"

He gave a start, and glanced down at the roll of stained parchment on his lap. "Oh, Marcus has made a fool of himself. Do you remember him, my dear? He came to a meeting of the Round Table last winter."

Gwenhwyfar remembered Marcus of Kernow well enough. A small, compact, rat-like man with dead eyes and a neatly trimmed little beard. He said little at the meeting - he was in the lowest rank of kings, being sub-king to Erbin of Dumnonia, himself sub-king to Artorius - but Gwenhwyfar had sensed an air of danger about the man. He was said to be intelligent and learned, and there were nasty rumours that he had murdered his brother, King Bedouin.

"What folly has he committed?" she asked.

"He has managed to stumble into a war against one of his bastard sons," replied Artorius, "a youth named Drystan. Marcus sent Drystan to Hibernia to fetch back a young bride. Instead the lad took it into his head to steal the girl for himself, slaughter her guards and carry her off to sea. She is very beautiful, apparently. The kind of beauty men kill for."

"Like Creiddylad," said Gwenhwyfar. The princess of Rheged, whose beauty had caused the recent war in the north, was now one of the ladies of the queen's household. An amiable, if not terribly clever girl, she appeared to have little idea of the blood that had been spilled over her.

Artorius nodded. "Yes, just like Creiddylad. God's teeth! If this goes on I shall have to shelter every pretty young girl of royal blood under my own roof."

"Why has Marcus written to you? Does he expect you to help him chase down the fugitives?"

Her husband picked up the letter again and slowly folded it into a square. "Yes, though the situation is more complex than that. This will be no ordinary man-hunt. Drystan took ship and fled to Amorica, where he claimed sanctuary from King Budic. Budic granted it, and keeps the boy and his stolen princess at court."

"Yet Budic is kin to Marcus!" Gwenhwyfar exclaimed, "why would he choose to offend his cousin?"

"Perhaps because he doesn't trust Marcus," Artorius replied with a shrug, "who can blame him? No man with half a brain could trust Marcus, not even his own kin. *Especially* his own kin."

His eyes narrowed. "Drystan is also Budic's kin, after all, even if the boy is illegitimate. Perhaps the King of Amorica means to depose Marcus and replace him with a relative he can trust. One who is also in debt to him."

Gwenhwyfar mulled over all this. "Why hasn't Marcus asked Erbin of Dumnonia for aid? Erbin is over-king of Kernow."

"He has. A messenger was sent to Erbin's court as well as mine. Marcus is furious. I think his rage against Drystan has unbalanced him. He will happily bring about a war between Britannnia and Amorica, merely to salve his own pride. If I let him."

"Then don't," Gwenhwyfar said firmly, "tell him to clear up his own mess. The High King does not get involved with such trivial local matters."

Artorius shook his head. "No. I cannot simply ignore

the matter. Marcus must know I am his ally. He may be a lesser king, but it would be foolish to squander his goodwill. At the same time I have other matters to attend to. The situation in Rheged, for instance. Bedwyr's reports inform me that he can barely keep the rival factions from each other's throats. He requests more troops to keep the peace."

"More troops," he sighed, "everywhere, more troops are needed. If only I could whistle them up from the earth."

"How will you help Marcus, then?" asked Gwenhwyfar.

"I'll send a token force of Companions. I doubt they can be of much use - any war between Kernow and Amorica, if it comes, will be fought at sea - but at least Marcus will be assured of my friendship and support. A few of our younger warriors can go. They need experience of battle, real battle, away from the drill-ground."

He turned to smile wearily at her. "This long peace of ours threatens to make us soft. Perhaps a little war or two is no bad thing."

Gwenhwyfar approved of his strategy. Marcus was not important enough to waste too much effort on, though at the same time he had to be appeased.

"Who will lead them?" she asked, "not yourself, I assume. Cei?"

"No," replied her husband. "Cei is too valuable to be sent off on some fruitless mission to the wilds of Kernow. Besides, you know how proud he is. He would consider it an insult. The same goes for Gwalchmei."

Gwenhwyfar pursed her lips. She had little use for Gwalchmei, whom she regarded as a vain, strutting peacock. In her opinion he was fit for nothing save wenching, drinking and decking himself in gold jewels and trinkets, like a costly male whore.

She knew better than to say as much. Along with Cei and Bedwyr, Gwalchmei was one of Artorius' oldest friends. He loved these three men like brothers. She privately suspected him of keeping Cei and Gwalchmei at Caerleon, when they could be doing useful work elsewhere, simply to ease his loneliness.

God knows, she thought with a stab of bitterness, *he seldom looks for comfort from me.*

"Llwch Llemineawg," said Artorius, "he will lead the expedition to Kernow."

Gwenhwyfar stared at him. She knew all about her husband's suspicions of Llwch, and how Cei's agents had kept a close watch on the man in recent months.

"I know," Artorius went on, "there's no need to look at me like that. Llwch is a risk. However, he has done nothing to rouse suspicion of his loyalty since we returned from Rheged. I cannot see into his heart, so he must be tested. This business in Kernow gives me the perfect opportunity to do so."

Again, Gwenhwyfar could see the sense of it. "If he fails..." she began.

"There is little room for failure," he said brusquely, "all I require of Llwch is that he leads our young men to Kernow, aids King Marcus in any way he can, and returns, preferably with life and limb intact. That will be enough to persuade me of his loyalty."

"For now," he added, "until some sterner test arises."

Silence fell. He re-read the letter, while Gwenhwyfar mused on the cruel nature of kingship. Even old comrades, sword-brothers who had fought alongside Artorius for decades, were not above suspicion.

Even I am vulnerable, she thought, *would he hesitate to strike me down, if my loyalty was in question?*

Not for the first time, Gwenhwyfar bore in mind the fate of Ganhumara, left to drown on a rock in the middle of the sea, and shuddered.

10.

Kernow

The sea-mist had lifted. King Marcus rested one hand on the dragon-head prow of his galley, and peered out at the grey waters.

His little fleet, twelve single-masted longboats, bobbed gently at rest. There was no wind. The sails hung limply, and a light drizzle swept the decks. Silence reigned aboard each vessel.

Marcus looked west. Somewhere to the north-east, lost to sight, was the southern coast of his kingdom. His fleet had taken advantage of a strong wind to venture out in search of prey. So far they had seen nothing save a couple of fishing boats and the fin of an occasional dolphin.

The king was patient. A sailor from childhood, he knew the whims of the sea. Nodens was the most capricious god of all, and might equally choose to rescue a ship or hurl it onto a reef.

He crossed himself and breathed a silent prayer. Nodens was an ancient pagan god of the sea. A false god, he reminded himself. The priests said it was blasphemy to invoke his name, even in jest. Marcus was a devout Christian, in a conventional sort of way, and had no wish to provoke divine wrath. He had suffered enough ill-fortune of late.

The ocean was still. Flat grey calm stretched away in every direction. The mist continued to dissolve, revealing broad acres of water.

"There, lord king."

Carrow, captain of the king's guard, pointed his spear to the north-west. Marcus looked, and spotted three long, narrow shapes drifting sluggishly through the murk.

Marcus gave a nod of grim satisfaction. "Well done," he said, clapping Carrow on the shoulder, "your eyes are younger than mine."

God had rewarded Marcus for his prayer. The shapes were longboats, most likely Amorican, on their way back from Hibernia. They seemed content to drift in the calm, oblivious of the predators lurking nearby.

"Oars," whispered Marcus. Carrow passed the word to the warriors on the oar-benches. The steersman waved at the other boats, who in turn dipped their oars into the water.

"Three more ships lost, Budic," the king muttered to himself.

He spoke of his kinsman, King Budic of Amorica, who had declared war on Kernow. Budic's ships frequently went back and forth across the sea to Hibernia, to trade with his allies among the Hibernian kings. They carried messages, weapons, goods and supplies, along with gifts of treasure and slaves.

Marcus was not ignorant of the trade, and took to the sea in person to disrupt it, harrying and plundering enemy vessels whenever he found them. It heartened him to know that his enemies had given him a nickname: *Cunomorus*, or Hound of the Sea. The name was hard-earned. While he ceaselessly prowled the trade route with his fleet, his mariners and workmen laboured like ants to build more galleys and longboats.

The coasts of Kernow were guarded by peasant levies and all the men he could spare from his war-band, reinforced by troops sent by the King of Dumnonia. The High King himself had responded to Marcus' plea for aid by sending thirty of his Companions, led by Llwch Llemineawg. It comforted Marcus to know he had the support and friendship of these two greater kings.

His bitterness and hatred for Budic, until recently an ally, knew no bounds. The slack-witted fool had succumbed to the youthful charms of Drystan - Marcus' blood boiled at the mere thought of his bastard son - and given the boy shelter instead of sending him back to Kernow in chains.

Now the traitors conspired to destroy Marcus and bring ruin to his kingdom. The dotard King Niall of the Uí Liatháin, who ought to have helped Marcus defeat the man who had abducted his daughter and slaughtered his warriors, stood aside and did nothing. Marcus suspected he was afraid of angering his fellow kings in Hibernia, who profited greatly from trade with Amorica.

The oars found their rhythm. Marcus' longboats darted like sharks towards their prey. His oarsmen worked in brisk silence, and the boats swiftly fanned out until they rowed in line.

Marcus clung to the prow. His heart thrilled to the steady rise and fall of the boat as it surged beneath him, the taste of salt spray in his mouth, the thought of the treasures aboard the Amorican longboats.

Too late, the Amoricans saw the danger. He grinned as chaos broke out aboard their vessels. The oarsmen panicked. Several dived overboard rather than stay and wait for death.

Two of the longboats wallowed hopelessly, oars thrashing feebly, like the limbs of a dying insect. The crew aboard the third kept their heads and tried to veer away west, back towards Hibernia.

It was a brave effort, but futile. Marcus' boats were already closing in a circle around the Amoricans. Arrows started to fly across the water. The enemy crewmen were of little value. They would all be slain, their throats cut and bodies dumped in the sea.

Marcus measured the distance between himself and the nearest Amorican boat. Not far now. He could make out the faces of the crew, bearded and pale with fright. A little closer, and he could leap across the water, sword in hand.

"Please, lord king," said Carrow, "stay aboard while we deal with the crew. It makes no sense to risk your life in a sea-brawl."

Marcus laughed at the anxiety on his bodyguard's craggy, weather-beaten features. They had had this argument before, many times, and it always ended the same way.

"Let men say what they will of Marcus of Kernow," he

cried, "but let none call him coward. Attack!"

His boat gave a final burst of speed, and Marcus almost lost his balance as the dragon-head prow crashed against the Amorican's hull. Timbers crunched, shouts of fear and alarm went up, a javelin whipped past his ear. Marcus laughed again, drew his sword and leaped.

Some of the agility of youth had deserted him. The enemy deck rocked violently as he tumbled aboard her, feet slipping on the damp wood. He almost dropped his sword, and yelled in fear at the thought of the precious blade, which had taken his smith weeks to forge, vanishing into the sea - swallowed up by Nodens, in revenge for the tyranny of Christ.

Marcus threw himself forward and fell into the belly of the longboat. He landed face-down on a heap of boxes and packets sealed in oilskin, rolled onto his back, screamed as the shadow of an Amorican loomed over him.

The Amorican wielded a long-axe in both hands. Sunlight glinted off the curved blade as he raised it high and planted his foot on the king's chest. Pinned to the deck, Marcus was helpless to avoid the death-blow.

"Carrow!" he yelled, "save me!"

Steel flashed before his eyes. There was a a thump, a gurgle, and something warm and wet splattered over the king's face.

The death-blow failed to land. Marcus cautiously sat up, blinked, and rubbed blood away from his eyes. The Amorican lay at his feet, twitching violently. A spear was buried in the man's throat. His blood splashed over the oilskin packets and the timbers of the deck.

Carrow grasped the king's wrist and helped him to stand. "Good throw," Marcus panted, "the dog almost had me."

"I warned you, lord," said Carrow, "now stand back and let your men finish this."

He kept a tight grip on Marcus' arm as more warriors of

Kernow leaped aboard the boat. Hopelessly outnumbered, most of the Amoricans threw down their weapons and pleaded for mercy.

"Kill them all," said Marcus. His men obeyed with relish, and the clean sea air was filled with screams and gurgles as the Amorican sailors were butchered like sheep, their bodies thrown overboard.

When the slaughter was over, Marcus ordered his men to unwrap the cargo. They dragged out the larger of the boxes and used their daggers to cut through the oilskin, revealing an oblong, iron-bound chest.

The lid was sealed tight, but had no lock. Two of Marcus' warriors wrestled off the lid to reveal tightly packed bundles of arrows and spear-heads.

Marcus nodded. Just as he suspected. The boats carried weapons, newly-made from the look of them, either in exchange or as gifts to equip King Budic's army in Amorica.

They will equip my men now, he thought. The storehouses at Caer Y Brenin were full of plunder taken from Budic's ships in recent weeks - grain, weapons, wine, even a few precious gold rings and arm-bands. If Marcus could hold off the invasion of Kernow until the onset of winter, and inflict enough damage on Budic's fleet in the meantime, he might yet achieve a kind of victory.

His hands curled into fists. No victory would be complete until Drystan and Esyllt were handed over to him. He wanted the boy in chains, and the girl on her knees, begging forgiveness.

In fairness to Esyllt, she might have been abducted by force. Yet she had made no obvious attempt to escape from Budic's court. He suspected the young couple were lovers. The shame was almost too much for Marcus to bear. It was his own fault. He should have some sent an older, more trustworthy man to Hibernia instead of his treacherous son.

I must be fair, he reminded himself, *I shall withhold*

judgement from Esyllt. For now.

There can be no mercy for the boy, even though he is my son. Flesh of my flesh be damned. I shall hang him, and throw his body to my dogs.

These bitter thoughts occupied Marcus until he sighted the black cliffs of his homeland. A wisp of smoke curled into the sky from the roof of his hall at Caer Y Brenin. His stomach rumbled at the thought of the feast his slaves would have prepared to greet their master's return.

A horseman was waiting at the sandy bay, enclosed by high cliffs, where Marcus and his warriors disembarked. The man dismounted and knelt in the surf before Marcus.

"Lord king," he said, his face pale, "thank God you have returned. A war-band has landed in Kernow."

Marcus almost tore at his hair. The longboats were a ruse! Budic must have sent an invasion fleet to Kernow while Marcus played pirate and left his coastline defenceless.

"How many spears?" he demanded, "where are they? Does Budic lead them, or one of his captains?"

The messenger swallowed. "No, lord king," he replied, "they are led by your son, Drystan."

11.

Esyllt cast another handful of dry twigs onto the fire and looked into Drystan's eyes.

"Let me tell you the story," she said, "of two lovers in my homeland. Their names were Mider and Étain."

"I should love to hear it," replied Drystan.

They sat opposite each other, cross-legged, on a grassy headland overlooking the sea. It was evening, and the bloody orb of the sun cast a spectral crimson glow over the waves.

"Mider was a warrior of great renown," said Esyllt, "and dwelled in a golden-roofed hall at Brí Léith in Tethbae.

He loved a woman named Étain, whose beauty surpassed that of any other woman in Hibernia. Her father, King Ailill, refused to let Mider wed his daughter, for he considered Mider low-born, and not fit to marry a woman of such noble blood."

"Ailill was a fool," murmured Drystan, "old men have no power over the hearts of the young."

He reached for her hand. Esyllt pulled away and carried on with her tale. "Mider would not be denied," she said, "and one night he abducted Étain and carried her back to his house. Furious, Aillill sent a witch named Fúamnach to seek revenge. The witch struck Étain on the head with her staff, and turned the girl into a pool of water."

"Curse all hags and witches," said Drystan.

"The heat of the fire in Mider's hall was enough to make the water seethe and boil," Esyllt went on, "it evaporated, and turned into a worm. The worm then turned into a fly. A swollen, hideous red fly. The size of this fly was the size of the handsomest man in Hibernia, and the sound of its voice and the beat of its wings were sweeter than pipes and harps and horns. Its eyes glimmered like precious stones, and its colour and fragrance could satisfy the hunger and thirst of any man."

"Magnificent insect," remarked Drystan. Esyllt held up a finger to silence him. He snatched at her finger, but she pulled away again.

"Fúamnach was not done with her witchcraft. She summoned a great wind, that blew the fly out of the hall and forced it to wander the land, alone and wretched, for seven years. At last the strength of the fly failed, and it fell into a river, where a giant trout swallowed it."

"The trout was caught by one of Mider's slaves, who took it back to his master's hall to be served in a great hall-feast. At the height of the feast, the marvellous fish was presented to Mider at high table. He carved open its flesh with his knife, and the corpse of the fly fell out. Mider recognised it as Étain, the woman he had loved and lost. He uttered a terrible groan, and his heart broke inside him. Thus he died. Thus ends the tale of Mider and Étain."

Esyllt waited nervously for Drystan's response. He was silent for a time and looked out to sea, to the south-west.

Below them, in a hollow at the foot of the headland, Drystan's men had pitched camp. Their white tents were laid out in orderly rows, or as orderly as possible on such uneven ground. Fires glimmered to the north, where sentries kept careful watch on the unfamiliar countryside.

The camp was quiet. Somewhere a deep voice sang, an Amorican lament for lost homelands. Many of the Amorican soldiers were the sons of Britons who had fled Britannia during the days of Vortigern, to escape the fury of the Saxons and seek refuge across the sea.

Esyllt listened sadly to the lament. She, too, was homesick, and longed to see Hibernia again. In her heart she knew that would never happen.

"Why do you tell me these parables of death and despair?" asked Drystan, still looking out to sea, "tell me stories of warriors and battles, of glory and victory and high endeavour. I look to you for solace."

"I would give you wisdom instead," said Esyllt, "Mider angered those more powerful than himself, and paid the price for it."

"Yes, yes," he said irritably, "I do understand the point of the tale. I am Mider, and you are Étain."

He reached for her hand again, and this time caught it between his own.

"King Marcus has no hag to call upon," he said softly, placing her hand flat over his heart, "nor does the High King, or any of our enemies. The last witch in Britannia died years ago. You have heard the tale of Bedwyr and Morgana?"

Esyllt nodded. Even in Hibernia the bards sang of Bedwyr the One-Handed, how he spent years in search of the evil witch Morgana, and finally slew her in a cave, high in the mountains. Esyllt always felt sorry for Morgana, and suspected there was more to the tale than the bards cared to say.

"We should have stayed in Amorica," she said, "we were safe there, under King Budic's protection."

Drystan rose with a swiftness that startled her, and pointed out to sea. "Out there," he replied, "beyond the sight of man, are a collection of islands. I met your uncle Morholt on the largest of them, and slew him in single combat. No-one made me do it. I volunteered to fight him, for my sake, and the sake of my people."

He knelt before Esyllt. "I was raised to fight," he said earnestly, "to flee, and hide my head under foreign suns, is not my way. I won you by the sword. I will win Kernow as well, and slay my father, or die."

Esyllt said nothing. Drystan spoke as though she was his possession. She felt more like a prisoner. Since her abduction, Esyllt had rarely been out of his sight.

She should have hated him. Certainly she feared him, his unpredictable moods and firm belief that most problems could be resolved with the sword. He had slain her uncle, insulted her father and treacherously slain a number of King Niall's warriors.

Yes, she should have hated Drystan. Longed for his death. Plotted to murder or betray him at the first opportunity, in revenge for the blood he had spilled. The trouble he had caused.

Yet she did not hate him. Drystan had done it all for her. The force of his devotion, his passion, was undeniable. He had yet to lay a finger on her, save when she let him, when another man might have used her as he pleased. Esyllt was entirely in his power.

More than that, he offered her glory. Power. If she gave in to him, agreed to become his wife, he in turn had promised to make her a queen. The Queen of Kernow and

Dumnonia. He meant to conquer both kingdoms and unite them under his kingship.

"After that," he would say, "the whole of Britannia will lie at our feet. Why not? Artorius cannot live forever. He will have to offer us a share of his power, or risk war. Thousands of warriors will flock to my banner, the whole of the south-west. Kings and warlords shall beg for my friendship."

These were the wild dreams Drystan had indulged in during the weeks of exile in Amorica. Esyllt listened to them with amusement, and more than a little trepidation.

Now he had an opportunity to make his dreams flesh. King Budic had given him a few ships, and spearmen from the king's own war-band. Along with his own loyal followers, Drystan had a hundred men under his command.

A hundred men, to conquer two kingdoms. Esyllt thought the venture hopeless, but still insisted on accompanying Drystan to Kernow.

"The women of the Uí Liatháin do not stay at home when their menfolk go to war," she had said, "we ride with them, and share their fortunes."

Her maid, Golwg, also refused to stay behind. Esyllt wished Ronan was with them, to calm her fears and absolve her sins, but Ronan was far away in Hibernia. She last saw him lying in the mud of the woods near her father's court, yelling curses and imploring the Almighty to burn Drystan with holy fire.

He cursed in vain, and now she found herself in Kernow, swept along by a fair-haired youth who meant to conquer kingdoms with a handful of men. They had already won a little victory: the rabble of ill-armed peasant militia who ought to have opposed their landing had fled without striking a blow, and left the invaders free to camp on Kernow soil.

Drystan went down on one knee before her. Esyllt was used to the gesture, and steeled herself for what came next.

"Marry me," he implored, "become my wife, and I will make you High Queen of Britannia. You shall sit on a golden throne in Caerleon, in place of Gwenhwyfar, and receive tribute from Britons and Saxons alike."

"No," she replied with a shake of her head, "we shall not marry, until you place the head of Artorius himself at my feet."

His white teeth flashed in a quick grin. "Done!" he cried, "the High King's head at your feet, stuffed and garnished on a silver platter, with an onion in his mouth!"

Drystan seemed to fear nothing. At dawn he roused his followers and led them north, deep into enemy territory. He knew Kernow well, having roamed the kingdom all his life.

Esyllt and Golwg rode beside him. At first glance they looked like young men, brothers even, clad in the same leather tunics, woollen cloaks and braccae as Drystan's warriors, and carried light spears and shields. Their faces were half-hidden under leather helmets, and their fair hair flowed loose and unbound to their shoulders.

Drystan's first target was a village, some three miles inland. It nestled inside a hollow between two bare hills, eight or nine roundhouses and a timber church guarded by a fence of sharpened stakes.

Esyllt feared he meant to slaughter the inhabitants. Fortunately the village was deserted - perhaps the fleeing militia had passed this way, and brought word of the invasion - though a few wisps of smoke still rose through holes cut into the thatched roofs. The pasture around the village was stripped of livestock, and the cattle pens stood empty.

"This place was abandoned in a hurry," remarked Goron, Drystan's closest friend and second-in-command.

Esyllt gave him a suspicious look. She disliked Goron, and he in turn made obvious his hatred and contempt for her, and all her race. Squat, thickset and almost bald, with a few shreds of ginger hair clinging to his greasy scalp, the ugliness of his character was writ large on his face. His eyes were small and puckered, his nose an oft-broken mess of misshapen bone and cartilage, his mouth a narrow, thin-lipped gash, usually twisted in a sneer.

"Abandoned or not, we burn it," Drystan said firmly, "burn it to the ground. I want my father to see the smoke, and know his lands are being put to the torch."

Esyllt laid a hand on his arm. "His lands are yours, or soon will be," she said in a low voice, "the people who live here are your people. Will you dispossess them, destroy their houses, leave them with nothing?"

Drystan shivered under her touch. "I am here to conquer," he replied, "no conquest was ever achieved with kindness. When Kernow is mine, and I sit in my father's chair at Caer Y Brenin, there will be time enough to make the people love me. For now, they shall learn to fear my banner."

He twitched his reins and rode forward, down the slope to the village. His men followed. Goron winked hideously at Esyllt as he cantered after his master.

The village burned easily. Drystan and his men took brands from the fires that smouldered inside a few of the houses, and tossed them onto the thatch. The flames caught with terrifying swiftness, leaped from roof to roof and spread fast through the bone-dry wattle and daub.

Esyllt watched the hollow rapidly fill with smoke. Drystan's men fled for the safety of the hillside. A few of the stragglers were scorched, and dismounted to splash water on their faces and cough out the fumes.

"Are you satisfied?" she asked Drystan when he rode up to her. His handsome face was flushed, and there were mild burn marks on his hands.

"Not yet," he grinned, apparently deaf to her sarcastic tone, "this is only the start. By the time we're done, every village from here to Celliwig shall be lit up like a row of candles."

Esyllt pictured the desolation: the blackened villages and farmsteads, the pall of greasy black smoke hanging over the fair green landscape of Kernow, the misery of the people.

She knew what he hoped to achieve by it. Drystan had told her of his plans before they left Amorica. Eventually King Marcus would be forced to deal with Drystan and his band of raiders, and ride out in pursuit. While Marcus was distracted, King Budic of Amorica had promised to land in force and storm Caer Y Brenin.

With his chief stronghold in enemy hands, and his kingdom in flames, Marcus would be forced to surrender.

"I don't trust King Budic," she said, "I think he will wait until you and your father have destroyed each other, and then take Kernow for himself."

Drystan looked at her with adoration in his eyes, and gently stroked her cheek. The reek of smoke on his skin almost made her recoil.

"You see dangers everywhere, my love," he said, "has not Budic been a good friend to us? He took us into his house, gave us all we could wish for. Food, shelter, arms and men and ships."

Esyllt didn't reply. Budic had been generous, true, yet there was something something untrustworthy about the young King of Amorica, with his sheep's face and oily, soft-spoken manner. He had lavished praise on Drystan and Esyllt, ordered his bards to compose hymns to their youth, courage and beauty, made all kinds of grand promises.

There was nothing she could say to instil caution in Drystan. His war-band rode east and carved a trail of blood and fire through the heart of Kernow. They encountered little effective resistance: once, a band of militia made a stand at a river crossing. Their shield-wall held firm against a hail of spears and javelins, until Drystan sent Goron upriver with a troop of Amoricans to find another crossing.

Esyllt prayed Goron would fail, and disgrace himself in

the eyes of his friend. Instead he took his men over the river and burst upon the enemy flank even as Drystan led a frontal assault. The ring of shields crumpled under the shock, and the militia fled for the safety of the woods. Esyllt watched in horrors as most of them were butchered.

"Easy work," laughed Goron, his broad face smeared with blood, "a few more skirmishes like this, and Kernow shall be ours inside a month."

Esyllt not only despised Goron, but failed to understand him. He often made drunken speeches around the campfire at night, of his pride in Kernow and how he loved his homeland above all else. Yet here he was, glorying in the slaughter of his own countrymen.

He is an animal, she thought, *a brute beast, incapable of true thought or judgement.*

Drystan, she told herself, was different. At least he took no outward pleasure in the bloodshed.

"It had to be done," he assured her afterwards, wiping his sword, "word of our victory will spread. Soon the militia will be too cowed to face us in the open. Peasants! Cowardly and stupid, only concerned with their own safety. They will hide inside their stockades, and leave us to deal with my father's warriors."

"You told me in Amorica that Marcus can muster three hundred spears," said Esyllt, "many more, if he calls upon Dumnonia and the High King for help. You can't face all of them in the field."

"Nor shall I," he replied carelessly, "the Swine of Kernow shall remain forever out of my father's reach. The horses Budic gave us are far superior to anything bred in Kernow. Marcus may pursue us from sun up to sundown, and never touch a hair of our heads."

"The Swine of Kernow?"

Drystan flashed one of his charming grins. "Every famous war-band has a name. I thought of ours last night, while I sat and watched the stars. We are the Swine of

Kernow, destined to ravage this land from one end to the other."

They moved on, dragged along in the irresistible wake of their captain. Kernow was sparsely populated, and for a whole day the invaders rode through wild, untamed country. They picked through ancient forests, bleak hills and narrow ravines, with only the occasional glimpse of smoke in the distance to remind them of human habitation. Every so often they passed the workings of an old mine, where the Romans had used slaves to dig for rich veins of tin and copper.

"There is still much ore to be found," said Drystan as they cantered past the narrow entrance to one such disused mine, "but my father and his predecessors were too lazy to re-open the mines. They allowed the kingdom to become poor and wretched, even though vast reserves of wealth lay just under their feet. When I am king, I intend to tap that wealth. The mines shall be active again, and trade re-stablished with Amorica and Frankia."

Esyllt warmed to his enthusiasm. This was the side of him she admired: the ambitious dreamer, full of grand schemes and adventures. In his company, she could believe almost anything was possible.

At last they neared Celliwig, a small hill-fort overlooking soft green hills and downs. The Swine of Kernow halted inside some woods, a mile or so from the fort. Drystan ventured forward with Goron and five men to scout out the land.

"The fort is still occupied," said Drystan when they returned, "it is held by Drem son of Dremidydd, one of my father's chiefs. He served my uncle too, King Bouduin, before Marcus slew him. Drem is a wily old dog. I saw the flash of spears on the ramparts. He won't be lured out to chase us through these woods."

"What must we do, then?" asked Esyllt, "we have too few men to attack the fort, and no siege equipment. Perhaps we should turn back to the coast."

"No," Drystan said, "we can't risk it. My father must have his men out by now. They will cut off the route back to our ships. Besides, I refuse to turn tail and run at the first setback."

His warriors stood in a circle around him. Esyllt noticed how drawn and tired they looked. Since landing in Kernow, Drystan had driven them hard, and a number of horses had almost collapsed of exhaustion. Now they found themselves deep inside enemy territory in a foreign land, cut off from the sea, with provisions running out and no obvious means of escape.

Their loyalty is not absolute, thought Esyllt, *if they lose faith in Drystan, there is nothing to stop them cutting his throat and coming to terms with King Marcus.*

She trembled. *They will also hand me over to the king. I can hope for no mercy from a man who assassinated his own brother.*

To her relief, Drystan's confidence didn't waver. "We wait here until nightfall," he announced, "Drem has kept all his men inside Celliwig. He cannot know of our presence. We shall approach the fort under cover of darkness, scale the walls and kill everyone inside."

The brutal simplicity of the plan appealed to his men. Goron uttered a bark of encouragement - *good dog*, thought Esyllt - which was echoed by a few others.

Some of the more grizzled, hard-faced veterans among the Amoricans still looked doubtful. Still, they said nothing, and their knives remained sheathed for now.

The Swine of Kernow settled down to wait for darkness. Fortunately it was dry, though cold, and the chill grew worse as evening drew on. Autumn was usually Esyllt's favourite season, but now she sat huddled in her cloak against the bole of a tree, and wished herself back in her father's court.

Golwg sat close to her. "There will be a throng in King

Niall's hall tonight," the slave murmured drowsily, "the mead-cup shall pass round, even as knife goes into meat, and the hearth blazes with warmth and light. Do you remember those feasts at the dark time of year, my lady, when I sat at your feet, and we listened to the bards sing of how the Uí Liatháin first came to Hibernia?"

"All too well," replied Esyllt, "hush, Golwg. Don't speak of the past. You will make me weep, and this is not a time for weeping."

"No. It is a time of fighting and killing. Of reaping souls. We have no place here."

Esyllt pulled her hood over her face. She knew what Golwg was going to say. They should have stayed in Amorica and enjoyed King Budic's hospitality, instead of accompanying Drystan on this insane quest.

She had other reasons for leaving Amorica. Budic was unmarried, and often cast lustful eyes at Esyllt when Drystan was looking the other way. If she had stayed at the Amorican court, with none to prevent the king doing just as he liked, Esyllt suspected Budic would have forced himself on her.

Dark clouds billowed over the forested hills to the west. *My life is ruled by the whims of men. Men dictate what I do and where I go. When I am a queen, it will be different. The only freedom is power. Power to rule over men, and follow my own path.*

Dusk brought with it more than shadows. The men on watch startled Esyllt out of her exhausted slumber as their voices, shrill with alarm, echoed through the woods.

"Horsemen are coming!" they cried, "riders in red cloaks!"

"How many?" demanded Drystan, "from what direction?"

"From the fort, lord," one of the men wailed, jabbing his finger in the direction of Celliwig, "we counted twenty, maybe thirty spears."

Drystan relaxed slightly. "Thirty men against a hundred," he said, "they are either fools, or ignorant of our presence here. Let us give them a warm welcome."

"We go barefoot," he ordered, "so as not to alert our guests. Carry only knives and bows. A few men will stay to guard the horses."

The Swine of Kernow moved through the trees in swift silence. Esyllt and Golwg followed in their wake. Both carried daggers. Esyllt's flesh was damp with sweat as she imagined the dark silhouettes of spear-armed horsemen tearing through the night.

Tales of Artorius and his Companions were known throughout Hibernia, ever since the High King left his mark on the island. The Companions were said to be unbeatable, flesh-eating demons rather than men, who slaughtered brave warriors and dragged their souls down to Hell.

They were also known to wear red cloaks. Had Artorius sent a troop of his famous killers to aid King Marcus?

They are outnumbered, she reminded herself, *and will be easy prey. There is nothing to fear. Not while Drystan is alive.*

Drystan's men halted on the edge of the trees. Beyond was a meadow, curving down to a thickly wooded valley before rising again to meet the outer ramparts of the hill-fort.

Esyllt sought out Drystan and knelt beside him. "There," he whispered, "do you see them?"

The breath caught in Esyllt's throat when she spied a band of horsemen in the meadow, some thirty feet away. They were little more than shadows in the fading light, though she caught a glimpse of their spears and blood-red cloaks.

"They must know we are here," hissed Goron, squatting in the long grass to Esyllt's left, "otherwise why do they stay?"

The horsemen came no closer. Esyllt thought they were

like so many statues, rooted to the earth.

"Let's loose a few arrows," said Goron, "either make them come into the woods, or drive them away."

Drystan didn't seem to hear. The young warrior's face was tense and pale, eyes narrowed, jaw clenched.

Then there was movement. The nearest horseman suddenly clapped in his spurs and trotted to the edge of the woods.

"He comes alone," whispered Drystan, "an envoy, perhaps. Let him be until I give the signal."

The rider halted. Esyllt studied his tall, slightly stooped figure, and what she could see of his face under the crested helmet.

It was a face lacking in mercy: long and lean and beardless, with a hardness to the little mouth and hooded eyes, and a nose like a hooked dagger. He put her in mind of a hungry falcon.

"Drystan son of Marcus," the rider called out in a flat, harsh voice, "stop skulking in those trees. Come out and speak with me."

Drystan cursed, and slammed his fist against the tree he leaned on. "They know we are here," he exclaimed.

"I am Llwch Llemineawg," the rider went on, "sent by the High King to fight on behalf of King Marcus. These men at my back are Companions."

Muttered oaths rippled through the woods. Everyone had heard of Llwch Llemineawg. He was one of Artorius' most famous captains, known for his skill and cruelty in battle.

"Come out, Drystan," Llwch said with a trace of impatience, "did you think your presence was unknown to us? We spotted your spears from the walls of Celliwig. Fortunately for you, Drem son of Dremidydd is an old woman, and prefers to skulk inside his fortress than ride out and fight. I got bored listening to his drivel, so thought to come in search of you."

"To hunt us, you mean!" shouted Drystan. His voice echoed across the meadow.

Llwch uttered a low chuckle. "Show yourself, my hero. No harm will come to you. I came to discuss terms, not fight."

"It's a trick," said Goron, "this man is one of the High King's war-hounds. He is steeped in blood. As soon as you show your face, he will cut you down."

Drystan chewed his bottom lip. "Maybe," he said, "but he risks his own life. He is within range of our bows. The moment he draws sword or gives the order to attack, shoot him."

Esyllt watched, heart fluttering, as Drystan stepped of the wood. He advanced boldly to meet Llwch and halted within a spear's length of the horseman.

"Well," she heard him say, "I'm here. What do you want?"

Esyllt listened intently to their conversation. "The bards already sing of you, lad," said Llwch, "the young champion who slew Morholt the Reaver, abducted the daughter of King Niall and invaded Kernow with just a handful of spears."

He folded his arms and looked Drystan up and down. "I must admit, I expected someone a bit more impressive. You're still a boy. A pretty boy. Did you really kill Morholt? That old pirate should have eaten you for supper."

Drystan took a step closer. "I rammed my sword into his guts," Esyllt heard him growl, "and gave my father his head in a bag. Show me a little more respect, Llwch Llemineawg, or you may go the same way."

Llwch threw back his head and brayed with laughter. "Good," he cried, "you swallow no insults. I hoped this would prove entertaining. Far more entertaining, at any rate, than watching Drem swill mead and piss himself in terror at your name."

"Old Drem really fears me?" asked Drystan, "he has

served two kings, and fought in any number of battles."

"As I said," replied Llwch, "you have a fearsome reputation. The only man in Kernow with the courage to fight Morholt. Now you've come to ravage your father's kingdom."

"Not ravage," said Drystan, "I am here to conquer. Your master Artorius would be wise to abandon King Marcus, and offer me his friendship instead. I will be the next King of Kernow."

"Yes," said Llwch, "my master."

He went quiet, twisted his head to look at his men, and then slowly climbed down from the saddle.

Esyllt tensed, half-expecting Llwch to draw his sword. Instead he unfastened his helmet and tucked it under his arm.

He started to talk. He and Drystan spoke low, and Esyllt was unable to hear what passed between them.

They spoke for a long time.

12.

Caerleon

"I will not be left behind!" roared Cei, "do you hear me, Artorius? This is my fight as much as yours!"

Cei, the High King's steward and one of his oldest friends, trembled with anger.

Artorius looked at him with pity. The years weighed heavy on Cei. Now forty-seven, he was still fearsomely strong, but had grown fat, and was losing the sight in his left eye. Artorius suspected his growing blindness was related to an old battle-wound he had suffered in Gaul, many years ago. Since then Cei had been a martyr to headaches, and his naturally sour temper grew steadily worse.

The king sighed. This would be difficult. He had to

make Cei obey orders, while at the same time soothe his fragile pride.

"I need you here in Caerleon," he said, "who else can I trust to govern the kingdom in my absence? Bedwyr is still in Rheged, and Gwalchmei is unfit for the task."

He glanced nervously around him. They were in his private quarters in the palace, where Artorius felt reasonably safe from spies. Even so, he prayed his words would not reach Gwalchmei's ears. He valued Gwalchmei as a friend and fighting man, but would never dream of giving the vain, strutting lecher any real power.

"What about Llacheu?" demanded Cei, "he's a man grown now, and needs some proper experience of leadership."

He wagged a hairy finger at Artorius. "It's no secret you plan to make Llacheu your heir. A fine High King he would make, if you died suddenly and he had no idea how to govern!"

"I agree," Artorius said calmly, "which is why I intend to name him regent while I'm gone. Under your supervision."

Cei sat and gently smouldered. Artorius knew he would submit eventually - the High King's word was law, even to old friends - but it was in his nature to resist.

Neither man spoke of the other option. Artorius might have left Gwenhwyfar to rule in his absence: she was perfectly capable, intelligent and educated, and knew how to bend men to her will.

Even so, he could not afford to leave his wife in charge of the kingdom. It would damage his reputation in the eyes of the sub-kings, none of whom allowed their queens a shred of power. There was also the danger they might not accept the dominion of a woman, and refuse to obey Gwenhwyfar's orders.

Cei was right. It was time for Llacheu, Artorius' second son, to learn how to rule without his father to guide him.

The young man was twenty now. Cydfan, his eldest son, had entered the church, and would be the next Bishop of Llandaff once the current incumbent had relinquished his stubborn hold on life.

I was already a seasoned captain at their age, thought Artorius, *my father appointed me Magister Militum, with effective command over his field army. Twenty years old, and I had seen more death and suffering than men twice my age.*

He thought of his foster-father, Ambrosius Aurelianus, rather than his natural father, Uthyr, the rough Votadini warrior he could barely remember. For Artorius, life truly began when Ambrosius walked into the smoky mead-hall at Curia, in the far north of Britannia, and smiled at him.

His sons had experienced no such hard upbringing. Artorius tried not to spoil them and ensure they grew into ruthless, capable men, well-equipped to survive when he was gone. It was difficult, though, to raise fighters in a time of peace.

Artorius constantly drummed into them the lesson that peace was an illusion, a happy dream, maintained only so long as spears remained sharp, and borders well-guarded.

Of his long-lost third son, Medraut, he tried to think of not at all.

Cydfan and Llacheu were dutiful and obedient, and seemed to listen. He hoped and prayed they did. The test would only come after his death. To Artorius, who desired supreme control over his kingdom until the end of days, old age and the grave were enemies he could not hope to defeat. They could, however, be staved off for as long as possible.

"Well, Cei," he said, "do you accept my judgement?"

The question was unnecessary. For all his pride and stubbornness, Cei was the most loyal of men, and never refused a direct order.

"You think I am old," muttered the steward, rubbing his bad eye, "old and done. A fat, half-blind greybeard, fit only to sit beside the hearth like an old dog and dream of better days."

"Of course not," said Artorius, though he did think something of the sort. Cei was not quite done, perhaps, but he didn't want to tax his friend's strength too much. In his heart, Artorius suspected Cei would only live a few more years. He had to be preserved for as long as possible.

"That is settled," the king went on, "I will go to Kernow and clean up the hellish mess King Marcus has made of his kingdom. You and Llacheu are in charge until I return."

"How many Companions will you take?" asked Cei, all business now. Artorius was glad to see him shake off his self-pity and concentrate on the matter at hand.

"Eighty," replied Artorius, "we can spare no more from the garrison. Our numbers are dangerously stretched as it is."

"Not enough," said Cei, "there are a hundred and fifty Companions left in Caerleon. Take them all. Our citizen militia can guard the city. Gwalchmei has drilled them well."

Artorius shook his head. "Absolutely not. No disrespect to the militia, but our enemies only fear the Companions. I won't leave Caerleon exposed."

For once, Cei didn't argue. He served as spymaster as well as steward, and well knew how many enemies, real and potential, clustered around the High King. The knives were out for Artorius, and only waited for a chance to strike.

"Promise me this," said Cei, "promise you will find Llwch and bring him back to Caerleon. Dead or alive. We don't abandon old comrades."

Artorius nodded. "Of course."

The disappearance of Llwch Llemineawg, and the chaotic situation in Kernow, compelled Artorius to once again ride out at the head of his Companions. Several days earlier, another exhausted envoy had arrived from King Marcus. The letter he carried was full of bad news. Budic of

Amorica had invaded Kernow.

Outnumbered, King Marcus had retreated to his stronghold at Caer Y Brenin, where he was currently under siege. Meanwhile his ally Drem made no effort to march to his aid from Celliwig.

Llwch and his young Companions were also stationed at Celliwig. He also made no move. This puzzled Artorius. It wasn't like Llwch, an aggressive fighting captain, to hide behind fortifications when danger threatened.

Then there was Drystan to consider. Artorius picked up the envoy's letter from the side-table where he had left it, and studied the name.

"I think this was written in Marcus' own hand," remarked the king, "he must have been in a rage at the time. Or drunk. The writing is shaky, especially when he comes to write Drystan's name."

"The boy has him rattled," said Cei, "hardly surprising. Marcus can't have predicted one of his bastards would cause such trouble."

"True. I almost admire Drystan. He may be a murderer and a traitor, but he has fire in his belly. For one so young, he knows how to lead men. His war-band has caused untold destruction in Kernow."

Uninvited, Cei reached for the wine-jug and poured himself a large measure. "A brave boy," he grunted, "no doubt of that. Shame he has to die. At another time, he might have been useful."

Artorius folded the letter and put it down. "Yes," he said quietly, "but die he must."

*

The High King rode out the next day. It was a raw, misted morning in late autumn. Artorius felt sluggish. The usual excitement of a fresh campaign, the once-glorious prospect of war, was absent.

He took Gwalchmei with him as second-in-command. The brawny, handsome warrior was several years older than the king, and there was a liberal salting of grey in his russet hair, yet he showed no sign of age or fatigue.

"I'm a soldier again," he said as they clattered over the stone bridge east of Caerleon, "thank God! A few more months on that accursed drill-yard, teaching farmers and tradesmen how to march in step, might have been the death of me."

Artorius looked at him with affection. He cast his mind back to their first meeting at Mons Ambrius, on the same night as the Treachery of the Long Knives. Hengist, the old war-chief of the Saxons, had summoned the British kings to a peaceful meeting at the ancient stone circle near the fort, and massacred them all.

Almost all. Gwalchmei's master, Eidol Cadarn, had escaped the slaughter and sought refuge inside Mons Ambrius. He owed his survival to his young slave, Gwalchmei, who broke the head of the Saxon warrior that tried to kill Eidol.

Gwalchmei, Bedwyr and Cei, thought Artorius, *the three men I love most in the world. Of them all, only Gwalchmei has retained something of his youth. I must draw strength from him.*

Artorius had mixed feelings about leaving Caerleon. The reborn Roman garrison town was the capital of Britannia. It was his duty to stay there, preside over justice in the Round Hall and continue the education of his sons.

A stern duty, and an unhappy one. There was little domestic comfort for him at Caerleon. He and Gwenhwyfar had become increasingly distant over the years, though they still consulted each other on political matters. The torments she endured at the hands of Diwrnach, and the necessary secrecy over her bastard child, all left their mark. Over the years she had become quiet and withdrawn, uncomfortable with intimacy.

All her passion was devoted to her son, Amhar. Artorius, who respected his wife and wanted to please her, foresaw trouble ahead. The boy was already much like the notorious Scotti warlord who fathered him - strong, violent, bad-tempered, coarse and grasping. He would grow into a difficult man. Unless Amhar proved loyal, Artorius feared he would one day have to deal with him.

If he is allowed to grow.

He shook away the evil thought. It would be easy to play the tyrant, and drown his fears in blood. Such a course only led to ruin. In his mind he heard the screams of Vortigern, as the hall-thatch collapsed on him and fire consumed his flesh.

The Companions rode south-east into Dumnonia. Artorius might have crossed to Kernow by sea, but he wanted to speak with King Erbin. Erbin had done little to restore peace in Kernow, even though King Marcus was both his ally and subordinate. Artorius smelled treachery, or at least negligence, and meant to remind Erbin of his duties.

He found Erbin holed up at Mons Ambrius, once the stronghold of Ambrosius Aurelianus. The King of Dumnonia held a number of hill-forts, and Mons Ambrius was the furthest north in his realm.

"Far away from the troubles in Kernow," Artorius remarked caustically as he rode under the timber gateway, "what a coward he is."

Gwalchmei grinned, exposing thick white teeth. "Don't protest too much, lord king," he said, "Erbin is what you expected him to be."

Artorius scowled, but had to to acknowledge the truth of this. Dumnonia was the largest kingdom still under British control. Only the King of Dumnonia possessed the manpower and resources to match the High King. To prevent such a threat, Artorius had given the kingship to Erbin, a weak and biddable man with a distant blood relation to old Dumnonian royalty.

Erbin was much as Artorius remembered, short and balding, with a weak cast to his features. He appeared more than usually nervous, and his face glistened with sweat as he knelt in the mud before the High King.

"We...welcome, lord king," he stammered, "I am honoured by your presence."

Artorius thought he could hear the man's teeth chatter. "Not so poor, Erbin," he said, looking critically at the king's fine robe of crimson wool, trimmed with fur, and the gleaming mail worn by his guards, "you are the very image of a king. A pity you don't behave like one."

Erbin cuffed some of the perspiration from his brow. "Lord king...I have sent fifty spears to reinforce King Marcus..."

Artorius interrupted him. "There are enough fighting men in Dumnonia to put five hundred spears in the field," he snapped, "where is your army, King Erbin? All I see here are your household guards."

Erbin offered no reply. Artorius roughly seized the little man's wrist, hoisted him to his feet and flung an arm about his shoulders.

"Come," he said in a friendlier tone, "let us eat together, and discuss the situation."

"I dare not march into Kernow, my lord," Erbin whined over the meal inside his hall, "the eastern half of the kingdom is lost. Almost every day my spies bring fresh news of another village burned, another army scattered, another hill-fort lost."

Artorius looked up from his beef, and wiped his greasy fingers on a cloth. "Have the Amoricans advanced so far inland, then?" he asked.

"No, my lord. King Budic concentrates all his forces at Caer Y Brenin. That young traitor, Drystan, and the Swine of Kernow are responsible for the carnage."

"The swine of what?"

Erbin looked on the verge of tears. "The name of his

war-band, lord king, as terrible a band of murderers and ravagers as ever landed in Britannia. They stormed Celliwig at night, killed everyone they found inside, put the place to the torch. Nothing remains of that fine court, only ashes and cinders and burned bones..."

He buried his face in his hands and wept. Artorius was appalled, as much by Erbin's behaviour as the dreadful news. The king was not only weak and cowardly, but lack-witted.

"I knew of the attack on Celliwig," he said, above the sound of Erbin's sobs, "what of my men who were stationed there? What of Llwch Llemineawg, their captain? They would never allow themselves to be taken so easily."

He tried to ignore the hard stares of Erbin's warriors, crowded on the mead-benches below high table. Their king's tears shamed them all.

Erbin lifted his head. "My scouts said nothing of Llwch," he mumbled, "but they did find men in red cloaks among the slain at Celliwig."

Artorius paled. His swollen and callused hands balled into fists. Drystan had killed his men. His young Companions, still raw and untested, slaughtered in their first battle.

I sent them to their deaths. I must avenge them.

"Erbin," he said, "how many spears do you have here at Mons Ambrius?"

The sub-king sniffed and wiped his tears. "Ah...thirty, besides my hearth-guard," he replied, "allow three days, and I can raise a hundred more."

"No. We must act fast to save Kernow. Give me your spears."

It was an order, not a request. Erbin hurriedly ducked his head in agreement, and Artorius turned his thoughts to war.

And revenge.

13.

Artorius gazed miserably at the destruction. Crops burned in the fields, the corpses of men and animals rotting under the autumn sun, cottages and outbuildings reduced to ash.

"This is the mirror of my youth," he said, "this is Britannia how it was, before we drove out the Saxons. I thought the past was expelled. I was wrong."

"This is Drystan's work," Gwalchmei said with his usual briskness, "fear not, lord. Once we've caught the little turd and mounted his head on a stake, we can set about repairing the damage to Kernow. Crops can be replanted, homes rebuilt."

If only we could do the same for the dead, thought Artorius, *close up their wounds, and bid them walk again.*

He kept this to himself. Artorius had come to rely on Gwalchmei's strength and optimism, his belief that nothing on earth was beyond redemption. To depress the man's spirits would be disastrous for Artorius' own state of mind.

They had ridden south-west from Mons Ambrius and crossed the border at midday, careful to give the Summer Country, that mysterious land in the heart of Dumnonia, a wide berth. Artorius had no wish to venture inside the gateway to Annwn again.

Kernow was a ruin. The Swine of Kernow had left not a cottage or farmstead standing between the border and Celliwig. Artorius was almost mesmerised by the scale of the destruction. Not since the days of Ambrosius, when Hengist's Saxons broke loose and ravaged the land from sea to sea, had he seen the like.

He wondered how many peasants still lived. If they watched, sullen and terrified, from the safety of the forests as Artorius rode past.

The High King, the famed Dragon of Britannia, who failed to defend them from one murderous youth and his pack of hirelings.

Then they reached Celliwig. Artorius had heard tales of

this court, said to be the fairest in Kernow, a place of bards, where Drem son of Dremidydd gathered the finest musicians in Britannia under his roof.

Celliwig was dark and quiet now. No more would the hearth-light bathe its walls in gold and illuminate the faces of laughing warriors.

Drystan's raiders had left the stockade and outbuildings intact. The hall, though, was a blackened shell. To judge from the bodies scattered about the floor, Drem and his household had been at meat when the Swine of Kernow struck.

The Companions picked through the ruins, heavy with the stench of death. "I knew this man," said Gwalchmei, kneeling beside one of the corpses by the doorway. "Tegfan, his name was. Just a lad."

Tegfan's body, hacked by a frenzy of spears, was draped in a red cloak. The fingers of his right hand were still curled about the hilt of his sword. A standard long-bladed cavalry blade, such as all the Companions were equipped with.

"There is dried blood on the sword," Gwalchmei, his voice heavy with grief, "at least he struck his blow before they killed him."

Tegfan was one of twelve Companions found dead inside the hall. Every one had died fighting, sword in hand. Artorius hoped this would comfort their families when be carried the terrible news back to Caerleon.

He would also carry the head of Drystan, impaled on a spear, and place it next to the skull of Diwrnach in the Round Hall. Let the enemies of Britannia see this grisly pair, and think twice before defying the High King.

Artorius leaned against a smoke-blackened pillar. "My boys," he said, "all slain. Brave boys. The best of the crop. I chose them to serve in the Companions. To help defend Britannia when I was dead. Yet they are dead, and I still live."

He forced himself to think. Twelve young Companions lay dead. He had sent Llwch to Kernow with thirty. Llwch himself was not among the slain.

"Perhaps the others were captured," said Gwalchmei, echoing his thoughts, "taken prisoner. Drystan might hold them to ransom."

Artorius mulled this over. It was difficult to imagine Llwch Llemineawg, whose pride almost matched Cei's, allowing himself to be captured alive.

"We will ride west," he said, "and flush out the Swine of Kernow."

Gwalchmei looked doubtful. "Are you certain, lord king? We don't know this country, and Drystan is clearly no fool. He might be anywhere among the hills and forests, waiting to ambush us. Why not stay here and send to King Erbin for more spears?"

Artorius wouldn't hear of it. He needed action, to have Drystan on the point of his sword, to dispel the storm of guilt and anger inside his head. Every moment of delay allowed Drystan and his allies to grow stronger.

"Caer Y Brenin may have fallen already, for aught we know," he said, "we must act."

Gwalchmei was not the sort to prolong an argument. The Companions rode west from Celliwig with the revitalised figure of the High King at their head. The thought of his men held captive by Drystan, of the torments they might be suffering, lent him new strength.

He would pay for it later, he knew, and be condemned to days of recuperation in the baths at Caerleon. Artorius cared little. He was oath-sworn to lead and defend his Companions, just as they were sworn to serve him and Britannia.

West of Celliwig, the land broke up into a series of wooded hills and valleys. Artorius sent five men forward to scout out the land, and two groups of ten apiece beyond the the flanks of the main column as it pushed carefully through the wilderness. Mindful of the need to spare the horses - there were no remounts - he ordered his men to advance at a slow trot.

"We need a native to guide us," he said after an hour or so, "there may be peasants hidden in these woods. Survivors of Drystan's raids."

"If there are, they won't show themselves," replied Gwalchmei, "not if they have any sense. To them we're merely another band of armed horsemen."

"They are my subjects," growled Artorius, "and should look to me for protection. I have ruled as High King for twelve years. Fought all my life to defend them. The sacrifices I have made, the blood I have shed! Does it count for nothing?"

Gwalchmei frowned. "The people of Kernow have never set eyes on you, lord king. You can't expect the poor folk hereabouts to recognise your face."

Artorius went quiet. He was in a sick and savage mood, and his heart was hot inside him. He wanted an enemy. Someone to fight, to kill, to carve into pieces. The civilised aspect of his nature faded, overcome by the wild blood of his Votadini ancestors.

Relief arrived in the form of two of his scouts. The Companions were advancing through a narrow, winding ravine when the scouts emerged from a belt of trees to the west. They rode hard to meet him, youthful faces flushed with excitement.

"We've found Llwch," they cried, "he waits just beyond the trees."

Artorius raised his arm as the signal to halt. "Why does he wait?" he demanded while the scouts gulped for breath, "is he alone?"

"He is guarded by three spearmen, lord king," one of the youths answered, "if he tries to escape, they will kill him. We didn't see his men. Llwch says that Drystan wishes to speak with you, and offer terms."

"Terms," Artorius spat, "I have only one kind of peace to offer Drystan of Kernow."

"It's an obvious trap," said Gwalchmei, "he's using Llwch as bait to lure us into those woods."

"We saw no sign of anyone else, lord king," said the scout.

Artorius pulled at his beard and glanced around at the steep flanks of the ravine. It was a perfect spot for an ambush, which was why he had sent out men to patrol his flanks.

All was silent, save for the occasional rustle of harness and neigh of a horse. Artorius had experienced the silence many times. It was the kind of unearthly hush that fell before a battle. The world held its breath.

"No," he said at last, "Drystan is shrewd, but this old badger won't be lured into his snare."

Artorius turned in the saddle. "Turn about," he ordered, "back to Celliwig."

"You were right," he added, with a nod to Gwalchmei, "I should have listened. We need reinforcements. I will send word to King Erbin, and order him to send as many spears as he can raise."

"What of Llwch?" Gwalchmei asked quietly, "once Drystan sees his ambush has failed, he may kill Llwch in revenge. And the others."

Artorius didn't reply. He was powerless to help Llwch, not without risking the destruction of his entire command. As High King, it fell to him to make such ruthless decisions. The lives of the few, no matter how valued, had to be set against the lives of the many.

The Companions and their Dumnonian allies turned about smartly - Artorius thought he could sense their relief - and rode back at a brisk trot to the eastern end of the ravine. Celliwig lay some ten miles away. With luck, they might reach the fort before nightfall.

A horn sounded from the western end of the ravine.

Artorius looked over his shoulder, and spotted a familiar figure on horseback, galloping hard towards the Companions from the woods. Three other riders were in pursuit, barely a spear's length behind him.

"Llwch," he cried. Gwalchmei followed as he put Llamrei to the slope and rode to meet his old comrade.

Llwch's red cloak was gone. He wore no helmet or mail, and carried a spear. He raised it as Artorius thundered down to meet him.

"Lord king!" he shouted in a hoarse voice. His eyes bulged, and his narrow features were twisted in a snarl.

He cast the spear. It plunged into Llamrei's neck. She screamed, threw back her head, twisted like a salmon on the hook, and hurled Artorius off her back.

The king landed heavily in boggy ground, rolled, struggled to his feet. Half-dazed, he instinctively reached for Caledfwlch. One word pounded through his head.

Treachery! Treachery! Treachery!

Llwch had betrayed him after all.

A clash of swords echoed through the ravine. Gwalchmei had put himself between Llwch and Artorius, and the two old comrades, who had fought side by side in countless wars, now hacked at each other.

Artorius looked around for Llamrei and saw the beast lying on her side in the mud. Her limbs thrashed feebly as the life-blood gushed from the wound in her neck.

His heart swelled with grief. Llamrei, his favourite mare, who had carried him to victory at Mount Badon. She had served him faithfully for over twelve years, never failed him, never swerved from a fight.

He tore Caledfwlch from its sheath and strode towards Llwch. More horns blasted through the woods - war-horns, a score at least, their deep notes rising and falling like a chorus of doom.

Artorius looked north, and saw his scouts in full retreat, flying down the sides of the ravine with a tide of horsemen in pursuit. Javelins plucked three of the scouts from their saddles. Their pursuers rode over them, trampling and mangling the bodies.

The High King forgot about Llwch. "Half the company will dismount," he shouted at his men, "and form a shield-wall. The rest a mounted reserve on the southern slope. Move!"

The Companions had often practised this strategy on the drill-ground, but never in battle. Artorius was relieved to see they kept their discipline, and deployed rapidly with no sign of panic. Many were veterans of the Saxon wars, his best men, the finest horse-soldiers in the West.

Llwch abandoned his duel with Gwalchmei and fled, accompanied by the three mounted spearmen who had pretended to chase him. "Leave them be!" cried Artorius, "we can deal with Llwch later."

Gwalchmei, red-faced and bleeding from a cut on his cheek, reluctantly obeyed. The world filled with baying voices and war-shouts as more warriors, mounted spearmen and men on foot, appeared to the west and north.

Artorius splashed through the bog to stand behind the half-circle of shields formed by his dismounted Companions. Their horses were taken to the rear by the men of the reserve, ready to use if and when the enemy broke.

To the king's horror, thirty of his horsemen suddenly broke ranks and galloped away, towards the trees. He was about to call after them, to order them back into line, but the words died on his lips.

Those were fled were Dumnonians, the men King Erbin had lent him. Artorius went cold. How far did this treason run? Was Erbin in league with Drystan? Had they planned this ambush between them?

"Turncoats!" howled Gwalchmei, who almost wept with rage, "cowards! Your heads shall rot on spikes!"

The Companions stood alone. Even now, abandoned by their allies, their composure held. Artorius did a rapid headcount of the wave of enemy warriors closing in on them: two hundred, maybe more, roughly half on foot.

Most of the enemy infantry had little discipline or training. They were peasants, scarcely a helmet or coat of mail between them, armed with pitchforks and sickles and other such crude weapons. Whipped and roared on by the horsemen, the undisciplined mob hurled themselves at the Companions on foot.

The shield-wall bent a little under the weight of bodies, but did not break. "Hold them!" shouted Artorius, "hold them!"

Gwalchmei, in command of the reserve, ordered the front rank into action. A score of Companions cantered down the slope and hurled their javelins over the heads of their dismounted comrades. Then they wheeled, split into two groups, and rode back to rejoin the flanks of the reserve.

Their javelins struck down at least a dozen peasants and caused the rest to falter. The Companions on foot locked shields and surged forward, spears stabbing at the eyes and guts of their foes. More peasants fell, blinded and disembowelled, shrieking in agony.

"On!" Artorius ordered, "on them! Forward - they fail, they fail!"

He resisted the desire to throw himself into the fight. Get some blood on his sword. Duty restrained him. Artorius was the High King. Everything depended on his survival. If he fell, his men would lose heart.

The wall of spears continued to advance. Step by step, the Companions rumbled forward, trampling the bodies of the men they slew. Artorius helped the men of the second line to cut the throats of the wounded.

He could only wonder where the peasants had come from, and why they fought on the side of Drystan. Had they been herded into battle, with the threat of death if they refused?

Drystan forced Artorius to fight and slay his own subjects, men he was sworn to protect. For that alone, the young man would suffer the slowest and most painful execution Artorius could devise. The death of Melwas would be merciful by comparison.

The horns boomed again. It was a signal to retreat, and the surviving peasants turned and fled in all directions like frightened sheep. They left over two score of their number stretched out on the ground. Artorius looked to his own men, and saw only a handful of red cloaks among the slain.

There was no respite. Two bands of horsemen, each some fifty or sixty men strong, swept in from both flanks to attack Artorius' reserve. Gwalchmei was alive to the danger. He split his command and led one half against the enemy to the east, while the other half charged to meet the threat to the west.

The Companions were outnumbered, but they were the finest cavalry in Britannia, far superior to anything Drystan could throw at them. Artorius warmed with pride as they carved into the enemy, shattering their loose ranks and sending men and horses tumbling to earth.

His joy soured when more men burst from the woods, light cavalry and spearmen. They swarmed in to encircle the mounted Companions, already engaged and unable to deploy.

"Mount!" ordered Artorius. The shield-wall broke up and his footmen ran to retrieve their horses, left behind by the reserve. As well-drilled as their riders, the beasts had remained calmly in position, undisturbed by the noise around them.

Artorius seized the reins of a spare horse and swung himself aboard. He saw the peasant levies were regrouping, lashed and bullied into some kind of order by officers on horseback.

His eyesight was keen as ever, and picked out a tall, blonde youth among the officers. The youth was a striking figure in silver ring-mail, one of the few among the enemy to carry a sword.

Artorius suspected this was Drystan. He measured the distance between them. If he led his Companions in a swift charge, was there time to slay Drystan before reinforcements could arrive?

The moment passed. Artorius cursed his hesitation. In his fiery youth he would have acted on instinct, not delayed to think. Now more horsemen closed up around the figure in silver mail, the turncoat Dumnonians among them, until he was lost to view.

Artorius swung his horse left. "To Gwalchmei!" he shouted, and led his men against the flank and rear of the enemy footmen.

Three vanished under his hoofs. Caledfwlch flashed into life, and hacked down two more. Warm blood splashed Artorius' golden mail. Roused by the scent of blood, the battle-fury descended on him. He cut a savage path, roaring curses, until he reached Gwalchmei.

His old comrade was breathing hard and spattered with gore. "Lord king," he gasped, "we must get out of this. Too many. Look there..."

He pointed his reeking sword to the ridge of the northern slope, where a dark mass of horsemen had assembled. Artorius made out eighty or ninety spears, and then stopped counting.

"How many are there?" he cried in despair, "have all the kings of the southlands betrayed me?"

Perhaps a score of his Companions had fallen, against three times their number of enemy dead. That left sixty spears. Too few to hold the field against Drystan's host. The most recent charge had scattered the enemy like leaves, but they were already re-forming on the edges of the ravine. Meanwhile the dense phalanx of horsemen waited on the ridge, like a storm waiting to burst.

"Retreat," he shouted, gesturing at Cilydd, who blew

the signal. Artorius turned east, straight at the infantry gathered there to block his retreat.

The Companions formed into a wedge, with Artorius at the apex, as they thundered towards the line of shields.

Had the infantry held, they might have withstood the shock of the charge. No horse, even one trained by the Companions, would willingly gallop into a line of spear-points.

As so often in war, Artorius gambled and won. The wall of shields disintegrated, and he was able to gallop straight through the gaping hole into the sparse woods beyond.

The ground was steep. Artorius struggled to prevent his horse from foundering. She was not so brave as Llamrei, nor as quick. Loose rocks slipped and tumbled under her hoofs

At last horse and rider gained the summit. To the north, the ground fell away to a broad, sweeping moor, studded with low hills and patches of forest. To the north-east, a river lay like a pale ribbon across the moor. It vanished behind the largest of the hills, which was crowned with a rough circle of trees. The grey sky hung heavy, shot through with drifting patches of cloud.

The earth trembled under the thunder of hoofs. Artorius looked back to check on the progress of his men, and saw Drystan's riders pour down the flank of the ravine in pursuit of the Companions.

"Hurry!" he shouted, "Gwalchmei, keep your company in order! Close ranks!"

His riders laboured up the slope. The enemy followed at furious, breakneck speed, the blonde youth in silver mail at their head. Now the Companions were forced to turn about and defend themselves, or be cut down.

A vicious brawl erupted near the foot of the slope. Gwalchmei was at the heart of it, bellowing futile orders as he laid about him. His already bloody sword thrashed two riders from their saddles, cut another's throat, lopped off a hand.

Artorius was tempted to charge back down the slope, lose himself in the grim delight of combat. Once again, he reined in his instincts. With Gwalchmei engaged, there was no other senior officer to take charge.

The Swine of Kernow fell back, leaving fifteen dead and wounded. A few of the Companions had fallen as well, but Gwalchmei's counter-attack had bought enough time to make good their escape.

Artorius led his company onto the moor. He knew this was a temporary respite. The enemy would give chase. Their horses were fresher, and the Companions couldn't hope to outdistance them over the long miles to Celliwig.

A flurry of horns echoed from the ravine. He swung his horse towards the hill beside the river. The Companions could make a stand on the summit. Forced to attack uphill, Drystan might be persuaded give up and withdraw.

In his heart he doubted it. The young warlord of Kernow was both clever and relentless, and appeared to care little for the lives of his men. Only his death offered Artorius a chance of victory.

Artorius risked a glance over his shoulder. The Companions were strung out behind him in full retreat, while the slope to the west was dark with horsemen. They gave chase like dogs after a wounded deer, howling for blood. Artorius glimpsed the fair-haired youth he thought to be Drystan, and spat a curse at him.

The Companions gained the hill. Artorius slashed at his horse's flanks, goaded her into one last burst of speed, and vaulted off her back the moment they reached the summit.

"Dismount!" he cried as the red cloaks streamed past him, "form two ranks!."

Gwalchmei repeated his orders. Again it was a practised manoeuvre, the product of years of drill. Again the discipline of the Companions proved its worth. Forty of his warriors dismounted and formed a double line of shields on the breast of the slope, while the remainder guarded the flanks and rear.

This time Artorius placed himself in the centre of the footmen, between Cilydd and Gwalchmei. He would fight, here, under the dragon standard, and show his face to those who meant to destroy him.

The Swine of Kernow did not pursue. Instead their horsemen milled about at the foot of the hill until their trumpeters sounded the retreat.

"They're running away!" cried Gwalchmei, his face flushed.

"No," said Artorius, "they wait for the infantry to come up."

He was right. The enemy cavalry retreated a little way, then spread out in good order. Meanwhile the mass of footmen straggled across the moor to join them, chivvied by mounted officers.

The youth in silver mail was everywhere. He galloped up and down the line of his cavalry, barking orders. His long, blonde hair rippled behind him, and his armour shone like polished diamonds in the pale winter sun.

"An angel of war," murmured Artorius. He saw something of his younger self in Drystan. The wheel turned, and the king stag could not rule forever. Here was the young stag, come to depose him.

He counted heads. According to the reports King Marcus sent him, Drystan had landed in Kernow with barely a hundred men. His following had now swelled to over three hundred.

Artorius wondered how Drystan had managed to triple the number of his war-band in just a few weeks. Men were easily attracted to the banner of a successful leader. The peasants had probably been forced into service, while a number of petty local chieftains may have been frightened or impressed enough to throw in their lot with the invaders.

He looked down at the host on the moor. There were

Amoricans and Dumnonians in their ranks. Artorius was at war with two kings, not just a brave adventurer and his crew.

His anger boiled again when a familiar figure rode forward, accompanied by a horseman holding a pole with no banner attached. This was the sign of a truce.

"Artorius," cried Llwch Llemineawg, "we have you trapped. Surrender, and your men can go free. Refuse, and all of you will die."

"You should know me better than that, oath-breaker," Artorius shouted back, "tell me, what did it take to buy you? What treasure was offered?"

Llwch was silent for a moment. "No treasure, lord king," he replied with a hint of sadness in his voice, "only the blood of my kin, which you refused to avenge."

Artorius sneered. "A poor excuse for betraying your king and killing your friends. I can almost smell your ambition from here. The stench is foul. Many Companions have died today. Your sword-brothers. How will you answer to God for their blood?"

"The same way I shall answer for yours," came the defiant reply, "you have ruled for twelve years, Artorius. Long enough. A new power rises in the land. I shall rise with it."

Artorius took a deep breath. "There is no more to be said. I will not surrender. Slay us if you can."

Llwch shrugged and rode back to his own lines. Artorius watched him confer with Drystan. He expected them to launch an immediate attack, but instead they parted to speak with their officers.

"The light grows dim," said Gwalchmei, "they will wait until morning, when their men are fed and rested."

"While ours are gnawed by fear," remarked Artorius, "courage eaten away by the terror and uncertainty of the night. We destroyed many a Saxon war-band thus, in the old days."

Llwch has advised Drystan of my own tactics, he thought, *the boy learns fast.*

It started to rain. Thunder rolled in the distance. Drystan's infantry began to throw up rude shelters on the moor, rough tents of animal hide, while the cavalry remained on guard. Artorius briefly considered a sudden downhill charge, a desperate effort to break free of the trap before it closed on him.

He dismissed the idea. His men were tired, as were their horses. Drystan would welcome such an attempt. As soon as they quit the high ground, the Companions would be surrounded and cut to pieces on the moor.

Artorius ordered half his men to stand watch, while the rest moved back into the safety of the trees, to eat their rations and get some rest. The horses were tethered here, and cropped hungrily at the thin grass.

"We might take them down to the river to drink," he said, "Drystan has not yet surrounded the hill."

Gwalchmei stared down at the rushing waters. "The current is strong," he replied, with a sidelong glance at his king, "strong enough to carry a man."

"You could yet escape, lord king," Gwalchmei added when Artorius gave him a shocked look. "When it grows dark, the enemy might not observe a single man borne away by the river."

"And leave my men to die?" Artorius exclaimed. "Never!"

Gwalchmei smiled bleakly. "Set aside your pride. You might have saved us already, by agreeing to give yourself up to Drystan. Not that the promises of traitors are worth much."

He spread his hands. "If you die here, Britannia will fall into chaos. Your men, including myself, are expendable."

Artorius gave a hollow laugh. "I suspect the men might disagree, Gwalchmei. Do you claim to speak on their behalf?"

"No, but I might. I will speak with them, and ask what they think is best."

The High King's mind churned while Gwalchmei passed among the Companions, and spoke to each trooper in turn.

It was almost dark by the time he returned. "There is agreement," he said, "the majority urge you to save yourself. Live, lord king, and avenge our deaths."

Artorius pushed past him to address the dark shapes of his men, gathered inside a clearing in the middle of the wood. "Is this truly your wish?" he asked, "you would have me run away?"

"Go, lord king," said a voice in the darkness. He recognised it as belonging to Dylan, one of his veterans. The voice was weary, but had no bitterness in it, and echoed by others.

"We're of a similar height and build," said Gwalchmei, "give me your armour. When Drystan attacks at dawn, his men shall mistake me for you. Let them rejoice over my corpse. By the time they realise their mistake, you should be far away."

"I see you have thought this over," snarled Artorius, though his anger was mostly directed at himself. He had led his men to this fate.

As ever, he was responsible. As ever, duty compelled him to a course both pragmatic and dishonourable.

He slowly removed his coat of golden mail, his cloak of imperial purple, and his dragon helm, and handed them over to Gwalchmei.

"What days we have known," the other man said cheerfully as he donned the mail. "I was glad to be your friend, Artorius."

He had not referred to the king by name since childhood. Speechless, Artorius could only embrace Gwalchmei and swear a private oath to the pagan gods of his youth - not Christ - that the blood of his men would be repaid a hundredfold.

They parted without another word. Clad in only tunic and braccae, Artorius picked his way down the slope to the riverbank. He had kept Caledfwlch, and carried the sword-belt slung over his shoulder. He was a strong swimmer, and thought he could carry the weight of iron.

He looked down at the black waters. The rain was heavy now, the boom of thunder almost directly overhead.

Artorius dived.

14.

The sun rose over a bleak, rain-soaked dawn. Drystan, who had slept on the ground in his mail under one of the hide shelters, woke early to rouse his men.

"Up!" he shouted as he strode eagerly among the rows of slumbering warriors and struck at them with the flat of his sword, "on your feet, you slugs! A red dawn rises, and we must rise with it!"

The joy of battle filled him like strong wine. Victory was at hand. His greatest victory yet, one that would glorify his name for generations. The High King and his little army were still trapped on the hillside. It only remained to put the wretches out of their misery.

Grumbling and cursing, his footmen staggered into line. The best of them were spearmen from the war-bands of the local chieftains who joined Drystan after his victory at Celliwig. Capable enough fighters, armed with spears and shields and leather helmets, but still expendable. The rest were peasants, dragged from their forest refuges and herded into battle. Their lives were of no account.

Horns echoed across the mist-laden moor. Drystan's cavalry were moving into position. He had ordered them to deploy on the flanks, ready to advance once the infantry were exhausted.

Drystan's tactics were simple: hurl waves of footmen against Artorius, kill as many Companions as possible, and then send in the cavalry.

Preserve Artorius until the end, lord, Drystan prayed silently as he buckled on his helmet, *let me slay him personally. Let me take Caledfwlch from his dead hand, and claim it for my own.*

His fingers shook with excitement. Once, not so long ago, he had dreamed of deposing his father and taking Kernow for himself. This seemed like a petty ambition now. A greater crown was in his grasp.

The tall, wiry figure of Llwch Llemineawg stalked towards him through the mist. Drystan's mouth went dry. He always felt nervous in Llwch's presence, and despised himself for it.

After their first meeting near Celliwig, where he had offered to betray Artorius and throw in his lot with Drystan, Llwch had justified his reputation for cruelty. A few of his men refused to join in his treachery and remained at Celliwig. When the Swine of Kernow stormed the fort, Llwch personally slew every one of the young Companions who chose to stay loyal to Artorius. Drystan would never forget the sight of him, red to the elbows with the blood of former comrades, hacking with grim ferocity at the corpse of the last man he killed.

"All is ready," said Llwch. He failed to salute. The grizzled veteran lacked respect, and seemed to regard Drystan as an equal.

When the time comes, I shall break him, thought Drystan, *or discard him. I can have no rivals.*

"You shall lead the infantry," said Drystan, "Goron and myself shall take charge of the cavalry."

Llwch gazed at him steadily. "I am a cavalry officer," he replied, "get some peasant to lead the militia. They're only spear-fodder."

Drystan welcomed the battle of wills. "I can see Artorius was too gentle with you," he said in a soft voice, full of quiet emphasis, "I am giving you an order, not a choice. Obey, or suffer the consequences."

The other man flung back his head and regarded Drystan through narrowed eyes. Drystan matched him stare for stare.

Llwch gave a sudden laugh, turned smartly on his heel and strode off towards the rabble of spearmen.

When he was gone, swallowed by the mist, Drystan allowed himself to relax slightly. He jumped as cold fingers touched his cheek.

"Peace, my lord," said a woman's voice. Drystan seized her hand and kissed it.

"Esyllt," he said, "I told you to stay in the rear with Golwg. When all is over, I shall bring you the High King's cloak as a gift."

Esyllt rested her fair head on his shoulder. "You owe me his head," she whispered, "let me see the face of the victor of Mount Badon. He was a great man. You can be greater still."

A shudder ran through Drystan. Esyllt had become much more than a useful trophy to him, a means to gain power, He loved her, worshipped her, would do anything to gain her praise and admiration.

Does she love me? He could only wonder. Esyllt had slowly warmed to him since the abduction, and did not discourage his advances.

She had yet to give herself entirely. He would not dream of lying with her until they were man and wife. For all his brutality towards men, Drystan would rather cut his own throat than force himself upon a woman.

She will come to me. When the time is right.

He leaned down to kiss his idol full on the mouth. "You are my inspiration," he murmured, "but for you, I would still be one of my father's bondsmen. Everything I am, everything I will be, is down to you. For you."

She smiled. Drystan studied her grey eyes, and wished he could know the thoughts behind them.

"Lord," said a rough male voice, full of impatience. Drystan sighed, and kissed Esyllt once more.

"Find Golwg," he said gently, "and stay well clear of the fighting. Afterwards, I shall bring you the head of Artorius, wrapped up in his cloak. We can be married then."

The first wave of infantry went in before the mist had lifted. Drystan wanted to preserve an element of surprise, and ordered the infantry forward in silence, with no drums or horns to signal their advance.

He watched the mass of spearmen jog up the slope. There was no cover on the bare hillside, and they were exposed to a shower of javelins from the Companions. Screams and gurgles tore the eerie stillness of morning to shreds as the missiles hit home.

Drystan waited patiently at the head of his cavalry. He could see little save a dark mass of bodies.

The armies met with a roar and the clatter of spears on shields. Drystan began to sweat. God had favoured him so far, he reasoned. Surely He would not abandon him now, at the crucial moment?

His infantry performed better than expected. The mist was almost gone by the time they broke and streamed back down the hill in bloody retreat. Men staggered past Drystan. Many bled from dreadful wounds. Some, maimed for life, leant on the shoulders of their comrades.

Drystan peered up at the Companions on the ridge. It was difficult to tell from such a distance, but he thought their line was broken in places. The dragon standard still flew defiantly over the helmets of the red-cloaked figures in the centre.

Under the banner stood Artorius. It was easy to pick him out in his purple cloak and golden ring-mail. Drystan drew his sword, the same sword he had used to slay Morholt, and held it aloft in salute.

Llwch was one of the last to return. His helmet was dented, and his mail smeared with blood, but he seemed unhurt.

"The men fought well," he said in his usual terse manner, "and managed to pull down a few Companions. We lost maybe twenty in return. Not bad."

Drystan nodded. "Rest awhile," he replied, "and see your men do the same. We'll need them again later."

Llwch strode away, and Drystan gave the signal for the second wave to go forward.

Nothing happened. Having witnessed the fate of the advance party, his infantry were reluctant to move.

Drystan turned on them. "Advance!" he screamed, "or I'll have every one of you flayed alive!"

He urged his white mare up and down the line of footmen, shrieking threats. At the same time his officers moved among the ranks of cowering peasantry, striking at them with clubs and spear-butts.

At last, goaded and bullied into action, the mob shambled forward. Above, high on the hill, Artorius and his men waited in silence. Drystan was both impressed and unnerved by their discipline. Few men, faced with the certainty of violent death, would have behaved with such composure.

Predictably, the second assault was less effective than the first. The Companions had no javelins left, and the compact wall of shields advanced a little way down the hill to meet the ragged charge of Drystan's infantry.

He kept his eyes fixed on the golden figure of Artorius. Caledfwlch whirled in the High King's hand. One spearman after another was cut down by the famous blade, until Artorius fought behind a knee-high rampart of corpses.

"Artorius lives up to his reputation," remarked Goron, "good. All the more glory and honour for us when he is dead."

"I will finish him," said Drystan, "understand? Artorius is my prey. Only a king should slay a king."

"As you wish," Goron replied with a shrug, "it should

be easy enough to finish him off. Even his sword-arm will tire."

All too soon, the footmen broke and fled. Drystan ignored the screams of the maimed and dying, and sent the first wave back in again, led by Llwch.

The sun cast a sickly radiance over the blood-slicked hillside. Artorius and his men still held the ridge, but not for much longer. Every fresh assault cost them more lives, and now barely two score of the red cloaks remained standing.

Before the stubborn fence of shields lay the wreckage of Drystan's infantry. Heaps of gory, broken bodies, spread-eagled in their own gore among the litter of discarded gear.

Still the dragon banner flew above the carnage. Still Artorius fought at the head of his men. The High King's sword-arm was red to the shoulder, and the shield on his left arm beaten to splinters. He had suffered no wound that Drystan could see. Fatigue didn't seem to affect him. Like Morholt, he grew stronger as the morning wore on.

When the shattered remnants of his infantry were once again pushed back down the hill, Drystan raised his father's sword. The blade caught the wan light, and a cheer rose from the throats of his cavalry.

This was the moment he had patiently waited for since dawn. The footmen were exhausted, and two-thirds of the Companions were slain. It was time to complete his victory.

Drystan drove in his spurs. Fierce joy swept through him as his mare leaped forward.

The earth quaked under the hoofs of his riders. Led by the fearless, silver-armoured figure of their chief, they swept up the hillside and crashed against the threadbare line of shields.

Drystan galloped towards the dragon banner. Artorius had vanished. Three wounded Companions, crouched behind their shields, stood between Drystan and the dragon standard.

He wheeled at the last moment and hacked at their

spears. The Companions were weary, else they might have stabbed at his horse's exposed flanks. Instead they retreated under the hail of blows, and Drystan was able to drive his horse between the shields and force them apart.

Now they were easy prey. He chopped one man's face apart, sliced the throat of another. The third bravely stood his ground, but his head was split open by one of Drystan's horsemen, who struck him from behind with an axe.

Drystan eagerly looked around for Artorius. He spotted the golden figure, less than ten feet away, down on one knee. The High King's head was bowed, and blood poured from his armpit. Caledfwlch was stuck in the ground next to him.

"Artorius! Guard yourself!" Drystan howled. The face under the dragon helm turned to look at him at the horsemen surging towards him.

The High King's eyes were brown, his mouth wet with gore. He snatched up Caledfwlch and struggled to his feet.

Drystan's sword flashed down. Artorius was too slow to parry, and the blade crunched against the side of his helmet. It left a dent in the iron. Drystan laughed as he struck again, and again, and again.

Artorius swayed under the relentless hail of blows. Caledfwlch dropped from his nerveless fingers. He toppled to the ground. Dark red blood leaked from under his helmet.

Drystan looked down on the twitching body of his rival. He paused to savour the moment. This was his greatest triumph. He had slain, man to man, the High King of Britannia, the victor of Mount Badon, whose name was famous from the shores of Hibernia all the way to distant Frankia. Never again, unless he marched on Constantinople and slew Caesar himself, would Drystan taste such glory.

The Companions would not surrender, so every last one was butchered where he stood, fighting back-to-back with his comrades. Soon the hillside was smothered with their bodies. They took a heavy toll before they died. Over half of Drystan's force was wiped out, and the exhausted survivors barely had strength to stand.

Goron and Llwch, both of them sore wounded, limped across the battlefield to join Drystan.

He stood over the royal corpse. "Here, Llwch!" he cried, "here lies your old master!"

"I gave him the death he deserved," he added modestly, "though, in truth, I thought he would be a more formidable opponent."

Llwch ran a hand through his sparse hair, rank with sweat, and gazed down at the huge body. Frowning, he knelt to study the bruised and battered face under the dragon-crested helmet.

"You thought to slay the dragon," he said, "you have felled a lion instead. This is not Artorius."

Drystan blanched. "What?" he snarled, "of course it's him. Who else?"

Llwch made a choking noise, and covered his face with his hands.

"This is Gwalchmei," he moaned, "Gwalchmei, one of the Three Chief Warriors of the Island of the Mighty. Gwalchmei, who rescued Bedwyr at Mount Badon and held off the vanguard of the Saxon host. Gwalchmei, the first of my sword-brothers, my greatest friend among the Companions."

"This is my reward. This is how God punishes the faithless. To let me live, and set before me the corpses of my friends."

"Impossible," said Drystan, "you must be mistaken. I took Caledfwlch from him."

He lifted the sword. The hilt was magnificent, richly furnished with a gold and garnet pommel, guards of beaten gold plates and with gold fittings on the hilt. The blade was decorated with intricate weaving patterns, and clearly the work of a master smith. It was a sword fit for any king to bear.

Llwch lifted his head. There was a haunted look to his

eyes, and tears glistened like snail-tracks on his sunken cheeks.

"No," he whispered, "that is Gwalchmei's sword. I saw him wield it in a dozen battles. Caledfwlch has a plain ivory hilt, stamped with Roman eagles."

"Tricked!" shouted Goron, "Artorius has made fools of us!"

Drystan turned away in disgust. The High King was an even shrewder and more ruthless man than he thought. Faced with certain death, he had dressed Gwalchmei in his royal armour, and slipped away during the night. Loyal to the end, his men had gladly died to cover his escape.

"He can't have got far," Drystan muttered, desperate for a straw to cling to. He looked around at the bleak moor. Save for the occasional clump of spindly trees, there was barely any cover.

Then he glanced down at the river. It seemed unlikely. Any man who entered those cold, fast-rushing waters would most likely drown, or be dashed to death against the rocks downstream.

Still...the river followed a winding course over moor and woodland for several miles. Did Artorius trust enough in God, and his good fortune, to take the risk?

"Mount!" shouted Drystan, startling a few of his weary men who lay nearby, nursing their wounds, "we have a king to hunt!"

15.

Caerleon

The Round Hall, usually packed with bodies when the High King dispensed justice, was more than half-empty. Only nine of the twenty-five seats at the Round Table were filled, and the voices of those present echoed hollowly in the rafters of the vast chamber.

Gwenhwyfar sat in her customary seat to the left of her

husband's throne. To the right sat Cei, nursing a flask of wine and glaring belligerently at the endless line of supplicants.

The throne was occupied by Llacheu, the High King's second son and unofficial heir. A slim, quiet young man, dressed all in black and gold, with his late mother's pale complexion and raven-black hair, he made a striking figure. Just twenty years old, he radiated a natural authority and confidence more befitting a man twice his age.

The queen couldn't help noticing that he treated the supplicants with rather more consideration than her husband. Artorius was irritated by fine detail and tended to rush to judgement, according to his instincts. His son, by contrast, listened carefully to each case, no matter how trivial.

Artorius had done well to leave Llacheu to govern as regent. The young man was eager to prove himself. Under his quiet exterior possessed inexhaustible reserves of energy and concentration. A skilled warrior, he was an even finer scholar than his elder brother Cydfan, who would one day become Bishop of Llandaff and head of the Christian church in Britannia.

"Next," grunted Cei. Two ragged peasants stepped forward and bobbed nervously before the throne, twisting battered leather caps in their hands. Llacheu rested his back against the hard wood of the throne, crossed one elegant, well-turned leg over the other, and gestured at them to speak.

"Come," he said in a kind voice, "don't be afraid. You look like honest men. Honest men have nothing to fear in the Round Hall."

The peasants swallowed, stared at the floor, and then started to talk in thick country accents Gwenhwyfar could barely understand.

She rolled her eyes. It seemed they had quarrelled over ownership of a cow, and come all the way to Caerleon to seek the High King's judgement.

Gwenhwyfar had listened to hundreds of such cases. She constantly had to remind herself that these were matters of vital importance to the low-born, whose survival through a rough winter or poor harvest might depend upon their livestock.

"It's a good cow, lord ki - my lord," mumbled one, his coarse, weather-beaten face flushed scarlet as he stumbled over the titles, "she's in calf as well. Can't afford to lose her."

"Nor can I," the other said quickly. Llacheu leaned forward slightly, laced his fingers together, and started to ask probing, thoughtful questions: how old was the cow? What breed was she? Who owned the herd she came from? Was she pastured on common ground?

Gwenhwyfar stifled a yawn. *Either Llacheu is a fine play-actor,* she thought, *or he is genuinely interested in the damned cow.*

She had to admit, if his interest was feigned, he feigned it with conviction. Not so Cei, who slumped in his chair, half-drunk and yawning between every swallow of wine.

He becomes a different man when Artorius is absent from Caerleon. A lesser man. God grant my husband returns soon, before Cei kills himself with sloth and drink.

She knew Cei was lonely. His wife had died two years ago, and they had no children. There were rumours of a bastard daughter somewhere - most warriors, even married men, fathered bastards - but he never formally acknowledged her.

There was little love lost between Cei and Gwenhwyfar, else she might have offered to find him a new wife. He had never ceased to blame her for the temporary disgrace of his lifelong friend Bedwyr, and spurned her cautious efforts to mend the rift.

Gwenhwyfar had given up trying to cultivate a friendship with him. The man was insufferably proud, and appeared to take pleasure in clinging onto ancient grudges, long after everyone else had forgotten them. At the same time she appreciated his worth. As steward and spymaster, Artorius relied on him to keep the peace at court and weed out conspiracies against the throne. To see Cei in such a state, permanently soaked in wine and apparently indifferent to the world around him, was alarming.

The queen decided to take action. When Llacheu had finished dispensing justice, she would request a private audience with him, and discuss what to do about Cei.

That evening, when the long day was done, Gwenhwyfar sent a servant to find Llacheu and summon him to her chambers. Mindful of any potential loss of prestige, she had no intention of begging an audience with her husband's son, even if he was regent.

"I am the High Queen," she said to her mirror, an oval of beaten and polished bronze, while she waited for Llacheu to arrive, "second only to Artorius, woman though I may be. I will not be treated as an inferior, or behave like one."

Llacheu was a stranger to pride. When there came a gentle knock at the door of the antechamber, another of Gwenhwyfar's maids opened it to find the regent alone in the corridor outside. He gave his easy smile, and stepped past the flustered girl before she could announce him.

Gwenhwyfar flowed to her feet. She was tall for a woman, and taller than Llacheu by half a head. The extra height made her feel more confident.

"Majesty," said Llacheu, executing a graceful bow.

He had doffed his cloak and wore loose-fitting black tunic and braccae. His pallid, almost translucent skin and slight figure made him look alarmingly fragile. Not for the first time, Gwenhwyfar wondered how he could possibly be a son of Artorius. At least his elder sibling, Cydfan, had inherited their father's burly frame and fair complexion.

It was said that Llacheu took after his mother, Ganhumara. Those bards who still dared to sing of the High King's former concubine described her as a slender waif with long, raven-black hair. If Llacheu and his brother harboured any resentment over her death, they were careful not to show it.

"Lord regent," said Gwenhwyfar, responding to his bow with a cool nod, "you came alone. That is unwise. We must always be on our guard, even in the palace."

Llacheu gave an offhand shrug. "I dislike being nursemaided," he replied lightly, "and cannot bear to have spearmen plodding after me all day. I must have some privacy. My brother encourages me to trust in the protection of Christ."

Gwenhwyfar was irked by his careless attitude. "Christ defends those who defend themselves. Prayers will not save you from a dagger in the hands of a Saxon assassin. Be wise, lord regent, and furnish yourself with an armed guard."

He bowed again. Gwenhwyfar thought she detected a hint of mockery in the gesture. "As you wish, Majesty," he said, "did you request my presence merely to hand out advice? I am tired, and my head aches from listening to peasants and freemen argue all day. A worthy creature, the British peasant, but he seems to think that his livestock and grazing rights are the most important subjects in the world."

Gwenhwyfar snapped her fingers at the maid, who ran to fetch wine. "I won't keep you long," said the queen, "you did well today. You showed far more patience than my husband. I think he grows a little bored with the peace we have made, and was only too glad to ride away to war again."

Llacheu laughed, and accepted a silver goblet from the blushing maid. "Father is a born warrior," he said after taking a delicate sip, "never truly happy unless in the saddle, spear in hand, and with an enemy to kill. That is his nature. Mine is very different. I wish for nothing more than order and harmony. Ripe harvests, full bellies, and the rule of law."

Gwenhwyfar cradled her goblet. "My husband is proud

of you," she said carefully, "very proud. He often says you and Cydfan are the two fixed stars of his life. If anything should happen to either of you, he would be distraught. Inconsolable."

There was a flicker of impatience in Llacheu's eyes. "You have made your point, Majesty."

"Not quite," replied the queen, satisfied with her little victory, "I sent for you to discuss Cei."

Llacheu looked surprised. "Cei? What about the old fire-eater? Who has he insulted this time?"

Gwenhwyfar gestured at her maid to leave. The girl hurried out, shooting a last glance at Llacheu.

He is handsome, thought Gwenhwyfar, *in a fey, poetic sort of way. He would not do for me.*

"Cei insults everyone," she said, "let us speak plainly. The man is becoming a drunk, and a liability. He always had a weakness for strong wine, but until recently it never affected his work."

"True," murmured Llacheu, "he is much like the Emperor Trajan in that regard."

Gwenhwyfar let this pass. Llacheu and his brother had received the finest education their father could provide, and liked to show it off.

"The point is," she went on, "my husband has always relied heavily on Cei. I'm sure you are aware of his more clandestine duties."

Llacheu gave a brief nod. It was no secret among the High King's inner circle that Cei presided over a complex network of spies and double agents. Their secret work was essential to Britannia's security. In their own way, they were more effective guardians of the state than a dozen war-bands.

"You must speak to Cei," said Gwenhwyfar, "be firm with him. Direct. Tell him that unless he drinks less and pays more heed to his work, he will be replaced. No man, not even one of my husband's oldest friends, is irreplaceable."

Llacheu almost choked on his wine. "You must hold my courage in high esteem, Majesty," he gasped, "far higher than I deserve. Tell Cei to stop drinking? I would rather place my head in the jaws of a hungry bear."

Gwenhwyfar did not smile. "This is no laughing matter," she said in her most austere tone, "much depends on Cei. Too much. He is growing old, of course, which may be part of the problem. It might be time to turn him out to pasture."

Uninvited, Llacheu crossed to the side-table to pour himself more wine. While he poured, he gave Gwenhwyfar a sly, searching look.

"Cei has never been your friend," he said, "I wonder, Majesty, do you act against him out of concern for the realm, or to serve your own interests?"

The queen stiffened. This was plain speech, too plain for her liking. "Learn to guard your tongue as well as your body, lord regent," she replied coldly, "or you may find one brings trouble for the other."

Her anger seemed to amuse him. Gwenhwyfar gained the impression he was toying with her. Using her as practice. This only added to her fury.

She was in the mood for an argument, but instead Llacheu backed down. "Very well," he said, "you are the High Queen, after all, and everything you say is perfectly true. Cei has degenerated of late. Between us, I suspect my father is wilfully blind to it."

Gwenhwyfar scented another victory. "You will speak with him, then?"

"Yes. Even if the old dog leaves his teeth-marks in my throat. However..."

Llacheu drank again. The High Queen waited for the price he would ask in return.

"Cei is not the only problem at court," he said, "there is also your son, Amhar."

Gwenhwyfar felt the blood drain from her face. This was unexpected. "What of him?" she demanded.

"Come, Majesty. You must be aware of his conduct. The boy has no discipline. He refuses to be tamed. Yesterday the drill-master tried to beat him for breaking the wrist of his sparring partner. Amhar snatched the master's stick and snapped it over his head."

"Then the drill-master is obviously unfit to be in charge of young warriors," Gwenhwyfar retorted, "dismiss him and find a new one."

"With respect, Majesty, that won't do. Amhar is big for his age, and vicious with it. He is also over-fond of hurting boys smaller than himself."

"They should learn to defend themselves better! Britannia needs strong fighting men, not brittle-boned weaklings. Do you expect me to discipline Amhar?"

"Not exactly. The boy is wild, and no amount of beatings or harsh words will change him. I propose Amhar should be sent away from Caerleon, to one of our garrisons on the border of the Debated Lands. There he can learn his trade among grown warriors, and practice his savagery on the Saxons."

Gwenhwyfar put down her goblet and advanced on him. "You would deprive me of my son?" she asked softly.

Llacheu stood his ground. "He may still be of tender years, Majesty, but has clearly outgrown his boyhood. There is another consideration."

"I am regent," he added, tapping his chest, "guardian of the realm until the High King returns. The well-being of the people of Caerleon are my responsibility. That includes our young men. I will not allow your little brute to run amok."

Gwenhwyfar lifted her hand to strike him. With a severe effort of will, she lowered it again. To lose her temper would mean losing the battle. This was a battle, she realised that now. Llacheu saw her as a rival for power, and rivals could not be tolerated.

His father's son!

"Amhar is not only my son," the queen reminded him, "but your half-brother. You are happy to send your own brother, a mere boy, to risk his life in the Debated Lands?"

Llacheu's smooth features might have been carved in marble. Terror stabbed at Gwenhwyfar's heart. How much did this cold, shrewd youth know - or suspect - of Amhar's true parentage? Did he want the boy out of the way to prevent the inevitable shame and outrage, should the truth ever get out?

"I came here to inform you of my decision," he said in a quiet voice. "Amhar will go to the Debated Lands. I am sorry if that causes you distress. You can, I hope, see the practical necessity for it. People in our position cannot afford to indulge in sentiment. We all make personal sacrifices for the good of the state."

Gwenhwyfar could no longer rein in her temper. "Don't lecture me, you mealy-mouthed little turd!" she cried, "I see your true motives!"

She stabbed a finger at him. "This is your revenge! Revenge for the death of your mother. All these years you have been so meek and obedient, pretending to be the dutiful son, obeying your father's every command, fulfilling his every wish. I always suspected you for a play-actor. Ganhumara was a deceitful woman who betrayed her husband. You are a sprig of the same rotten branch!"

The insults slid off Llacheu like rainwater. "Majesty, please," he said mildly, "calm yourself. The servants will be listening."

"Let them! Let all the world know your true nature!"

Gwenhwyfar looked around wildly for her dagger. It lay in its sheath on the wolfskin coverlet of her bed. She took a step towards the bed.

She stopped. The black clouds in her mind ebbed a little. The consequences of assaulting Llacheu were unthinkable.

"You wrong me, Majesty," he went on in the same

unruffled tone. "My father has always been good to me. I bear him no ill-will. I think only of the good of Britannia. Perhaps you should do the same."

His quick footsteps thumped on the carpet, and the door slammed shut even as Gwenhwyfar's dagger whirled through the air and rebounded off the timber.

16.

Artorius was strapped to a wheel. The wheel turned, the straps broke, and he was flung head-first into a pit of snakes.

The fangs bit into his flesh. Every muscle in his body flared with pain. He sank into a heap of squirming, glistening bodies.

His struggles were in vain. He could not escape. Their coils were wrapped tight about him. The air was crushed from his lungs. His body was dragged into blackness and suffocation.

He tried to scream again. Only a raw, scraping noise came from his throat. Artorius fell into shadow. The serpents closed about him.

They dragged him down, down into the deepest circle. Some other burden clung to him, a weight he could not endure. Instinct screamed at him to cast it off. He tore one hand free of the coils,

That was not the end. He swirled amid the darkness, conscious only of movement, unable to see or speak or hear. Something slammed into his gut. He gaped in silent agony, and the random eddies of the pit hurled him towards a speck of light.

The speck rapidly increased in size. Soon the pale light flooded him, blinded him, filled his mouth and nostrils. The serpents fell away. He was able to move again.

Artorius broke the surface and floated in calm waters. A branch swirled lazily past. He grabbed it and clung tightly while it carried him west, following the course of the river.

Then he was in the shallows, half-drowned, washed up among a patch of reed beds. He lay on his back in the soft mud and blinked up at grey skies. A light rain fell from the clouds scudding across the arch of the world.

When enough strength and sense had returned to him, Artorius coughed and rolled onto all fours. He struggled through the waterlogged reeds until he reached firm ground. There he collapsed onto his face.

One thought drummed through his head.

I have lost Caledfwlch. I have lost Caledfwlch. The sword of kings. Caesar's sword. Lost in the river.

Artorius had misjudged his own strength, and the force of the river. The weight of the sword-belt had threatened to drown him. He had no choice save to cast it off. Now the famous sword was lost somewhere on the river bed, and his honour and prestige lost with it.

His second thought was for his men. Eighty Companions, eighty of the finest soldiers in the West, many of them his friends. Slaughtered due to his own folly.

My men. I abandoned them. They chose to die for my sake. I should have died with them. Their blood is forever on my head.

Gwalchmei's face rose before him: Gwalchmei as a cheerful, freckle-faced boy, when Artorius first met at him Mons Ambrius. Dead, cut down by traitors who thought they had slain the High King.

The boyish face was replaced by the narrow features of Llwch Llemineawg. Artorius drew in breath to scream hatred at the face of a man he had once loved and trusted, and was racked by another coughing fit.

When he had recovered, he forced himself to stand. His legs wobbled under him, but he was able to stay upright and look around.

The river had carried him into a thickly wooded valley. He vaguely recognised the landscape, and reckoned that

Celliwig lay not far to the west. Not that the deserted stronghold was any kind of refuge now. Once he realised Artorius had escaped, Drystan would send out riders to hunt down the fugitive.

Still half-stunned, Artorius struggled to think. Drystan's huntsmen would follow the course of the river. It passed close by Celliwig, too obvious a hiding place for them to miss.

His only hope was to stick to the wild. Avoid highways - there were few enough of those in Kernow - and head for Dumnonia. If he could reach friendly territory, there was a chance Artorius might reverse this appalling defeat, and avenge the sacrifice of his men.

He set off into the deep woods. At least he had some rations, a crust of bread and a few slivers of dried meat, stuffed into a drawstring bag tied to the strip of leather that served him for a second belt. Enough to last him a day or so. He could drink from the river.

Many years had passed since Artorius last roughed it. He was young then, and life in the wild had seemed part of a grand adventure. Nor was he alone. There had always been comrades to laugh and sing and dice with, share the discomfort of a chill winter's night around a warm campfire.

To stumble through the dark, alone, with naught save a few mouthfuls of bread and meat between himself and starvation, was no kind of adventure at all.

He had nothing save his bare hands to defend himself. Despite his best efforts as High King, the wild places of Britannia were still plagued by wandering bands of robbers and outlaws.

A born horseman, Artorius was not used to travelling any great distance on foot. After an hour or so he began to appreciate the torments of his infantry when on campaign, forced to march for miles along bad roads. No wonder they were often too weary and footsore to fight at the end of it.

The woods were silent, full of hidden or imagined terrors. Artorius was still wet from the river. He needed to find warmth and shelter, quickly, before the damp got into his bones.

After another hour of so of groping through the dank, shadowy forest, his teeth started to chatter. *God help me*, he thought, *is this how it ends? The High King, heir to Ambrosius, found dead in a ditch somewhere in the wilds of Kernow?*

God was kind. Just when he thought the forest would go on forever, a light glimmered through the trees. Ever cautious, Artorius crept warily towards the dim yellow glow. At times he went on all fours in the thickest of the undergrowth, ignoring the briars and thorns that snagged at him.

He reached the edge of a little clearing. Much of it was occupied by a cottage, a poor dwelling of thatch and wattle, with a couple of outbuildings beside it. Artorius heard the whinny of a horse from inside the larger of them. To the north, a narrow track dwindled away into the forest.

The light shone from the cottage's only window. There was a fire inside, and smoke drifted from the hole cut into the thatch. Artorius thought he heard the murmur of voices.

He chewed his lip. This was the sanctuary he needed. How to deal with the occupants, though? They were unlikely to welcome some ragged stranger to share what little food they had.

His eye was drawn to a neat stack of logs under the lean-to propped against the northern wall. An axe lay against them. The blade looked good and sharp.

Artorius circled around the edge of the clearing, until the window was no longer in his line of sight. He padded on the balls of his feet towards the lean-to and snatched up the axe.

The weight felt good in his hands. At last he had a weapon. He pressed his back to the wall and edged around the side of the cottage. Mindful of being seen, he ducked under the sill of the window and knelt beside the door.

He took a few deep breaths and listened to the voices inside. One belonged to an old man, harsh and cracked.

"My foot is swollen with gout," the elderly voice whined, "thanks to this accursed weather. How can I work if I cannot even stand?"

"Work?" snapped another voice, a woman's this time, high-pitched and indignant, "when did you ever work, Morgant? What do you know of work? You were born idle."

"Aye," he retorted miserably, "never fear, my death will not be long in coming. This winter shall be the end of us..."

Artorius rolled his eyes. It would almost be a mercy to kill them both. As it was, he only meant to rob them.

He put his boot to the door, a flimsy object of half-rotted timber, kicked it down and marched inside.

The old woodcutter and his wife screamed in unison. Morgant tried to rise, and fell off his stool into the hearth, raising a cloud of sparks. His wife, who had more presence of mind, reached for a long knife on the table.

"Wait!" cried Artorius, "I don't want to hurt you. Just give me food and shelter for the night. There need not be any..."

The old woman gnashed her blackened gums and stabbed clumsily at his face. Artorius jerked his head aside.

"For God's sake," he muttered. She sliced at him again, forcing him to retreat. He well knew how much damage a knife could do, even in the hands of one with no training.

"Out!" she squawked, "out, you hairy thief! You think we are so poor and defenceless? Easy prey? Out of my house, this instant, or I'll spill your guts over the floor!"

Artorius put a swift end to the farce. When she stabbed at him again he caught her wrist and squeezed. Her fingers sprang open and dropped the knife. Still game, she clawed at him with her other hand.

He brought the stave of his axe down on her head, just hard enough (he hoped), to knock her out for a while.

Her eyes crossed, and she collapsed. Artorius caught her thin body - it was like handling a bundle of twigs - and gently lowered her to the floor. There were no carpets or rushes, just bare earth.

There was a moan of despair from the hearth. "Rhian! You have slain my wife!" wailed Morgant. The spindly old man tried to crawl towards her, dragging his hideously swollen foot behind him.

"She isn't dead," said Artorius, "I just put her to sleep for a while. Let me help you stand."

"No! No! Don't touch me!"

Morgant cringed, and scrambled away when Artorius offered his hand. The High King shrugged, picked up Agnes and laid her in a seated position against the wall.

He took stock. The cottage was a cramped, single-room affair, with a ladder leading up to a loft where the aged couple slept. Other than the table and two stools, there was no furniture. An old broom rested against the wall, and there was a clay jug on the table, full of water. The remains of a supper fire smouldered inside the hearth, itself a rough circle of stones.

Morgant's fall had knocked aside a griddle laid over the hearth. The cakes baked for supper were now scattered over the floor.

Artorius coughed. The air was rank with smoke. He wiped his streaming eyes, picked up one of the cakes and took a careful bite. It was a simple mixture of flour and water, with no fruit or even honey to sweeten the bland taste.

Still, at least it was warm, and filled a gap in Artorius' stomach. While the greybeard watched him in terrified silence, he blew on the fire until it glowed again, righted the griddle and gathered up the rest of the cakes.

"There," he said, placing them back on the griddle, "nothing like a warm meal, eh?"

Morgant continued to watch him from the shadows. Artorius fastened the thin wooden shutters on the window, picked up the broken door and wedged it into the doorframe. Now the light from the fire would be hidden from prying eyes in the woods. Artorius knew he should allow no fire at all, but he was still wet through and needed the heat.

He seated himself on one of the hard stools. An uneasy silence fell. Artorius chewed slowly on a cake and strained his ears to listen for the dreaded sound of hoofbeats.

Time passed. The rain pelted down outside. He almost pitied Drystan's men, stumbling through the wet and darkness. They would be tired from the battle, some of them wounded.

Rhian groaned and lifted her head. Her eyes flickered open. She looked around dully, unable to focus, one hand tugging feebly at a strand of grey hair.

Artorius gave a silent prayer of thanks. He had feared the old woman was too weak to survive the blow he gave her. Of all the deaths on his conscience, that would have been the heaviest.

Her husband dragged himself across the room. They clung to each other like a couple of frightened children. She was still half-dazed, and sobbed in pain when he gently probed the lump on her brow.

The axe rested across Artorius' knees. A terrible thought struck him.

They have to die.

It was the only sensible course. Otherwise, after he left, they might betray him to Drystan in hope of reward. To still their tongues, and hide the bodies in the woods, was the safest way.

His hosts might have been ignorant, but they were no fools. "If you mean to do it, do it," said the man, with more courage than Artorius would have credited him with.

"You are cruel," he hissed when Artorius didn't respond, "I see it in your eyes. You have done many evil things in your time. Taken many lives. Why do you hesitate? You have a good axe. I have slain wolves with it. Strike, and have done."

"Eat," said Artorius after a moment, nodding at the cakes on the grill, "both of you. Before the fire goes out. There is water in the jug. Dip a cloth into the water and hold it against your wife's brow."

Morgant did as he was told. Artorius watched him, wary of any sudden movement. He had forgotten to pick up the knife. It lay on the floor where Rhian had dropped it, within reach of the old man and his wife.

They have to die.

The woodcutter was right. What difference did two more deaths make? Artorius had long ceased to count the people he had slain, on the battlefield and off it. As High King, he was sometimes obliged to condemn men - and women - to the gallows. True, they were thieves and murderers, mere scum, the dregs of the gutter. That didn't stop their faces haunting him at night.

His first duty was to protect his subjects. Was not a thief his subject? What protection did Artorius offer him? The priests would say that hanging a thief rescued his soul from damnation.

Priests lie. They tell me pretty falsehoods to soothe my conscience, and win my favour.

They are not alone. Every man wants something from me. Bit by bit, piece by piece, I am picked apart. What shall remain of me by the end?

At least the cottage was relatively warm and dry. The thatch was old, but kept out the rain. Artorius waited until his clothes were merely damp. Then he stood up.

"Strip," he ordered Morgant. He kicked off his boots and peeled off his woollen tunic.

The old man gaped stupidly at him. "Strip," Artorius said again, "we're going to swap clothes. Don't worry. You have the best of the bargain. This is fine wool."

A dim light of understanding dawned in Morgant's clouded eyes. He tugged off his ankle-length smock, hooded mantle and braccae and handed them to Artorius.

The garments were loose, soiled and patched in places, and a surprisingly good fit on Artorius' burly frame. Old age and ceaseless hard labour had bent Morgant's back and bowed his legs, but he had clearly been a large, powerful man in his youth.

"Now," said Artorius, "put my clothes on and sit close to the fire until they are dry. Can't have you catching a chill."

Despite his earlier flash of defiance, Morgant was obedient as any child. He pulled on Artorius' damp garments, knelt beside the hearth and warmed his gnarled hands over the flames. Occasionally he cast anxious looks at his wife. She in turn stared at their guest with pure malice in her little eyes.

All through the night Artorius sat and fought a silent war with his conscience. He didn't dare sleep. Morgant might be a broken reed, but Rhian still looked keen to slit his throat if she got the chance. The fire burned low, filled the room with shadows. Eventually it spluttered out altogether.

By this time the grey light of dawn had started to filter though cracks in the shutters. The old couple dozed against the wall, huddled up together. Artorius, who had stood more night watches than he could remember, was wide awake. His bones ached - how he longed for the baths at Caerleon - but he was still alive and whole.

They have to die.

He ran a finger along the blade of the axe. Morgant kept it good and sharp. Two swift, clean strikes, and the thing would be done.

It would be a mercy. How long could they live? Another year, at most. They are doomed to die of starvation, or cough their lungs out by the fire.

Once again, Artorius refused to step into darkness. To slay men on the battlefield, or send criminals to hang, was quite different from the cold-blooded murder of two defenceless peasants.

Artorius rose, wincing at the stiffness in his joints, and carefully placed the axe beside the door. Morgant and Rhian slept on while he took an old leather bag from a nail on the wall. He found half a loaf of coarse rye bread on a shelf, along with a piece of hard cheese, and stuffed these into the bag.

He slung the bag over his shoulder, pushed the broken door aside and stepped outside. It was a grey, tattered morning, the unearthly silence of the forest broken only by the rustle of rain among bare winter branches.

I hang men for horse-stealing, Artorius thought wryly as he entered the tiny stable. The creature inside was in better condition than he expected, a dappled grey mare in the prime of life. Artorius spoke gently to the mare, stroking her mane and neck.

There was a pile of saddlery in the corner. The mare was quiet as he fitted the reins and saddle to her.

With a last look at the smoky little cottage, he climbed aboard the saddle, dug in his heels and cantered away into the forest.

No-one who saw the burly vagrant in the grubby smock, his sullen face hidden under a hood, riding alone through the forests of Britannia, could have imagined this was Artorius, the High King.

The stolen bread and cheese, and what remained of his rations, lasted him three days. He kept to the wild, following the stars, and on the fourth day crossed the border into Dumnonia.

Still there was no sign of pursuit. Perhaps Drystan's men had given up or been recalled. Save for King Marcus at Caer Y Brenin - assuming he still held out - the whole of Kernow was now in enemy hands. Drystan and King Budic would need all the spears they could muster to hold down their conquest.

On the fourth day after his defeat, the forests thinned out and Artorius found himself wandering alone through a sea of marsh and low-lying fen. The skies hung heavy, tinged with yellow, and a storm forever threatened on the horizon.

His belly rumbled with hunger. There were only a few morsels of bread and cheese left in the bag. He saved these for the last extremity, and drank brackish water from the marsh. The mare was in better condition. He was careful not to push the animal too hard, and led her on foot over rough ground.

The air was warm and thick as soup. It grew warmer as he toiled further north, following an erratic path through the treacherous bogs and whirlpools. There was no sun, yet Artorius feared he might roast. Sweat rolled down his body and dripped off his brow.

Flies. Artorius tried to fight them off, but there were too many. Endless clouds of flies, buzzing and crawling under his hood, into his sleeves, over his skin. Strangely, they left his mare alone. He panicked.

They will eat me alive!

He knew where he was. Without meaning to, he had stumbled into the Summer Country, that strange, shifting land in the heart of Dumnonia. It was said to be the gateway to Annwn, the Otherworld, where the old gods still ruled and the laws of man and nature were overturned.

The Summer Country was the home of the Painted People or Hill Folk, the last dregs of the oldest inhabitants of Britannia, driven into these marshes by the ancestors of the Britons. As High King, Artorius let the Hill Folk alone, and forbade any of his subjects from entering their realm. Those who did seldom returned.

Artorius had been here before. With a courage fuelled by outrage and humiliation, he led his cavalry into the

Summer Country to hunt down Melwas, the traitor who abducted Ganhumara from Caerleon. Artorius slew Melwas in single combat before the gates of his hill-fort, and then...

No. I will not think of it.

Even now, so many years later, Artorius was haunted by his treatment of Ganhumara. He had loved her, in his way, and allowed jealousy and wounded pride to get the better of him. The thought of being cuckolded - that Ganhumara had gone willingly with her abductor - drove him to an act of terrible cruelty. He had placed Ganhumara aboard a boat with a single oar, and let her drift out to sea with no provisions.

She had almost certainly drowned. He often pictured her frail, lifeless body, washed up on the sands of some remote beach. Her death was not only a crime, but a mistake. Artorius had always known that one day God would punish him for it.

Perhaps this was his punishment. To end his days in defeat, after so many triumphs, cut off from his men and all he loved, forced to wander the trackless wastes of the Summer Country until he collapsed or was devoured.

I lost Caledfwlch.

The loss of his sword, ultimate symbol of his power and authority, spelled the end of his good fortune.

Then the voices started. Artorius had heard them before, during the hunt for Melwas: ghostly voices in the marsh, the sound of lost souls or forgotten gods, doomed to wander the Summer Country and mourn the torments they had suffered on earth.

"It is hard to leave you, my love, but at least there will be no more pain..."

"Bury me next to our child...promise me you will bury me next to her in a peaceful place, where the wild flowers grow, and our bones can lie entwined for eternity..."

"Wretch! You come before me now, when I no longer have the strength to hurt you. What a coward I have

nurtured...what a fool I am..."

"Please, no, please...I have prayed endless hours, I have founded a church in your honour, and still you take them from me...is it all for nothing then?"

"All for nothing...no salvation, no bliss beyond death...nothing save the dust of the tomb...those who loved us will soon forget...the cold grave and worms in our flesh..."

"The promises of Christ are false! Christ the Deceiver and his lying priests! The nailed god has betrayed me....the pain!....no rest, nothing but pain and eternal pain..."

"I would not be alone....never alone...dear God, I shall run mad with loneliness...mad, mad, mad...."

The miserable, soul-rending chorus was unbearable. Artorius stopped his ears against it and staggered on through the haze and flies. His eyesight blurred. It seemed to him the perpetual sun melded and reformed into twin pillars of flame, burning like twin candles on the dim horizon. Their hellish glow lit up the meaningless, dreary wasteland of the Summer Country, a mockery of light and life, while the voices rose to a storm and the clouds of flies savaged his flesh.

He spied a pool of clear water surrounded by a ring of twisted, leafless trees. The water appeared to simmer in the heat. He let go of his horse's reins and staggered towards it, wrenching at his clothes. He wanted to plunge into the water and drown the flies that clung to him like parasites, feeding on his blood.

A loose stone twisted under his foot and sent him headlong into the dirt. Artorius fell on his face, crawled blindly towards the pool. The flies were in his eyes now, as well as his mouth and nostrils. He could neither see nor breathe.

"Artorius."

A dry, throaty voice. At the sound of it the cloud of flies suddenly dispersed. Artorius was able to see and breathe again.

He blinked, and saw a man squatting on one of the dead branches near the pool. The man might have been handsome, once, but years of privation had left their mark. He was painfully thin, his skin burned nut-brown, his face a leathery, wrinkled mask. A pair of fiercely intelligent eyes peered out from hooded and puckered lids, and a straggly beard, like a growth of dirty moss, reached down to his waist. His hair was grey and scanty, with faded streaks of reddish-brown.

His long, bony arms clutched a staff, similar to the one Morgana, Artorius' foster-sister, used to carry. It was made of some kind of dark wood, almost as gnarled as its owner. The stranger's only garment was a long woollen robe, tied at the waist with a bit of string. He went barefoot, and the nails of his feet were black and broken.

Something about him reminded Artorius of Nudd, the ugly dwarf who had guided him to Caer Thannoc, the hidden stronghold of Melwas.

"You know my name," said the king, climbing to his feet, "how? I don't recall seeing your face before. I'm not likely to forget it."

The other man's hideously lined features cracked into a grin. "You speak plain, Artorius. Good. No more or less than I expected. I have seen you often, from a distance. A very great distance."

Artorius looked at him sharply. Was this man an enchanter? Perhaps he was no man at all, but some demon or malicious god. The Summer Country was said to be full of such unearthly creatures, survivors of Britannia's pre-Christian past.

The wizened stranger seemed to read his thoughts. "It is no use wondering," he said with a chuckle, "I often wonder myself. There are all kinds of stories. One tale insists I am the son of a woman raped by the Devil. Or else I had no parents at all, but am forged of the elements. A creature of earth and water, with a lump of cold iron for a heart. Yes, all kinds of stories..."

His voice trailed away, and his eyes took on a faraway look. "Memory fades," he added, "yet I recall a battle on a moor, far to the north...the shield-walls clashed, the war-yells rose, and one side had the victory."

"My sweet lord was slain in the fight. He died, and his sons, and his noble hall-troops. All fell victim to the grim spear-play. The sorrow drove me mad, and I fled to wander in the wild. Alone, feared and despised. A lunatic, some called me, others a prophet, others a magician. They stoned me when I approached their villages, and drove me out with sticks and curses, and would have drowned me in the river..."

"The river, yes. That is where the old god found me. Where I was cleansed, and renewed, and restored to life. For a while. A little while."

He levelled his staff at Artorius. "The gods sent me here to find you, Artorius. To watch you, and shepherd you, and see you come to no harm."

Artorius had listened carefully to the man's odd manner of speech. He tended to speak in triads - *he died, and his sons, and his noble hall-troops* - which was the sign of a bard. The battle in the north sounded real enough (there were always battles in the north) and any number of hermits, saints and madmen wandered the hills and forests of Britannia.

"Give me your name, old man," he said, "since you make so free with mine."

"I have several," replied the other, with a hint of pride, "the one I like most is Myrddin Wyllt. It has a certain ring to it, no?"

"You have come a long way from your homeland, Myrddin Wyllt," said Artorius, "and for no clear reason. Why should your pagan gods wish to help me? I am a Christian king."

Myrddin rose from his branch. He was tall, far taller than he first appeared, and towered a clear head above Artorius.

"The gods see into your heart, lord king," he said, "yes, you worship the nailed god, called the Christ, the carpenter of Galillee. Or pretend to. Yet it was not Christ who chose you as the saviour of Britannia. It was not Christ who gave you Caledfwlch, the Red Death, the Hard Hitter, to wield against Britannia's enemies."

Artorius hung his head. "I lost Caledfwlch," he muttered, "the river took it. I am unworthy."

"What the river takes, it can also restore. Am I not living proof of that? Step into the pool, lord king."

Artorius eyed the water suspiciously. "What for?" he demanded.

"To be reborn. You passed the test."

"Test? What test?"

Myrddin hugged the staff to his thin chest. "You spared the woodcutter and his wife. There is compassion in you, Artorius. You hold to your oath. The king stag is still fit to rule, and must live a while yet. Who will defend us if he falls?"

Despite his misgivings, Artorius found himself drawn to the water's edge. A yellow haze still shimmered over it. He slowly removed his borrowed clothes and stepped naked into the pool.

It was pleasantly warm. Artorius waded in up to his neck, basking in the effect of the heat on his tired muscles. For a moment he forgot where he was, and allowed his head to slip under the water, just as he did in the bath-house at Caerleon.

The pool was deeper than he thought. For a while he floated, suspended in the blue depths. Above him the pale yellow light of the Summer Country sparkled on the surface. Artorius thought he glimpsed a ring of golden stars, slowly orbiting a much larger sun. He knew this was impossible.

The sky here was featureless.

He emerged to find that Myrddin had gone. In his place, leaning against the twisted tree, was a sword.

The sword rested inside a red leather scabbard. Artorius gasped when he recognised the worn ivory hilt, stamped with a pair of golden Roman eagles.

He dragged himself out of the water, dressed quickly and ran to fetch his horse. She had waited obediently for him while he spoke to the enchanter.

"Remember, lord king, there are other powers in this world..."

Myrddin's voice was like a breath on the wind. Artorius looked around, but saw no sign of him.

He approached the tree and reached for the sword. His fingers closed around the hilt and slowly drew the blade from its sheath.

This was Caledfwlch. The same weight and balance, the same grip, the same notch two-thirds up the blade where it had once rebounded off a Saxon helm. A wave of exhilaration swept through Artorius. The gods had forgiven him!

He swung aboard his mare. If her strength held, within two days he could be out of this strange realm and near the border of Gwent.

"The king stag is still fit to rule...who will defend us if he falls?"

These words thundered inside Artorius' skull as he drove in his heels and urged the mare into a gallop.

He was king again, and had a kingdom to save.

17.

Cotyaeum, Phrygia Epictetus

Both armies were set out like thousands of chess pieces. The broad plain they stood on, flat and featureless, served for a board.

I am one of many pawns, thought Medraut.

He was positioned on the extreme left flank of the Roman army, though it was Roman in name only. Most of the troops were Gothic foederati. Eight thousand horse and foot, sent by the Emperor Anastasius to chastise the troublesome Isaurians and drive them back into their mountains.

Those mountains loomed to the west under massive blue skies. Shreds of white cloud hovered over the distant peak. This rocky and inhospitable terrain was the gateway to Isauria, now officially a rebellious province. The Eastern Empire had fallen into civil war.

The war promised to be a long and gruelling one. Even if Rome won here, and defeated the Isaurians in open battle, the province itself would still have to be reduced. There were any number of fortified outposts and little towns hidden away up in the hills. It was the unenviable task of the Roman generals to conquer them all.

A cold wind rippled across the plain. Thousands of colourful pennons fluttered in the breeze. It was almost spring, yet winter clung stubbornly to the high places of Anatolia.

Medraut had been on campaign for months, and could not remember what it was like to be truly warm. Even inside his coat of ring-mail, with a leather tunic and woollen under-shirt beneath it, he shivered.

Perhaps it was fear of death. And of failure. He glanced over his shoulder at his men. Ten light auxilia, spear-armed Gothic troopers mounted on swift ponies. He was a decanus now, a junior officer in charge of ten men. His superiors saw great potential in him, or so they claimed.

The men looked steady enough. Bearded, hard-eyed faces stared back at him from under ridged helmets. They were young, none older than twenty, anxious to prove themselves.

"Remember your orders," Medraut barked at them for the tenth time that morning, "keep to the left, and follow my lead. Advance and retire on my signal. Otho, do you hear me?"

Otho, a red-bearded trooper with startling green eyes, gave a nod. "Good.," Medraut finished lamely, "If I fall, you take command."

He coughed to hide his embarrassment, and turned back to study the enemy. Doubtless his men thought he was an old mother hen, forever clucking over them, and laughed at him behind his back. Let them. They were raw, full of the arrogance and swagger of untried youth. When the real fighting started, they might appreciate his experience.

The Isaurian host filled the western half of the plain. Medraut was both impressed and appalled by their courage. Led by Longinus of Cardala, a former senior imperial official deprived of his rank by Anastasius, they had come down from their mountains and attacked the towns and cities of nearby provinces. For weeks they plundered, burned and looted at will. The skies of north-west Anatolia were still bruised by the smoke of their conquests.

Faced with a Roman army, Longinus had decided to risk a battle instead of retreating into the hill country, where he might have led his enemies a merry dance for years. His confidence was understandable. Some ten to fifteen thousand Isaurians were drawn up opposite the Roman lines. Medraut's eyes ached as he tried to take in the long lines of infantry in the centre, rank after rank of spears and shields and steel helmets, a teeming forest of bright banners. Their cavalry, mostly light auxilia, were arrayed on the wings.

Longinus clearly meant to fight a defensive battle. His army had started to deploy before first light, and placed overturned wagons at regular intervals along the front line of his infantry. Behind them waited his archers and slingers, ready to unleash a hail of missiles on the Romans.

Medraut's heart lurched inside him as trumpets sounded

to his right. For almost an hour messengers had galloped back and forth along the Roman lines. It almost seemed as though the fight would never begin. Part of him hoped so. Medraut had witnessed enough violent death to fear the onset of another battle.

Another, greater, part of him loved the glorious ceremony and spectacle of war. His soul thrilled to the sight of the heavy cavalry on the left flank of the Roman army moving forward with heavy tread, pennons blazing in the silvery winter sunshine. Five hundred veteran troopers in burnished ring-mail, their officers in lamellar armour: coats of overlapping steel plates or scales laced together. Tougher and more rigid than mail, lamellar offered greater protection against blunt weapons such as maces and axes.

This is the stuff of my childhood dreams, thought Medraut as the cavalry rumbled past. The earth shook under the weight of their passage, and the hoofs of their big horses kicked up clouds of dust from the stony plain.

Medraut raised his sword as the signal to advance. While the heavy lancers ploughed straight towards the Isaurian right flank, his troop was one of several detachments ordered to advance in support.

The squadrons of enemy spearmen contracted as the Goths bore down upon them. An ear-splitting chorus of trumpets and bugles sounded the charge. The horses shifted into a canter, then a gallop.

Medraut, stuck out on the far left, watched the phalanx of steel-clad riders thunder into the enemy lines. The Isaurian auxiliaries scattered rather than meet the charge head-on, and swarmed in again to cast their javelins from distance.

"Forward!" shouted Medraut. His task was to help drive off the skirmishers and keep them occupied while the Isaurian infantry were cut to pieces.

His men spurred into a gallop and spread out either side of him. Medraut drew back his first javelin and hurled it at the nearest Isaurian. It took the man in the chest and pitched him from the saddle. Medraut's pony leaped over the writhing body. He reached for his sword.

There was no need. The Isaurian skirmishers fled for sanctuary behind the second line of their infantry. Medraut wheeled his pony away from the hedge of spears and signalled at his men to fall back.

They were well-drilled, and followed him to the edge of the plain, where the land started to curve upwards to a series of barren ridges. He was pleased with their discipline, and gave Otho a nod of approval.

His troop was one of the few not to take the bait. Most of the rest of the Roman light horse had given chase and become entangled with the Isaurian footmen. Medraut winced as he saw men pitched from their saddles, their horses hamstrung or butchered. The Isaurian hillmen made superb infantry, probably the best in the Eastern Empire, and cut down the Goths with savage, practised efficiency.

Meanwhile the heavy cavalry made little impression on the Isaurian shield-wall. Unable to press home their charge against a wall of spears, they drew back and hurled javelins and axes into the tight-packed ranks of footmen. Some Isaurians fell, but the gaps were quickly plugged by men from the second line.

"What should we do, sir?" asked Otho. The young Goth's voice quivered with excitement. He and his comrades were like dogs straining at the leash, teeth bared, eyes bright and feverish. Given the chance, they would hurl their bodies into the press without a second's thought.

"Wait," said Medraut. They were at a safe distance from the battle, and he wanted to see how it progressed before making a decision. He hadn't survived ten years as a fighting soldier by doing anything rash.

The cavalry attack on the left had failed, but that was merely the first wave. A tremendous shout rolled across the plain as the Gothic infantry surged forward, some eight thousand spearmen formed into three gigantic phalanxes. Detachments of lightly-armed archers loped in their wake.

The Roman generals hurled them against the Isaurian footmen in the centre, and the hideous noise threatened to split Medraut's eardrums: horns and bugles and trumpets, the crack of shield-wall against shield-wall, the clash of spears, the thump of iron on wood, the screams and shouts and curses of thousands of men locked in deadly combat. The sky was darkened by a storm of stones, arrows, darts and javelins from both sides. Within moments the plain was carpeted with dead and wounded, and the air filled with screams.

Medraut gnawed at his lip while the outcome hung in the balance. The Isaurians were less well-equipped than the Goths - they fought in plain leather tunics and were armed with spears and daggers, while the Gothic footmen wore ring-mail and carried swords as well as spears and axes - but they were tough, stubborn, and fought in defence of their homeland.

Otho plucked at his cloak. "We can't just sit idle, sir," the young man pleaded, "I've got friends among the infantry. Some of them will be in the front line. We have to help!"

Medraut's hand moved swiftly. A second later, and the edge of his sword was against Otho's throat. "You do nothing unless I order it," he said in the quiet, firm voice his men had come to know and fear, "understand?"

The other man was sensible enough to back down. Medraut was fond of Otho, but wouldn't hesitate to cut the Goth's throat if he thought it necessary.

He heard rather than saw the Roman cavalry launch a charge on the right flank. The thunder of hoofs was a distant storm, heralded by another squall of trumpets.

Our generals are too cautious, he thought, *we should have thrown everything at the Isaurians, infantry in the centre and cavalry on both flanks, all at the same time. A single determined charge would have swept the hillmen away.*

A shudder rippled down the Isaurian line. Their infantry started to give ground. Medraut sensed the Gothic cavalry had broken through, heaping pressure on the Isaurians in the centre.

What would Longinus, the enemy general, do next? Medraut thought his only choice was to throw in his reserves and hope they shored up the breach. Otherwise the day was as good as lost. His infantry might hold their ground for a while, for the sake of pride if nothing else, but eventually crumble.

"They fail!" cried Otho, "their flank has gone!"

He was right. The Isaurian archers and slingers started to desert their posts and run towards the foothills to the east. A troop of reserve horse tried to stop the fugitives and herd them back towards the fight.

"Fools," murmured Medraut. To get in the way of men fleeing for their lives was always a mistake. He shook his head as several of the mounted officers were dragged from their saddles and knifed or beaten to death on the ground. Their comrades turned about and joined the rout, until the entire left wing of the Isaurian host had disintegrated.

A fresh blast of trumpets drew Medraut's attention to the south, where the survivors of the Gothic cavalry on the left rallied for another charge. The heavy cavalry stormed forward again, an unstoppable tide of steel and flesh, supported by the remains of the auxilia.

"Now, sir!" Otho begged, "let us go forward!"

Still Medraut hesitated. He caught a brief glimpse of Longinus, a tiny doll-like figure in golden lamellar mounted on a white horse, surrounded by his staff officers. The Isaurian general bawled at the officers and waved his sword at them, his face red under the crested helm.

He has panicked, thought Medraut, *and blames others for the crisis. His nerve is gone.*

Longinus' words had little effect. Most of the officers abandoned him and fled with the rest of the cavalry. Those who stayed tried to reason with the general, who rewarded their loyalty by screaming insults and beating them with the flat of his sword. One of the men he struck almost fell from the saddle, blood pouring from his nose and mouth.

The Gothic cavalry struck home. This time the battered Isaurian shield-wall could not deny them, and was crushed under the sheer weight of men and horses. One hillman after another simply vanished under the flailing hoofs, while the mailed Goths rode at will through the shattered enemy ranks, singing crude war-chants as they hacked and speared the Isaurians into bloody ruin.

Now the battle was won, Medraut judged it safe enough to join in. "On!" he cried, gave his reins a jerk and galloped towards the shambles of the Isaurian flank.

Here a billowing sea of dust, tinged with red, coated the warriors of both sides. Medraut rode straight into the maelstrom and threw his last javelin at the nearest Isaurian, who was on his knees in the dirt trying to hold together the shattered remnant of his jaw.

The javelin pierced the man's heart and killed him outright. Medraut drew his spatha and cut down two more Isaurians as they tried to flee past him. It was like killing rabbits: panic had infected the enemy host, turning brave men into cowards. Here and there a few stubborn groups of spearmen fought on, but the majority threw down their weapons and took to their heels.

Spears, shields and fallen banners littered the plain. More than one horse stumbled over the abandoned war-gear. Medraut was careful to slow his pony to a trot and guide her away from the worst of the slaughter. Roman officers, especially junior officers like himself, could not rely on the commissariat to supply them with fresh horses if their own beasts died or were lost.

Medraut had lost contact with his men. He lifted his

helmet to get a better view, but saw no sign of them among the mass of bodies. The Isaurians were now in full retreat, horse and foot streaming away towards the east, hotly pursued by the Goths. No Roman officer made any effort to restrain or recall their men. Medraut had witnessed routs like this before. He expected the killing would continue for hours, or until the Goths were too exhausted to pursue further. Some would chase the Isaurians too far into the foothills, and be ambushed and slain in their turn. Such was war.

It occurred to Medraut that he would seldom have a better chance to desert. In the chaos of the rout, all discipline had fallen away, and for the moment it was every man for himself.

He had often pondered this moment in recent weeks. The army could teach him little more, and he had no ambition to climb up the ranks and become a senior officer. His time among the Romans was merely part of his essential training. A means to an end. After so many years of exile, he was at last ready to return to Britannia.

To face his father in battle, and exact revenge for his mother's death.

Plenty of spare horses wandered over the battlefield, or stood next to their fallen riders, mournfully nuzzling at the bodies. He would need a spare mount for the journey ahead. Medraut guided his pony towards the nearest and snatched at the beast's reins before it could bolt.

To his relief, the other horse yielded, and allowed herself to be led away. While chaos and slaughter raged around him, Medraut quietly left the field of blood and struck out alone.

West, towards his far homeland.

18.

Caerleon

The return of the High King, a lone, bedraggled fugitive, exhausted and half-starved after several days on the road with little sleep and less food, was greeted with disbelief. At first the sentry on the gate struggled to recognise Artorius, and took him for a madman.

"Here is the proof of my sanity," Artorius croaked, holding up his sword. The sentry's mouth dropped open at the sight of Caledfwlch.

Shortly the gates swung open. Artorius wearily urged his stolen mare forward and trotted into the familiar streets.

Cei was there to greet him, along with the sentry and a dozen Companions. The steward's good eye widened with shock as he beheld the pitiful state of his master.

Now he was safe and among friends, the last of Artorius' overstretched stamina gave out. Cei and two of the Companions rushed forward to support him as he sighed and pitched forward into nothing.

Artorius woke on a couch inside a large, rectangular room with pillars at each corner and colourful murals painted on the walls. He vaguely recognised it as one of the antechambers inside the palace. Thanks to the hypocaust, always kept at full heat during the cold months, the chamber was blessedly warm.

A ring of concerned faces gazed down at him. Gwenhwyfar was among them, as well as Cei and both his sons. His head was propped up on soft pillows, and his naked body lay under a warm blanket with a wolfskin coverlet. It was the first real comfort Artorius had known for weeks. His head felt as though it was stuffed with wool, and all he wanted to do was sleep.

He forced himself to stay awake. "Water," he rasped. Gwenhwyfar beckoned at a slave, who filled a cup with red liquid from a jug and handed it reverently to the king.

Artorius swallowed the contents with relish. Watered wine, tinged with some medicinal herb or other. When he was done, he smacked his lips and let the cup fall to the floor.

"Well?" growled Cei, "now you've quenched your thirst, perhaps you might like to give us an explanation. What happened in Kernow?"

Artorius almost smiled. For all his aggressive insolence, Cei couldn't hide the anxiety in his voice.

"I was beaten," he replied, "lured into a trap, and utterly defeated. All my men were slain. I only survived thanks to the favour of God."

The gods, he added silently.

"All?" Now there was a tremor in Cei's voice. "How can that be? What of..."

"All dead. My entire command was destroyed. Gwalchmei died to save me. I ought to have died with him. I was afraid. I fled. The others persuaded me I had to live, that Britannia could not survive without Artorius as High King. But it was fear that compelled me."

Silence greeted this. To his surprise, Gwenhwyfar took his hand and stroked it. Her eyes were wet. No such moment of tenderness had passed between them for months, even years.

His sons looked grave. Stout, red-haired Cydfan, holy as ever, grasped the little silver crucifix hanging from his neck and mouthed silent prayers. Llacheu stood with his arms folded, tall and masterful as ever, forbidding in his black tunic and black cloak fringed with gold thread.

Cei turned to the slave. "You heard nothing," he said, wagging his finger under the boy's nose, "you did not hear the High King say those words. You will not repeat the words you didn't hear to anyone outside this room. If you do, I will hear of it. If you want to keep a tongue in your head, keep it still. Understand?"

The slave turned white, and gave a mute nod of agreement. "Good lad," said Cei, patting him on the cheek, "make yourself scarce."

"Now," he added, once the slave had padded out, "we may speak plainly. Artorius, explain in detail what happened."

The High King told them, of the storming of Celliwig, the treachery of Llwch Llemineawg - Cei fouled the air with curses when he heard of this - and the ambush in the ravine. Artorius spared none of the details of the last stand on the hillside, and how Gwalchmei persuaded him to use the river to escape.

"Drystan's men had the hill surrounded," he finished, "I left under cover of night, and the river carried me away. I have little doubt our men were all slaughtered at first light. Gwalchmei wore my cloak and armour to deceive the enemy."

He told them nothing of his wanderings in the Summer Country, or of the encounter with Myrddin Wyllt. They would not understand or even believe it. All that mattered was his survival, and how to restore the situation in Kernow.

When Artorius had finished his account, Llacheu spoke for the first time. "We should act quickly," he said, "Bedwyr must be recalled from Rheged and ordered to bring all the troops he can gather, including the garrison at Wroxeter. Envoys sent to all the loyal sub-kings. Cadwallon Lawhir and Caradog Freichras can muster eight hundred spears between them. With the remainder of the Companions and the other allied war-bands, we should be able to muster over fifteen hundred men. More than a match for anything Drystan and his Amoricans can put in the field."

Artorius was impressed. The pressure of leadership and responsibility had turned Llacheu into a man. Faced with disaster, he reacted with cool decisiveness, and refused to give way to panic or rashness.

God be thanked, thought Artorius, *I have bred a king.*

"Llacheu speaks sense," he said, "our best hope is strike back quickly. Send messengers to Rheged. Tonight. Now."

Artorius ordered a slave to allow him only two hours' sleep while Cei and the others plotted the campaign ahead.

The slave woke him on time. Still groggy, he heaved himself off the couch and saw a table laden with food. Light-headed and almost delirious with hunger, he slavered at the sight of the bread and cheese and fruit laid out on a silver platter, and a great heap of sliced beef. There was also a goblet and a silver flask of wine.

He dragged up a stool and set about the meal with furious relish. When the pit in his belly was adequately filled, he belched, drank down the last of the wine and wiped crumbs from his beard.

Two spearmen in red cloaks guarded the door. One approached the king and gave a respectful bow. He carried a blue woollen tunic, braccae, sandals and a fur-lined cloak.

"Lord king," he said nervously, "these clothes are for you."

This one is young, Artorius thought sadly. *Too young.*

His guilty mind summoned up an image of dozens of red-cloaked corpses, strewn over a desolate hillside in Kernow. Among them lay Gwalchmei, the friend and companion of his youth, clothed in golden armour and a purple-fringed cloak.

"What's your name, lad?" he asked quickly. The youth swallowed and looked away from the king's nakedness as he handed over the clothes.

"Gareth, lord king," he stammered in reply.

"My thanks, Gareth," said Artorius. He donned the tunic and cloak, belted on Caledfwlch, and lumbered out into the corridor.

The spearmen followed him like a couple of obedient hounds as he made his way through the maze of shadowy, torchlit passages and galleries into the great hall at the heart of the palace.

Here, where the Roman tribune of old and his advisers once sat, a table had been set up. A map of southern

Britannia was rolled out on the table. Cei and Llacheu, along with several lesser officers from among the Companions, talked quietly as they pushed wooden counters over the map.

Gwenhwyfar was also there. Artorius had no objection to her presence. She spoke more sense than many of his generals, and had a keen grasp of strategy.

"Have the messengers to Rheged been despatched?"

The others, with the exception of Gwenhwyfar, jumped at the sound of his voice. He grinned. It took a great deal to startle her.

Cei was first to recover. "They have," he snarled in return, "and why in God's name are you on your feet? You look like something crawled from a freshly dug grave. Back to your bed."

Artorius limped over to the table. "I am the High King," he said mildly, "remember to address me as such, old friend."

He ignored Cei's glower, and glanced down at the map. The round wooden counters represented his garrisons scattered up and down the frontier of free Britannia, as well as the strongholds of the various sub-kings.

His gaze fixed on Viroconium, a Roman colony town in the north of Powys, now refortified and used as a garrison base. Eighty Companions were permanently stationed there to act as a mobile reserve in case of any Saxon incursions from the east.

"It's a risk, father," said Llacheu, "our northern garrisons will be left with no support if we strip Viroconium of troops."

He echoed Artorius' fears, but there was no help for it. The Companions had suffered severe losses in Kernow. Their military reputation, previously invincible, was dented. Only they could restore it. Artorius would gather the Companions together into a single body, as of old, and lead them as the spearhead of the counter-attack.

His mind turned to Cerdic, that subtle and mysterious man, whose motives Artorius often struggled to fathom. For the past decade the Bretwalda of the Saxons had sat quietly in the ruins of Londinium, and made no effort beyond a few small-scale raids to test the defences of the British kingdoms.

Artorius had his spies in Londinium, just as Cerdic doubtless had his in Caerleon. It was a game the two kings played, with the lives of their agents as the stakes. Recent reports suggested that Cerdic was still training his young men for war.

Unlike many kings, Cedric hoarded his warriors like precious gold. He used them as garrison troops in the Debated Lands, and to quell any protests or feuds among the Saxon tribes. Otherwise he was careful with their lives.

Artorius could only surmise that the massacre of Saxon warriors at Mount Badon cast a long shadow. Under Cerdic's cautious leadership, his people would never again attempt the wholesale conquest of Britannia.

Unless his enemies handed him an opportunity. Artorius tried to shut out the image of Saxon war-bands wreaking havoc in his lands while the bulk of the British army was absent, chasing shadows in Kernow.

"The risk must be taken," he declared, "Drystan will be hunted down, and the shame of our defeat wiped out."

19.

Kernow

"I won't fight the High King in person," said King Budic, "my quarrel is with Marcus of Kernow, not Artorius."

The young, smooth-faced monarch, as persuasive and reasonable as ever, spread his hands. "Consider, my friends. To make war on the High King is to make war on all the sub-kings of Britannia. I cannot fight so many enemies at once."

Drystan glared at him with loathing. "So you will sail away with all your men," he spat, "and abandon us to face Artorius. You make a poor ally, Budic of Amorica."

Another man might have bristled at the insult. Budic merely looked sad and toyed with the gold ring on his middle finger.

"It is no shame to withdraw in the face of heavy odds," he said, "you are welcome to accompany me back to Amorica. Next summer, when we have gathered fresh troops and supplies, perhaps we can try again."

He raised a delicately plucked eyebrow at Drystan. "I would advise you to quit Kernow while you can, my friend. Your chances of negotiating a truce with Artorius and Marcus are not great."

Budic and Drystan made an equally handsome pair. The King of the Amoricans was still in his mid-twenties, tall and lean and muscular, with long, curling black hair, combed and oiled in the Eastern fashion. He wore a coat of silver ring-mail under his heavy cloak, and a band of red gold forged in a pattern of interlaced oak leaves adorned his brow.

There was a certain elegance about Budic, his languid manner of speech, his slow, graceful movements. He put Drystan in mind of a cat, sly and lithe and cruel, and about as trustworthy.

They had met for a conference of war in the king's pavilion, pitched on the wind-blown fields outside Caer Y Brenin. After weeks of siege, King Marcus of Kernow was still holed up in his stronghold. Drystan's father had stuffed the fortress with enough provisions to hold out for months.

After returning from his victories in the east, Drystan urged Budic to throw all his men at the walls in a direct assault. The Amorican king politely declined. He preferred to sit outside and wait for Marcus to beg a truce.

"A king must be careful with the lives of his men," he

was fond of saying, "after all, his power relies on them. The defences of Caer Y Brenin are high and strong. Your father is a fine soldier, and will fight for every foot of ground. No, my friend. I understand your high spirits, but we must be patient. To recklessly spill blood is to invite defeat."

King Erbin of Dumnonia was also present at the conference. The timid, rat-like little man had been in secret correspondence with Budic for months, and finally screwed up the courage to openly rebel against Artorius after the defeat of the Companions in Kernow. He had brought five hundred spears from Mons Ambrius, so now the allies had some two thousand men encamped before the timber walls of Caer Y Brenin.

Drystan had little respect for Budic, and none at all for Erbin. To him the Dumnonian was an opportunistic coward, a fair-weather friend who would abandon the cause at the first sign of difficulty.

"What say you, Erbin?" asked Drystan, eyeing the little man with distaste, "should we raise the siege, and scatter like frightened birds before the approach of the dragon?"

He hardly needed to ask. Erbin had been seized with fright ever since messengers galloped into camp, just after dawn, with the dreadful news that the High King had mustered a fresh army at Caerleon.

Artorius had gathered his fleet at the port, and seemed intent on invading Kernow via sea rather than land. This was either brave or incredibly foolish, since Britannia was in the depths of winter. Even a short crossing in rough weather was dangerous.

Drystan could scarcely believe Artorius had escaped his trap. His warriors, exhausted as they were from battle, had followed the fugitive's trail to the borders of the Summer Country, where it ran cold. No matter how much Drystan threatened and cursed them for a pack of superstitious fools, none would agree to enter the gateway to Annwn.

Erbin's long fingers twisted together. His brow was

damp with sweat, and his teeth chattered as he forced out a reply.

"I...ah...I feel we should send envoys to ask for terms. Favourable to us, of course. Artorius doesn't want to fight a war inside his own territory, against his own people. If we offer peace - any kind of peace - I believe he will snatch at it."

Drystan was surprised. Erbin's advice was typically craven, but not without a degree of sense.

He glanced suspiciously at Budic, and wondered if he and Erbin had secretly met beforehand and discussed the matter without his knowledge.

"You are both frightened of a reputation," he sneered, "yes, Artorius won some battles in the past, when our fathers were still young. What of it? Even Caesar grows old."

He smacked his fist into his palm. "I have beaten Artorius and his supposedly invincible Companions in the field. One of his most famous captains is a turncoat in my service. Let us march out to face him. Together. This time our victory will be final. His head shall adorn a spear, and his crown be trampled in the dust."

Drystan, a far more subtle creature than he pretended, saw the gleam in Budic's eyes. Mention of the crown had sparked the Amorican's interest, as he knew it would.

All three men in the pavilion dreamed of the High Kingship. Drystan was well aware of this, and played on it. Even Erbin, who shuddered at the mere name of Artorius, could muster a little courage at the thought of a golden crown. Especially if it rested on his head.

He struck again, before the courage of his allies wilted. "Give me six hundred men," he urged, "and I'll ride north to oppose the High King's landing.."

"That will leave you with more than enough spears to keep my father cooped up in his den," he added when Budic and Erbin still looked doubtful.

It was a calculated ploy. He offered to put himself between them and the wrath of Artorius. By appealing to their innate cowardice, Drystan hoped to persuade them to stand firm.

His allies briefly glanced at each other. Drystan sensed an understanding pass between them.

"Done," said Budic, "you may take five hundred of my Amoricans. Erbin will supply the rest. Won't you?"

The corner of Erbin's mouth twitched. For a moment Drystan thought he was about to protest, but the frightened little man evidently thought better of it.

"Of course," he said with a weak smile, "take them with my blessing."

Drystan sought out Esyllt before he left. She wasn't difficult to find. As usual when the weather allowed, she stood on a hilltop above the allied camp, overlooking the sea to the south and Caer Y Brenin to the north.

There was a single tree on the summit of the hill, bent and blasted by centuries of sea-winds. Esyllt and her slave Golwg stood together near the tree, two slender figures in dark blue hoods and cloaks, inseparable as always. Drystan often wondered what they spoke of together.

Me, most likely, thought Drystan as he laboured up the steep hill. He sometimes envied Golwg's intimacy with Esyllt, and wondered how much the girl knew of his efforts to woo her mistress. Far too much, he suspected.

Esyllt saw him approach and signalled at Golwg to make herself scarce. The slave, almost Esyllt's twin in appearance, obediently retreated out of earshot.

Drystan's heart turned over when Esyllt turned to face him. Her face was paler than ever, and her eyes too bright, as though she suffered from a fever. In recent weeks, ever since they came to Caer Y Brenin, she had kept him at arm's length. Her coolness pained him deeply, but he still adored Esyllt too much to press his company on her.

"I came to say goodbye," he said awkwardly, "I'm

going north. Artorius means to invade Kernow by sea. He must be stopped. Budic and Erbin won't face him, so the task falls to me."

"I can win," he added when Esyllt failed to respond, "Artorius won't escape me this time. You once asked me to bring you his head. In a few days I will lay it before you. I promise."

The ghost of a smile played across her lips. "What are your promises worth, Drystan?" she asked softly, "you once promised to marry me, if I would have you, and make me Queen of Britannia."

"That promise still stands," he replied.

She bowed her head and folded her arms in their heavy sleeves. Drystan's heart skipped as he waited for the rejection. How could he expect anything else? To Esyllt he was a bloody-handed killer who had slain her uncle, murdered her father's followers, and forcibly taken her from all she knew and loved.

Since then he had pitched her into a civil war against Artorius, the greatest soldier of the age. If their luck turned sour, even her white neck would be forfeit.

Drystan's spirit refused to accept defeat. Once again, he went down on one knee before Esyllt, careless of the mud, and stretched out his hand.

"Marry me, Esyllt," he said brokenly. "I shall raise you above all the women on earth."

Esyllt kept him waiting. He wondered if any of the soldiers below watched him, and laughed at his expense. Perhaps even his father witnessed his embarrassment from the timber ramparts of Caer Y Brenin.

At last she moved forward and enfolded his hand between hers. The soft warmth of her touch made his head swim.

"Come back to me, with or without the head of Artorius," she said, "and I shall wed you."

Drystan went north with a light heart, convinced that

the fulfilment of all his dreams was close at hand. At his back were three hundred mounted Swine of Kernow, with Goron and Llwch Llemineawg as his sub-officers, and a thousand infantry. He rode under a standard of his own design, a yellow lion with red eyes, rearing against a green field. Drystan saw himself as the lion, ready to tear down the dragon.

The long lines of horse and foot marched through a devastated landscape. While King Marcus sat inside Caer Y Brenin, trapped by superior numbers, his enemies had sent out freeriders to lay waste to his kingdom. Every field stood empty, the livestock stolen to feed the invaders, every village, farmstead and timber hall reduced to charred gables and post-holes.

Drystan regretted some of the devastation. This was the land he meant to rule, after all. He had tried to persuade Budic to show a little restraint, but the King of the Amoricans kept sending out bands of horsemen to plunder, slay and harry.

He suspected Budic wished to destroy Kernow as a rival power. To burn the crops in the fields, destroy every home, kill or drive away the people and livestock. The kingdom would take years, maybe generations, to recover.

Once the grim work was completed, Budic would place Drystan on the throne of Kernow as a useful puppet, and sail away to leave him in charge of a profitless, depopulated wasteland.

The sly King of the Amoricans was deluded if he thought he could use Drystan. Once Artorius was slain and Caer Y Brenin taken, Drystan planned to turn on Budic and drive him into the sea.

King Marcus would be executed: Drystan had no qualms about putting his estranged father to death. As for Erbin of Dumnonia, he could be relied on to throw his weight behind whoever was strongest. His spears would be useful in the war of conquest that followed. There would be plenty of hard fighting before Drystan reigned supreme as High King.

He welcomed the trials to come. In his mind Drystan pictured himself seated on the throne in the famous Round Hall at Caerleon. The golden wreath of the High King adorned his brow, and he wore the purple cloak of the Caesars. Queen Esyllt, her belly full with their son (the first of many) sat to his left, terrifyingly beautiful in a silver crown and silken robes, imported at great expense from Constantinople.

In place of the slaughtered Companions, Drystan's own trusted warriors and loyal sub-kings filled the seats of the Round Table. Heralds from distant lands flocked to Drystan's magnificent court to win his friendship with honeyed words and golden promises, and an endless stream of tribute - jewels, weapons, horses, cattle, slaves, all a man could desire - poured into the new capital of the West.

A new age, a new dawn, a new order. Drystan was born to fulfil this destiny. The strength and hope and vigour of youth coursed through his veins as he galloped north, straight as a spear, hair streaming in the wind. His horse ate up the miles of the fair green country he yearned to make his own, until the rugged, rain-lashed coastline of northern Kernow stretched before him.

As soon as word reached him of Artorius' preparations, he had ordered scouts to ride north and watch the coasts. Two of them came to meet him now, their horses racing before a furious south-west wind blowing in off the grey seas.

"No sign of any sails, lord," they reported, "we keep watch night and day, as you ordered."

Drystan shaded his eyes to gaze out at the splintered waves. The weather was like to grow worse during the night. To the south, the sky was thickly painted with black clouds, and rain fell in sheets.

"If Artorius puts to sea," said Llwch, "that strip of

beach to the north is perhaps the likeliest spot for a landing. His fleet will follow the coast south-west from Caerleon."

The traitor's face dripped with moisture. His lank hair was plastered to his skull. He had lost weight since Gwalchmei's death, and now resembled a living cadaver.

"You know the High King better than all of us," said Drystan, "will he dare sail? A squall is blowing up. Even the hardiest fisherman would think twice before challenging Neptune in these conditions."

Llwch looked out to sea. "Artorius has braved the elements before," he said quietly, his voice almost drowned by the hiss of rain and boom of distant waves, "at Lindum we rode into battle against the Jutish war-host in the middle of a storm. I remember the play of lightning on our spears, and the roar of thunder overhead. The men were afraid, but Artorius drove us on. He feared nothing. *Nothing*."

"We swept the Jutes into the marshes, and hunted them down like deer. Artorius was more than a man that day. He was Mars himself, the moving spirit of war. No spear could touch him, no arrow, no hard-forged steel."

Drystan was outraged. "You still admire him," he said accusingly, "in your heart, you long to be his man again, and ride with the Companions. You are a double traitor!"

Llwch's long face was engraved with lines of misery and doubt. "No, lord," he replied sadly, "I have chosen my path, and must follow it to the end. God forgive me. If Artorius lands, I shall stand by your side in the shield-wall."

Drystan was unconvinced, but this was no time to quarrel with his most experienced officer. He gave orders for his men to pitch camp, though there was little cover for miles along the bleak headland. In the end the Swine of Kernow were forced to take refuge in the lee of a hillside, where they crouched in their flimsy tents, eating comfortless suppers of bread, beans and watered ale.

Their commander shared these hardships. To do otherwise was to risk forfeiting the loyalty of his men. He remembered his father, King Marcus, sleeping in a gaudy pavilion while on campaign and feasting on good red meat while his troops shivered and starved. They hated him for it.

In spite of the cold, he started to feel drowsy. As always when he grew tired, thoughts of Esyllt started to drift through his mind. He lay down on his thin bedroll and pictured her in a summer forest, laughing as he crowned her with a garland of flowers. They lay down together in the sticky heat. She allowed him to kiss her, and peel off her gown.

Her naked body stretched out on the grass. Her grey eyes yearned up at him, devoid of their usual gentle mockery. Her red lips parted. They reached for each other.

Drystan woke with a start. The roof of the tent sagged above his head, heavy with rainwater. He heard a harsh voice raised in song outside. One of his men, warbling some filthy marching tune.

"Silence!" Goron's voice. The singer wisely fell quiet. Drystan muttered a curse and closed his eyes again.

"Lord!"

Llwch's guttural voice roused him from the sweet dream of Esyllt. Drystan groaned, reluctant to be torn from her arms, and opened his eyes.

It was still dark inside the dank, stuffy cavern of his tent. Outside the rain still fell in torrents, and the wind moaned across the cliffs like an army of lost souls.

"Lord, rouse yourself!" Llwch shouted, "the fleet is sighted!"

Drystan had slept in his mail, with his cloak for a pillow. He snatched up his helmet and sword-belt and crawled out of the tent. The grass was soaking wet, and his belly cramped with hunger.

It was almost dawn. The sky was dark blue, with patches of grey in the east. He looked around him blearily. Gaunt, hollow-eyed officers moved among the scattered tents, yelling and kicking the men to life.

"Where?" he mumbled, lacing on his helmet. Llwch, who looked ghastly in the merciless light of early morning, his face pale and haggard, with deep bags under the eyes, pointed at the cliffs.

"North," he said abruptly. "Artorius must have put to sea during the night, in the very teeth of the squall."

Drystan heard the note of awe in Llwch's voice. This time he didn't remark on it. It was impossible not to admire the High King's courage. His entire fleet might have easily been sunk or smashed to pieces on the jagged reefs off Kernow. Drystan knew a little of Artorius' career. Time and again, he took appalling risks in order to confound his enemies. Time and again, God or the Devil ensured fortune was on his side.

"Where is Goron?" Drystan asked. A soldier came jogging up with his horse. The beast, wet and bedraggled and flat-eared, had spent a miserable night huddled in the open with the other horses, guarded by a troop of luckless spearmen who drew lots for the task.

"Already gone to defend the beach," replied Llwch, "Artorius may have landed by now. His ships came out of the sea-mists and caught our scouts unawares. Goron only has fifty men with him. They can't hold for long."

Drystan patted his sodden horse's neck and carefully swung himself into the saddle. She wouldn't carry him far in her present exhausted state, but the beach was only a short ride away.

The dismal note of a war-horn sounded through the camp. Drystan's throat was dry, and he had to work up some phlegm to make himself heard. "On your feet!" he cried, "the High King is upon us. You can sleep until Doomsday once I have his head on a spear. Follow my banner!"

Llwch urged his tired horse into a canter. Drystan and his standard bearer followed him towards the beach, a narrow smear of shingle under rain-lashed black cliffs.

They reached the crest of the hill, which then swept downwards in a long, elegant curve towards the cliff-line. The cliff-tops were almost hidden under a heavy cloak of gloom and mist, and the sea was a vast, boundless expanse of charcoal grey.

Drystan's heart missed a beat when he spotted his rival's ships. Seven galleys with graceful prows and snow-white sails bobbed at anchor inside the bay. Twice as many longboats, packed with soldiers, rowed the short distance towards the beach.

"The track down to the beach is narrow," said Llwch, "we have to dismount and lead the horses down, or leave them. I suggest we put some archers on the headland. I know Artorius. He will put his head down and come at us like a wild boar. Our archers can rain missiles down on his men as they wade through the surf."

Drystan's doubts over Llwch ebbed a little.

"Stay here and wait for the infantry," he ordered, "meantime I'll go to the beach."

He ignored the sceptical look on Llwch's face and urged his pony down the narrow, twisting track that led between the steep sides of a gully to the shore. His standard bearer and a handful of riders followed him.

Drystan knew he should have waited for the rest of his troops to come up. He lacked the patience, and wouldn't allow Goron and his fifty spears to face the might of the High King's host alone.

The track was littered with loose stones, rolled down from the heights above. Drystan cursed when his pony stumbled, and swung himself out of the saddle to lead her on foot. He couldn't risk the beast going lame. If the worst befell, he would need her to carry him to safety.

Drystan was determined not to be taken captive. Artorius might plan to parade him in chains through the streets of Caerleon, in grotesque military of a Roman military triumph. He would fall on his sword rather than endure such a humiliation.

His men also dismounted to spare their horses. They turned the last bend of the track, where the flanks of the gully opened out onto the beach. Drystan's blood pounded as he heard the defiant shouts of his men, and the ominous thump of spears on shields.

He stopped dead. Before him the scene was spread out like a tapestry. Goron's spearmen were ankle-deep in the surf, deployed in a single line of shields that almost covered the length of the beach. The sturdy figure of their captain, in his ring-mail and boar's crest helmet, was easy to pick out in the middle of the line. He and his men drummed their spear-butts on their shields, roaring chants and insults at the boatloads of enemy warriors.

"Plant my banner here," Drystan ordered his standard bearer, a scarred veteran with a livid purple sword-slash where his right eye used to be.

The golden lion banner was stuck firmly into the earth. Drystan glanced up at the cliffs looming overhead. They were lined with slingers and bowmen. The rain still fell heavily, but his archers had kept their coiled bowstrings dry inside their caps.

Horns boomed through the early dawn mist. The first of Artorius' warriors jumped from their longboats and started to wade eagerly ashore. They were Companions, faces hidden under steel ridged helmets with dangling cheek-pieces, red cloaks trailing in the water. Every man carried an ash spear and a heavy round shield.

Drystan looked for Artorius among them. In place of the High King the Companions were led by a squat, bull-necked man in a heavy mail coat and a battered old helmet. He wore a black leather patch over one eye, his shaggy white beard trailed down to his bulging waist, and in place of a spear he carried a double-headed battleaxe.

"Loose!"

Llwch's harsh voice echoed from above. The sky was

briefly darkened by a flight of arrows. The iron-tipped shafts fell among the Companions as they struggled through the waves. Here and there a man fell, but most were saved by their armour.

They seemed to take heart from the presence of the figure in the leather eye-patch. He led them on in grim silence, splashing through the shallows, the wan light of dawn glinting off the blade of his fearsome axe.

Drystan heard the Companions chanting a name. He sucked in a deep breath as he realised the identity of the one-eyed man.

"Cei! Cei! Cei!"

Cei. The most famous of the Companions. Cei of the sharp tongue and foul temper, who had slaughtered Picts by the dozen at the Battle of Eburucum, and torn down the King of the Northlands.

Drystan drew his gold-hilted sword. *I slew Gwalchmei*, he told himself. *I can also send Cei to the long house, and his master.*

Over a hundred red cloaks stormed ashore. Led by Cei, they tore into the thin line of shields. The notched axe rose and fell in a murderous arc. Drystan winced as it clove into a spearman's head, sliced easily through his leather helmet and the fragile skull beneath.

The sea was dirtied with blood and brains. A wordless roar of triumph filled the morning air. Goron's spearmen retreated before the onslaught, shoved backwards by weight of numbers.

More arrows poured from the cliffs, mingled with a hail of stones and javelins. Llwch's archers did all they could to stem the tide. Still the Companions drove forward.

The longboats were empty now, and had turned about to row back to the galleys. Drystan caught the glimmer of scores of spears and helmets aboard. Once the boats had fetched reinforcements, Drystan's men would be hard-put to stand their ground.

He felt a stab of doubt. The odds seemed hopeless. Should he quit the beach, and get away to safety with most of his army still intact? It meant deserting Goron, his oldest friend, as well as fifty good men.

The ground shook under him. He looked over his shoulder, and saw his own reserves flooding down the gully. The Swine of Kernow, mostly on foot, followed by hundreds of infantry.

Relief washed through him, followed by anger at his brief cowardice. Without waiting to see if any followed, he lifted his sword and ran towards the fight.

Goron's men had almost vanished under the deluge of red cloaks, the shield-wall smashed beyond repair. Drystan looked for Goron, and spied him fighting off two Companions at once.

He bled from a spear-gash on his cheek. More blood oozed from another slash on his thigh. The Companions drove him back relentlessly, trying to drive their spears into his face. Goron held them off with more luck than skill. He cried out as one of the spears opened a deep cut on his sword-hand. The blade clattered onto the shingle, and he was forced to crouch behind his shield, face crimson with effort.

Drystan raced to Goron's aid. He ducked and weaved through the press, felt something whip past his head, sensed rather than saw the javelin fly at him. He flung up his shield, gasped at the bone-jolting impact of the missile as it ploughed into the timber, almost lost his balance on the wet shingle.

Suddenly the one-eyed warrior loomed before him. Drystan twisted aside from the terrible axe, already soaked with blood, and fell back into a crouch, body well behind his shield, sword ready to thrust into his enemy's gut.

"Cei! Cei! Cei!"

The frenzied war-chant of the Companions mingled with the crash of distant waves and the mournful cry of gulls. Drystan and Cei faced each other. The one-eyed warrior was far too canny to blunder within reach of Drystan's sword. He stepped back, grinned, and crooked his finger at Drystan.

"Come at me, you little turd," he grunted.

Drystan's mouth dried. Cei was twice his size, and obviously strong. His slanted shoulders were wide as a barn door, and he wielded a battle-axe most men would struggle to lift. On the other hand, he was old. There was a sluggishness to his movements. If Drystan could dance around him long enough, the big man would tire...

Then the random tides of battle flung a wave of fighters between Drystan and Cei. A corpse fell over Drystan. He was crushed under its weight. Foul breath gusted over him. Warm blood pumped from a vicious cut that had neatly carved the dead man's face in half. The stuff splashed into his mouth and eyes and nostrils. He gagged, choked, heaved the body off him with desperate strength.

The iron rim of a shield smashed against Drystan's chin. His jaw throbbed, and one or two teeth were loosened. Purple stars wheeled before his eyes. He was unable to stand. Whimpering, he crawled on all fours, spitting blood and the shattered fragments of a tooth.

A trumpet-blast sliced through the chaos all around him. A high, pure note. Three times it rose and fell, and was echoed and redoubled by the shouts of the Companions.

Drystan's strength returned. He rose, though his legs shook under him, tried to ignore the steady pulse of agony in his jaw.

The trumpet had sounded from the west. He turned groggily to look in that direction. West and east, the narrow beach was hemmed in by high cliffs. The cliff-face to the west was not quite so precipitous, and a man with no fear of death or broken bones might attempt to scale its heights. If he slipped, his body would be smashed on the slimy black rocks beneath.

A band of Companions had made the hazardous climb. Their longboats, now empty, bobbed on the waves below the cliff. Drystan counted at least thirty red cloaks clustered on the summit. Among them was a burly figure in a white cloak fringed with purple. He wore no helmet, and his head was adorned with a laurel wreath forged of gold.

Artorius.

The High King and his men made their way along the ridge of the escarpment, and stormed towards the archers on the cliff. To Drystan's dismay, the lightly-armed bowmen took to their heels. A handful stood their ground - Drystan thought he saw the tall figure of Llwch Llemineawg among them - but were swiftly overrun and cut down.

Meanwhile the Companions on the beach pressed their attack. More troops poured from the longboats. Drystan's men, outflanked and outnumbered, were driven back to the gully.

A swordsman leaped at Drystan. Still dizzy, he managed to parry the slash aimed at his head, and punched with the boss of his shield. It smashed into the other man's chest and knocked him down.

Scores of Companions rampaged over the beach, now littered with bodies, slaying almost at will. The Swine of Kernow were in full retreat, and the morale of their allies was shattered. Drystan shouted in vain at his spearmen to hold firm.

"Rally!" he screamed, "rally to me! Form line, form line!"

Buffeted by the crowd of fugitives, he clung to the pole of his standard. Where was Goron? The men were mortally afraid of his brutish second-in-command. Only Goron might restore a semblance of order.

His friend had vanished among the throng. So had Drystan's horse. The young officer tasked with her holding the reins lay dead with a spear in his throat. His eyes stared blankly up at the sky, both hands curled around the iron stuck in his flesh.

Drystan was faced with a stark choice: flee with the rest, or fall on his sword. Consumed by the shame of his first defeat, he might have done the latter, but the thought of Esyllt prevented him. He would not leave her to struggle through life without him.

He abandoned his standard and joined the men stampeding like frightened cattle up the track. They shoved and trampled each other in their blind desperation to escape.

Drystan was carried along with the tide. An elbow smacked into his bruised face. Blood flowed freely from his nose. He cursed, slipped, almost twisted his ankle on the rough ground.

The fugitives blundered into a killing ground. Artorius and his men were waiting at the summit of the cliff to greet them with a shower of spears. Drystan dived to the ground as bodies fell all around him.

He tore off his helmet, flung it away along with his shield, and scrambled to rejoin the scattered crowd of fugitives.

The High King made no effort to block their retreat. Instead the burly figure barked an order, and he and his Companions parted ranks.

One man at least would not escape. Drystan caught a brief glimpse of Llwch, on his knees near the edge of the cliff-top, guarded by two Companions. His wrists were tied behind his back.

Llwch would certainly die. Drystan was determined to live, and found one last burst of strength to propel himself up the hill.

To safety.

20.

Llwch had aged since Artorius last saw him. The High King wondered how old he was. Thirty-eight, perhaps? Forty? The years passed so quickly. It seemed barely months had passed since Llwch first caught his eye as a promising young cavalry officer, when Ambrosius was still alive.

The man who stood before him might have been in his late fifties. There were fresh lines in his hawkish face, and streaks of grey in his sparse black hair. His narrow shoulders were bowed, as though crushed by some heavy weight.

Guilt, thought Artorius. He recognised the symptoms.

They stood on a high ridge overlooking the sea. The slope and the gully below was carpeted with bodies. Artorius' men wandered among the human wreckage, stripping the dead of their clothes, armour and weapons. When that grisly task was done, the corpses of enemy warriors would be piled into a great heap and burned. Those few Companions who had died in the battle, and their allies, would be given honourable burial.

Artorius sat cross-legged on his shield and looked up at the prisoner.

Their eyes met. Neither spoke for a long while. Llwch was no danger - his wrists were still bound, and two grim-faced Companions stood behind him - yet there was still a spark of defiance in his sunken eyes.

"Well, my friend," Artorius said at last, "you have rolled the dice and lost. What remains?"

Llwch's shrivelled mouth worked. For a moment Artorius thought the man would spit on him. It would be in character. Under his quiet, unassuming exterior, Llwch had always been a coarse brute who took too much pleasure in killing. Artorius remembered the screams of Jutish prisoners he captured in the fens of Lindum.

"Death," said Llwch, "death remains. By rope or sword. I care not which. I have reached the end of my thread in this world."

Artorius gnawed on a strip of dried bacon. His feet were sore. He had taken off his boots to brave the scramble up the treacherous cliffs and outflank Drystan's men on the beach. It was a clever move, if dangerous, and won the battle.

One of the men who also braved the hazardous climb was Bedwyr, lately come from Rheged. The one-handed warrior sat nearby, drinking more ale than was good for him and glaring balefully at Llwch.

Artorius strove to keep his temper in the face of the traitor's careless attitude.

It was difficult. The stench of dead men was everywhere. They might still be alive, friends and enemies both, if Llwch had kept to his oath.

"I have questions," he said, "but I won't ask why you betrayed me. I know already. Because I refused to avenge your kinsmen in Rheged."

Llwch stared at the ground. "That was the tipping point," he admitted, "I knew then you were unfit to rule as High King. It confirmed a suspicion I harboured for years. God had placed the wrong man on the throne. You are unfit to rule."

Bedwyr snorted. "Let me put him to the question, lord king," he muttered. "I'll made the whoreson squeal before we kill him."

Artorius held up his hand. It pained him to hear the hatred in Bedwyr's voice. These men had once been closer than brothers. Now their old fellowship was destroyed forever.

Cei had deliberately busied himself elsewhere. "If I clap eyes on that turncoat, I'll strangle him," he said with typical bluntness. Artorius understood, all too well, and let him go.

"Why am I unfit to rule?" the king asked quietly. Caledfwlch rested in its leather sheath beside him. He resisted the urge to snatch up the blade and bury it in Llwch's stomach. This had to be done properly. The High

King performed justice, not murder.

Llwch seemed unmoved by Bedwyr's words. "You try to enforce Roman law," he replied, "and see yourself as a little Caesar, sitting in the shell of an old Roman palace, clinging on to the shreds of empire. The Caesars are gone, Artorius. They deserted Britannia in our grandfather's day and left us to fend for ourselves. It is time we broke free of Rome for good."

"Mount Badon was an opportunity. We could have pushed east and driven the Saxons back into the sea, reclaimed the Debated Lands, severed our last ties with the Roman government in Gaul, or what is left of it. Instead your threw up barriers. Now the island is divided in two, and the Saxons will never be uprooted. They enjoy the best land. More of their foul kin come to our shores every year. Meantime we skulk in the west behind long lines of earthworks and hill-forts. How long will those defences hold, once Cerdic and his allies have built up their power again?"

He spoke with fierce conviction. Artorius, who had never suspected Llwch of harbouring such bitter thoughts, was taken aback.

"You never complained of my policy before," he replied, "am I to believe your treachery was motivated by concern for the realm? That is why you betrayed our young soldiers at Celliwig, and conspired with Drystan of Kernow to entrap me and slaughter my warriors? No, I will not believe it. You were selfish, blinded by the glint of gold."

"What promises did Drystan make?" demanded Bedwyr, "how much did it take to buy you, and agree to slit the throats of your brothers?"

"I was not bought," Llwch answered steadily, "nor was I made any promise of lands or gold. It is Drystan who desires your crown, Artorius. I would not carry such a burden for any price."

"Liar," spat Bedwyr.

Artorius swallowed his morsel of bacon. He regretted failing to kill or capture Drystan during the rout. The boy, unmistakable in his silver mail, was spotted among the fugitives, but had seized a riderless horse and made his escape.

No matter. Drystan could wait for another day. Once Artorius' men had rested, he would march south and sweep his enemies out of Kernow.

"Tell me about Drystan," he said, "what kind of a man is he?"

"He has the fearlessness of youth," replied Llwch after a moment's thought, "and no concept of his own limits. He thinks the world is there for the taking. Until today, he had never tasted defeat."

And he will be the wiser for it, thought Artorius.

He nodded at the spearmen behind Llwch. "No," said the prisoner when they laid hands on him, "let me do it myself."

Artorius frowned. "Suicide? And risk your soul's damnation?"

"My soul is damned already. At least let me die with honour. I cannot be shamed before the Companions, dangling on the end of a rope like some common thief."

Bedwyr stood up and hobbled towards Llwch. "Here," he snarled, drawing his sword, "use this. At least I can say you died on my blade."

Artorius was overwhelmed by melancholy. *That it should come to this.*

"Take him down to the beach," he ordered the spearmen, "untie his wrists, and let him die with his face to the sea."

Llwch was marched away. The warriors of Britannia watched in silence as he was escorted down the winding track to the shingle beach, still littered with corpses, and made to kneel at the sea's edge.

His wrists were untied, and Bedwyr's sword placed in his hand. Artorius stood to watch the end.

Llwch's head was bowed. He muttered a final prayer. Then he pressed the tip of the sword against his stomach, gripped the hilt in both hands, and threw all his weight forward.

They left his body on the shore for the carrion birds to pick over. Bedwyr retrieved his sword from Llwch's flesh, washed it in the sea, and stalked away without a backwards glance.

The host marched south, towards Caer Y Brenin. At the High King's side rode Cei and Bedwyr, and those of the sub-kings who had answered his summons. Caradog Freichfras and Cadwallon Lawhir, his staunch allies, were foremost among them. Their two hundred cavalry and six hundred spears made up over half his army.

The lesser kings of Rhos, Brycheiniog and Ergyng had not come. Artorius knew these men were jealous of his power, and resentful of his efforts to curb the blood-feuds and cattle raids they regarded as part of their natural existence. King Erbin of Dumnonia had betrayed him, and Marcus of Kernow was cooped up in his stronghold.

Britannia was crumbling. Artorius had to move swiftly, and destroy or scatter the enemy host at Caer Y Brenin. His rivals would take heart if he failed to win a quick victory. Between them, the lesser kings could muster a host large enough to attack Caerleon.

Meantime, while the Britons tore each other to pieces, the enemy in the east continued to gather strength. When would Cerdic make his move? How long could the Bretwalda afford to wait? His own chieftains might force him to act. The Saxons were always ravenous for more land. Britannia's garrisons were weakened, her borders ill-defended, her kingdoms sliding into civil war.

Cerdic will never have a better chance, thought Artorius, *this is his time. His father Hengist would have been ravaging our borders by now. If he advances west with all his power, only Llacheu and a few hundred militia will stand in his way.*

He pushed such nightmarish thoughts from his mind and force-marched his men south. There was no protest from his Companions, who still thirsted to avenge their comrades. The victory on the beach, and the death of Llwch Llemineawg, had only gone a little way to slaking that thirst. Nothing less than the head of Drystan, mounted on a spear and paraded before them as a trophy of war, would satisfy it.

Artorius could have wept at the ruin of Kernow. It was the old days come again, days of fire and devastation and the smoke of burning thatch on the hillside. The stench of charred corpses in the air. Everything his foster-father, Ambrosius, had fought to prevent.

Artorius had tried to carry on his predecessor's work, and won a few years of peace. Now all was undone, thanks to Drystan.

Drystan! The youth had come out of nowhere, an obscure bastard princeling. King Marcus ought to have drowned him at birth.

Artorius realised he had been too merciful. Too trusting. He should have executed Gwythyr, the northern prince who waged war on Rheged, and all his warriors with him. Nailed their heads and limbs to stakes and displayed them along the Wall, so the barbarian tribes would think twice before invading British soil again. For that matter, he should have killed Llwch months ago, instead of giving the man a chance to prove his loyalty. Where had such merciful intentions led to? Civil strife, the slaughter of good men, and the near-destruction of free Britannia.

He would never make such a mistake again. Artorius had done his best to follow Ambrosius' example, and rule with justice and mercy. From now on, he would follow his instincts.

His troops marched through the night. Shortly after dawn, the earth and timber ramparts of Caer Y Brenin rose through the mists that enfolded the land to the south.

Artorius sent Bedwyr forward with the pick of the Companions to look for the enemy camp. They returned at the gallop, far more quickly than he expected.

Bedwyr's seamed face was a picture of dismay.

"They've gone, lord king," he said, "all gone."

21.

Horsemen came from the north, bearing word of defeat and disaster.

"Drystan is slain. All our host is destroyed!"

These dreadful tidings spread like fire through the camp of the Amoricans and their Dumnonian allies. King Budic immediately gave orders for the siege of Caer Y Brenin to be raised.

Esyllt stood on the hillside, beside the lone tree, and watched the army disperse. Men scrambled over the plain below her like so many frightened ants. Tents and pavilions were taken down, fires doused, supplies and war-gear piled aboard wagons with feverish haste.

She saw the King of the Amoricans ride south, towards the coast, followed by his bodyguard. His white cloak flapped about him as he drove his horse into a gallop, sleek black head bent over her neck, careless of his royal dignity.

"He is a coward after all," she murmured, "run away, little king. Run away to your ships, before the dragon comes to gobble you up."

Golwg touched her mistress's arm. "We should go too, my lady," said the slave, "King Budic may allow us to sail back to Amorica with him."

"Go if you wish," Esyllt replied, "you have my permission. For myself, I will go north, and look for Drystan."

"My lady, Drystan is dead. You heard the messengers. He was killed in battle."

"So they say. I will believe it when I see his body with my own eyes. Not before."

She started down the hill. Golwg trotted after her. Esyllt was touched at the girl's loyalty, and her courage.

We put the menfolk to shame, she thought.

The news of Drystan's death had hit her like a blow, and left a dull ache in her heart. Esyllt's attachment to a man she ought to have despised had only grown since he left.

Out of a sense of loyalty to her father, she had tried to spurn his advances, and keep him at a distance. Her coldness only enflamed him. Twice he had promised to lay the head of the High King at her feet, and raise her above all other women in the land, if only she could consent to marry him.

The promise of a crown, of almost unlimited power and freedom, overrode all her other passions. Even guilt. She prized freedom above all else. Drystan had promised, time and again, that he would not treat her as other men treated their wives. So long as Esyllt returned his love, she would be able to live on her own terms, and rule the kingdom as her husband's equal.

Esyllt knew her reasoning was entirely selfish. She was cursed with a man's heart, and a man's desire for independence, trapped inside the weak and malleable shell of a woman. Even a woman of royal blood could not hope to escape the constraints of marriage, the brutal dominance of a husband, and the terrifying dangers of childbirth.

Did she love Drystan? A form of love, perhaps. Esyllt was more practical than her would-be husband, and suspected that love in its purest form was an invention of poets. In a relentlessly harsh and cruel world, people needed each other in order to survive. She needed Drystan, and would not give him up until she knew for certain he was gone.

The tent she shared with Golwg was pitched near the

foot of the hill, at a respectable distance from the soldiers. Their ponies were tethered to a wooden rail nearby.

Esyllt stopped. The two spearmen King Budic had ordered to guard the women had vanished, doubtless fled in the general chaos. A young soldier was sawing through one of the tethers with his dagger.

"Please," said Esyllt.

The soldier spun around at the sound of her voice. He was young, with a fuzz of yellow beard on his pale cheeks, and had a lean, nervous, wolfish look about him.

Trumpets blared around them as the soldier and the princess stared at each other. Men streamed past, some mounted, some dragging their horses by the reins. None spared Esyllt so much as a glance. King Budic's ignoble panic had infected the entire army.

"Please," Esyllt repeated, "don't take our ponies. We are lost without them."

"Tell me your name," she added, "and when I am queen, I shall remember it, and reward you."

The soldier's eyes bulged. He ran his tongue across his lips. An older man might have laughed her promise to scorn, but this one was scarcely more than a boy, and frightened out of his wits.

"I...I am Syfwlch," he stuttered, "of Dumnonia. My master King Erbin has fled, and all our men. They left me behind."

Golwg stepped in front of her mistress. "Have mercy, Syfwlch of Dumonia," she murmured, "there are plenty of spare horses."

His eyes flickered between her and Esyllt. He lowered his knife as Golwg took another step towards him.

Golwg was quick. Steel flashed in her right hand, and the edge of a hidden knife carved a thin red line across Syfwlch's throat.

The boy dropped his knife and raised both hands to the fatal wound. Bright blood pumped down his neck. It spread over his white tunic like the petals of an obscene rose, while he choked and fought for breath and buckled to his knees.

With a nod of approval to Golwg, Esyllt walked past the dying youth and grasped the tether of her pony. The beasts were skittish, alarmed by the noise and panic, but a few soothing words calmed them again.

The two riders struck out north. They were careful to give Caer Y Brenin a wide berth. After weeks of being cooped up in his stronghold, Marcus would burn for revenge on those who had humiliated him and waste to his kingdom.

Esyllt tried to put aside the dire thoughts of her fate if she fell into his hands. Esyllt had heard rumours that the men of Kernow burned unfaithful wives at the stake. She could almost picture the flames, and smell her own flesh roasting.

She goaded her pony into a gallop. The beast fairly flew across the hills, leaving the timber walls of Caer Y Brenin far behind. Golwg could barely keep up, and for several miles they rode in silence, following the tracks of Drystan's army.

They weren't difficult to follow. The passage of hundreds of horses and men had churned up the ground, and the recent rains had not quite washed away the imprints. For half a day Esyllt and Golwg rode through quiet, frostbound forests and barren hills, stopping only once to allow their ponies to rest and drink from a stream.

When dusk they came on, they started to encounter survivors from the battle in the north. First, a riderless horse, still bitted and saddled, wild with fright, blood oozing down a spear-cut on his neck. He neighed at the sight of the riders, tossed his head, and cantered away into the nearest woods.

They encountered a few more riderless horses. Then, as the sky darkened and rain threatened in the west, Esyllt spied a dead man. He lay curled up at the foot of an oak tree, one hand pressed over a ragged hole in his side. He had escaped the battle, only to fall from his horse and bleed to death, alone, in the wilderness.

Young, thought Esyllt as they rode past his body, *almost as young as the boy Golwg slew...*

Esyllt could not waste time on sentiment. They saw no more corpses, and the shadows of night were rolling across the land when the sound of faint hoofbeats reached her ears. By now they had left the woods far behind, and cantered over a flat plain with wooded hills to the north.

"My lady," cried Golwg, "they could be the High King's men. We should turn back."

Some instinct drove Esyllt to press on, confident in the knowledge that Golwg would follow.

The hoofbeats grew louder, and the dark silhouettes of six horsemen appeared before her. They came on fast, the last rays of the dying sun reflected off their crested helms and ring-mail.

Their leader wore no helm, and his long fair hair rippled in the wind as he galloped closer. Esyllt cried out when she recognised him.

"Drystan!"

At the sound of her voice, he brought his horse to a halt. The men behind him also reined in. Drystan looked exhausted, his face damp with sweat and spattered with dried blood.

"Esyllt?" he croaked, dashing the back of his hand across his brow, "it can't be...."

She slowed to a trot and pushed back her hood. The haunted look in Drystan's eyes vanished. He spurred towards her.

They embraced. He buried his face in her neck, murmuring her name over and over. She held him close, ignoring the stench of blood and violent death that rose off him.

"God has sent you," he whispered fiercely, "my one salvation. My only reason to live."

Esyllt kissed him on the cheek. "What happened?" she asked softly.

"We were beaten," he moaned, "beaten like whipped dogs. We met the Companions on the beach, but they outflanked us. Llwch was taken. Scores of my men lie dead. The Swine of Kernow are shattered. It's over."

Esyllt looked over Drystan's shoulder at his companions. She vaguely recognised them as members of the Swine of Kernow, and could almost sense their loyalty ebbing away.

Men follow a leader for as long as his victories last, she thought, *but no longer.*

"What of Goron?" she asked.

Drystan lifted his head. Seen at close quarters, his face was ghastly pale, and there was a nervous twitch in the corner of his bloodshot left eye. "I don't know," he whispered, "I saw him fighting on the beach. He was outnumbered. I tried to reach him..."

Esyllt strove to hide her relief. She had loathed Goron, but he was Drystan's oldest friend.

From now on, he has only me.

"How did you escape?"

Drystan wiped away his tears. "These men saw me in the rout," he said, nodding at his companions, "my horse was gone, but they found me a spare. Otherwise..."

His eyes took on their haunted quality again. He stared past her, at some unimaginably horrible fate.

"Lord," said one of the warriors behind him, "we must go. Now. The enemy will be out looking for us."

Drystan snapped back into life. For a moment he was his old, decisive self.

"Yes," he said, "you're right. South, to Caer Y Brenin and the camp of King Budic. He and Erbin of Dumnonia have enough men to make a stand against Artorius, if I can pour a little fire into their bellies."

"My love," said Esyllt, "when news reached the camp

of your defeat, Budic and Erbin lifted the siege and fled back to their own lands. The only troops at Caer Y Brenin belong to your father."

Drystan gaped at her, and then his face took on a hard, shut-in quality. "Then it truly is over," he said, "Artorius has the victory, and we must leave Britannia and hide our heads in exile."

The little band of fugitives rode south-west, in the hope of reaching the coast and a boat to take them to Amorica. There was no refuge for them in Kernow, and Esyllt dared not return to her father's court in Hibernia with Drystan in tow. Even the mild-mannered King Niall would be roused to anger at the sight of the man who had murdered his warriors and abducted his daughter.

Amorica was their only safe haven, even though King Budic had proved a weak and unreliable ally. "Let us hope he welcomes us again," said Drystan.

Or he might think to cut off our heads, thought Esyllt, *and send them to Artorius in the hope of buying the High King's forgiveness.*

She kept this notion to herself. It would only plunge Drystan further into despair. His courage already trembled on a knife-edge. She was amazed how easily his spirits were roused or depressed. He was unstable as well as fragile, and might easily crumble without her support.

The weather turned foul. Pelting rain and howling winds buffeted the riders as they forced their horses along muddy, uneven roads. Drystan knew the route to the coast, and the nearest port, but the elements conspired to drive them off-course.

As they struggled through the murk, one of Drystan's warriors cried out in alarm.

"Spears!" he shouted, his voice hoarse as he struggled to make himself heard, "spears to the east!"

Esyllt turned and strained her eyes to see through the rain. Her heart skipped a beat when she spied a troop of horsemen on the crest of a hill, barely quarter of a mile away. She counted thirty spears on the hill. More than enough to overwhelm Drystan and his little band.

"Perhaps they won't see us," she said.

It was a futile hope. One of the horsemen raised his sword, and he and the others started to move down the hill.

They came on at speed. Ten of them peeled away to block the road to the south, while the rest thundered straight towards the fugitives. Their war-cries were carried on the wind like a chorus of angry ghosts.

"My father's men!" shouted Drystan, "we must not be taken. I will not be his prisoner!"

He turned his horse's head and plunged away east. Esyllt and the others followed, desperately urging their tired horses into a gallop.

They hurtled across a wet and barren moor. A row of grey hills loomed through the mist to the west. Drystan steered his horse towards the largest of them.

Esyllt could barely see through the rain and the spray of mud and stones kicked up by her pony's hoofs. She clung tightly to the reins, shut her eyes and prayed. The prayers were unlikely to be heeded. Esyllt knew she had done more to earn divine wrath than favour.

In truth, she cared little for God, and had only ever paid lip-service to her father's beloved church. Only the fear of her soul's damnation, dinned into Esyllt from infancy by the priests, had stopped her from turning to the old gods her uncle Morholt had worshipped. Their wild nature appealed to her, and she often dreamed of joining the ancient spirits as they danced freely across the land.

She wiped her eyes as the grey curtain suddenly parted, revealing a gigantic fortress of stone, piled up on the largest of the western hills. Esyllt cried out: even her father's court in Hibernia, or King Budic's palace in Amorica, were mere cattle-byres in comparison to this massive stronghold.

The base of the hill was encircled by a ditch, thickly

overgrown with weeds and full of dirty water. Drystan's horse leaped the gap and raced up the slope towards the gates of the outer wall.

Esyllt's own horse had just strength enough to jump the ditch - she closed her eyes as he soared over - and almost tumbled her out of the saddle when he landed on the other side. Before he collapsed, she slid off his back and led him up the steep ridge on foot.

Golwg dismounted beside her, while Drystan's warriors streamed past them. Their pursuers were just visible on the moor, perhaps half a mile to the west, riding at a leisurely canter.

"They don't need to wear out their horses," said Golwg, "they can see where we are. Drystan has led us into a trap."

"Be silent," snapped Esyllt. Golwg went pale and bit her lip. The pair usually spoke to each other with sisterly affection, though Esyllt always bore in mind that Golwg was a mere slave, to be used and disposed of as such.

In their present situation, Esyllt had little patience with a slave who complained, and dared to speak ill of her betters. They laboured up the hill in tense silence, neither looking at the other.

Esyllt was dismayed when she reached the entrance. It was a gaping archway, wide enough for two horsemen to enter abreast, with the gate itself and a number of stones missing from the arch.

The rest of the fortress was in a similar state of ruin. It was clearly ancient, and had not been inhabited for generations. Long-dead workmen had carried tons of locally quarried stone up the tortuous slope, to pile up crude defensive walls with more enthusiasm than skill.

Time, neglect and weather had done their work, and now most of the stones lay scattered about in heaps. The walls were barely waist-height in places, fallen away completely in others.

Head bowed against the wind, Esyllt dragged her

reluctant horse through the gate, towards the remainder of the inner wall. She passed the foundations of several roundhouses, rough circles of stones, barely large enough to accommodate two or maybe three people.

The inner wall was in slightly better repair, and more defensible. It contained the foundations of three more roundhouses, with a larger structure in the middle. This was also roughly circular, and had perhaps served as the chieftain's hall. Unlike the other buildings, much of it was still intact.

Esyllt and Golwg took their horses inside the inner circle of defences. "Put them in there," said one of Drystan's warriors, pointing at the hall.

They did so, and found themselves inside a vast grey shell, large enough to house fifty or sixty warriors. The thatched roof was gone, and rain pattered on the overgrown green floor where ancient princes had once held court.

The rest of the horses were already stabled inside. They stood clustered against the northern wall, steam rising from their sweat-soaked hides. One warrior was left to guard them. He gave the women a respectful nod as they left their beasts with the others.

Esyllt ducked under the entrance and looked around for Drystan. She spotted him perched on the rampart of the inner wall, peering west. Two of his warriors stood beside him, while the other three crouched miserably against the stonework, wrapped up in their wet cloaks and doubtless brooding on their fate. They looked like dead men already.

Pitiful, thought Esyllt, *is this what all our grand dreams have come to? Perhaps I should have consented to marry King Marcus, and found what happiness I could in my gilded cage.*

She pushed away the bitter thought. They were not dead. Not yet.

Drystan leaped down from the wall and strode towards her. "They won't attack," he said, "instead their captain has left twenty spears to watch the fort, and led the rest away. They rode west."

"Towards Caer Y Brenin?" she asked.

"I think so. To inform my father, I expect. He will come with all his power to smoke us out of here. Perhaps Artorius as well."

Shadows played on his still-youthful face. "I won't be taken," he said with cold determination, "I won't be their trophy."

He moved closer to Esyllt and caught her hands. "Come," he whispered, "let us find some quiet place, lie down together and open our veins. Let them find us mingled in our blood, beyond their reach forever. It will be my last victory."

"*Your* last victory," she said angrily, pushing him away, "I want none of it. Shame, Drystan. What has happened to you? One setback, and your courage goes all to pieces. Where is the man who defeated my uncle in single combat? Who invaded a kingdom with a hundred men? Who defeated Artorius himself in battle? *That* was the man I fell in love with."

He gaped foolishly at her. "I won't lie down with you and slit my wrists," she added before he could respond, "if blood must flow, then let it be the blood of our enemies."

"But," he said, gesturing helplessly to the west, "we are beaten. Surrounded. There is no way out of this."

"There is always a way."

Esyllt turned away to run her eye over the ruined defences of the fort. "What is this place?" she asked abruptly, "why did you bring us here?"

"I don't know its name," he answered. "I used to come here with my friends when we were children. This place is old. Very old. I brought us here because it was our only hope of escaping my father's soldiers. They would have caught us otherwise. Our horses were too tired to outrun them."

"You bought us time," she said, "only a little time, perhaps, but enough."

"Enough for what? A few last prayers?"

Drystan's voice was drained of hope. Despair and lack of sleep had reduced him to a scarecrow figure. There were black smudges under his eyes and a grey pallor to his skin.

Esyllt folded this beaten man in her arms and kissed him. The kiss lasted until she felt Drystan wrap his arms tight around her. "See," she breathed, "you are not done yet."

"Not while you live," he said in a husky voice, full of pent-up desire.

She toyed with a lock of his greasy hair. "The last time we parted, I promised I would marry you. The promise still stands, though you have not reminded me of it."

Some colour returned to his cheeks. "You would marry me? Now? When all our dreams are dust?"

"Yes," she said with simple conviction, "even if I burn for it."

His tired eyes lit up with joy. "Here...?" he exclaimed.

She gave a shrug. "Where better? I would rather marry you in the open, under the honest sky, than in some gloomy church."

"We have no priest."

"Good. I want no priests. Let us make our vows to each other, and keep them in the privacy of our hearts, where Christ cannot touch them."

22.

Myrddin remembered little of his former life, save in dreams. When he slept, the golden-haired bard he had once been lived again. His deep, rich voice once again filled the hall, accompanied by the sweet music of his lyre.

He slept now, on the dirt floor of his little cave, and dreamed of the last battle. Even now, the memory caused him pain. He kicked and whimpered in his sleep, and clawed at empty air. Slow tears dripped down his sunken cheeks.

In his dream Myrddin crouched on the edge of a wood, somewhere in the remote north, far beyond the Wall. Bards were not permitted to fight, but he had secretly followed the war-host so he might watch the battle.

A spectral voice echoed like a trumpet in the purple skies:

"This is the place where was slain Gwendolau,
The son of Ceidaw,
The pillar of songs,
Where the ravens shrieked for blood."

Myrddin stopped his ears against the terrible voice. His heart broke at the sound of his dear lord's name. Gwendolau, the ring-giver, generous master, peerless warrior, staunch friend to bards and seers.

Gwendolau was a prince of the Old North. Myrddin, too, was a northerner. His family were slain in some raid or ambush, and Gwendolau's father Ceidaw had raised him as a foundling. He must have been very young, since the faces of his parents were mere shadows in his mind. Shadows, and a dim memory of love.

This much Myrddin could remember. The rest of his youth was buried in the deepest pit of memory, never to be recovered. Sometimes he recalled sensations - the smell of fresh-baked bread wafting through the mead-hall, the touch of a lover's skin in the darkness behind the kitchens, the shrill yelping of wolfhounds when they were led out to hunt. That was all. The tragedy of Arfderydd had destroyed his memory, along with his wits.

Arfderydd.

Myrddin shuddered in his sleep. This was the place. The

accursed name. Arfderydd, where all his friends died. He crouched on the edge of the wood and beheld the plain, the storm-blasted heath where it happened.

He saw again the flash of spears on the horizon. A cloying smell filled his nostrils. The rival war-bands drank honeyed mead before the slaughter, and the air was filled with its sickly sweet odour.

The enemy host, a horde of foul and malicious pagans, outnumbered Gwendolau's men. The rumble of their chariots swept like thunder across the heath. Myrddin knelt, clasped his hands and prayed to the Almighty for deliverance.

His prayers came to naught. The pagan spears rushed to attack, and the host of Gwendolau waited bravely to meet them. Hard-honed blades set for war, shields locked together, they stood firm against the shock of the charge.

Myrddin chanted poetry in his sleep, the words of the last poem he ever composed, on the edge of the wood at Arfderydd:

"Men went to Arfderydd, mead-incited,
The heady bliss of battle, with eager laughter,
They slew with spears and swords,
Gwendolau, a giant in battle, the son of kings,
Did great slaughter by the deeds of his hand.

Men went to Arfderydd, swift was the host,
Fresh mead their delight, their poison too.
Six hundred engaged three hundred,
The pagan host attacked, cruel in battle,
And after the spear-joy, there was silence.

Men went to Arfderydd, glory-seeking,
It would be wrong not to praise them.
Sturdy and strong, the war-hounds fought fiercely,
Blood-red blades struck in dark blue sockets,

In tight formation, their fears left them.

Men went to Arfderydd; only one returned.
Friends I had; faithful I was.
Slain in the struggle, it grieved me to leave them,
The bravest ones had their lives cut short.
Red their swords, let them never be cleansed,
White their shields, their courage stainless.

Men went to Arfderydd with the dawn.
They stained their spears, splashed with blood.
Those pagan blades the cruellest in all the world,
A blood-bath for my friends, death to them.
Before the army of the heathen, they went down,
Made certain the death-bed of Gwendolau.

A man went from Arfderydd, sorrow-laden.
He had sung sweetly at midnight feasts.
Wretched, the lamentation for his friends,
His wits were scattered at the break of day.
In the strife, his lord fell.
After that death, the lone man was broken."

When the poem was finished, the dream of Arfderydd mercifully faded. Myrddin's old self went mad with grief, and wandered alone through bleak hills and shadowy forests. He stumbled - or was drawn - into the Summer Country, the natural home of wanderers and madmen.

There he saw a vision, in a round pool of clear water surrounded by a ring of twisted, leafless trees. The water showed the death of Morgana, the last Seer of Britannia, slain in her cave by a one-handed warrior.

The warrior, who wept as he slew her, cut off the dead woman's head. Her body was left for the wolves, and the vision of the cave faded, replaced by the image of a walled town beside a river. Banners flew from the turrets, displaying a red dragon against a white field.

Caerleon, city of the High King.

These words ghosted through Myrddin's fractured mind. He watched the one-handed warrior carry the head into the town and lay it before a man seated on a carved wooden throne.

Artorius.

The man on the throne was a burly, scarred figure, uncomfortable in his purple-lined cloak and golden crown. He gazed sadly at the battered head of Morgana, her raven locks crusted with dried blood. A slave bore it away, and Artorius embraced Morgana's assassin.

A high-pitched squeal shattered the vision. Myrddin awoke with a startled cry and rolled onto his haunches.

He reached for the gnarled staff propped against the wall of his cave. Then he relaxed when he saw the tiny creature standing in the narrow entrance.

"Mab," he sighed, "foolish imp. One of these days you will frighten me to death."

Mab was a little black piglet. Myrddin had found her wandering alone in the forest, and snatched the beast before she could run away. He suspected her mother had been killed during a boar-hunt.

Myrddin, who had eaten no flesh since Arfderydd, had no intention of eating Mab. Instead he kept her for a companion. She listened patiently to his mutterings and ravings, and never complained or tried to escape. He gained far more pleasure from the company of a pig than his own kind: on the few occasions Myrddin had attempted to approach a village or farmstead to beg for food, the inhabitants had driven him away. Once, he was beaten so badly he almost died. At another time, the villagers tied him to a stake and threw him in a river.

Myrddin beckoned at Mab, who trotted over to nuzzle at his filthy hand, grunting happily.

"The gods preserved me," whispered Myrddin,

scratching Mab behind the ears, "didn't they, imp? Abandinus plucked me from the river, so I might prove a useful servant."

Abandinus was an ancient British river god. All but forgotten now, save for a few votive offerings and inscriptions on stones scattered about the land. He and his kin had long been replaced by Christ the Nazarene.

The gods of Britannia were mere whispers now, feeble shades, jealous of the power they had lost. Yet they still watched over the land they had once ruled, and sought out human servants to guard it.

Morgana had been their servant. When she was slain, they looked for another, but there were few in Britannia now who willingly served the deities of old. The mad bard, Myrddin Wyllt, was chosen to do their bidding. Once a Christian, he had thrown aside his old faith at Arfderydd, where the power of Christ failed and the pagans had the victory.

He wandered out into the noonday sun. It was a bright, brittle winter's day, with a faint hint of spring on the breeze.

Myrddin yawned and stretched until his joints clicked. A tall man, the roof of his cave was too low for him to stand upright in. In consequence he had developed a slight stoop.

His belly rumbled. Myrddin could live on remarkably little, but he still needed to eat. With Mab cantering at his bare heels, he delved into the forest to hunt for a meal.

Myrddin had survived for almost a year in the wild. In that time he learned, often through painful experience, how to forage, and feed himself on a diet of wild plants, nuts and berries. He knew to avoid the plants that gave off milky or discoloured sap, and those with spines, fine hairs or thorns, along with other dangers.

"Beans, bulbs and seeds inside the pod," he chanted as he rooted through the undergrowth, "bitter-tasting leaves, and grain heads with pink and black spots. These things are no good for us. They drive needles into our belly and make us vomit. Don't they, imp?"

Mab nuzzled in the earth, searching for grubs and other tasty morsels. Myrddin gave her an affectionate tap on the head and returned to his work. His long, claw-like hands, disfigured by broken and dirty nails, seized clumps of edible roots and ripped them from the earth.

At length he loped back to his cave, carrying an armful of wild oyster mushrooms, roots, nettles, and dandelion. He left them in a heap just inside the entrance and fetched some dry grasses and mosses from his store of tinder at the back of the cave. Then he set about building a fire.

Myrddin's most precious possession, especially in the winter, was the steel blade of his dagger. The dagger had been a Christmas gift from Gwendolau, in the happy days when Myrddin stood high in favour at his lord's court.

There wasn't much left of the blade now. Myrddin placed a tattered square of cloth over the pile of tinder, crouched over it and held the worn length of metal between his thumb and index finger. In his other hand he grasped a piece of flint, with the sharpest edge pointed at the steel.

Grunting with effort, he struck the blade against the flint with swift downward strokes. The friction raised yellow sparks from the steel, which were deflected onto the cloth. Myrddin chuckled happily when the cloth caught light.

The nascent flames quickly spread to the tinder. Thankfully it was a still day, with no breeze and little chance of rain. While the fire leaped and crackled, Myrddin went to fetch water from the little burn that flowed close by his cave.

He took a rusted iron helmet with him. Myrddin had found it while exploring one of the gigantic ancient barrows scattered over the Summer Country. The barrows were the tombs of ancient princes. They were said to be haunted by evil spirits, and sensible people avoided them. Even the Hill Folk gave the barrows a wide berth.

Myrddin, who feared little since Abandinus saved him from the river, liked to explore the subterranean vaults of the dead. Many were full of old treasures: weapons and bowls and amulets, carvings of forgotten gods, all stacked neatly beside the dusty bones of their former owners. Some of the oldest treasures were forged of bronze, from before the time when man discovered the secret of iron.

He knew it was unwise to steal from the barrows. That he risked incurring the wrath of the spirits. Myrddin, however, feared little in this world or the next since Arfederydd.

The old helmet served him for a bowl and a cooking vessel. He knelt by the burn, scooped up water until the helmet was full, and returned to his fire. He placed the helmet upside down over the flames, grabbed a handful of the foodstuffs he had collected and dropped them into the water. Then he settled down on his stringy haunches to wait for the water to boil.

He gave a lump of raw mushroom to Mab, who snatched it in her jaws and chomped it down. While Myrddin watched the little creature eat, it occurred to him that he should cast the stones.

The stones were held in a little leather bag on a string around his neck. He had found them inside one of the burial chambers deep inside a barrow, arranged on a gaming board. The rules of the game were now long-forgotten, but he had taken the stones for himself. They were his way of interpreting messages from the gods, and of scrying the future.

He untied the string and upended the bag, scattering the stones over the ground. There were five, all different colours. Each colour represented a different value: white, blue and yellow for good, black and red for evil.

Myrddin peered down at the stones. The pattern they formed when they landed on the ground was all-important.

They had fallen in a similar pattern for several days

now. The red stone landed in the middle, with the black and white either side of it. Blue and yellow landed at a distance from the others.

Red for war, thought Myrddin, *white for peace, or virtue? Black for malice, and a shadow I cannot see.*

He closed his eyes, sucked in a deep breath and laid his right hand palm-down over the three central stones.

Myrddin gasped as pictures flashed though his mind. He saw a battlefield - any number of battlefields, hosts of spears, forests of banners and rivers of blood; his ears were filled with shouts and screams and braying war-horns, the neighs of terrified horses and triumphant yells of victorious warriors as they drove their enemies from the field.

One battle was fought over a dry, arid plain, with mountains in the distance. Myrddin's Sight, his supreme gift from the gods, roved over the field and picked out a single warrior. A tall, hard-faced man in a coat of iron plates shaped like leaves, his youth burned away in the fires of war, his eyes hard and merciless.

Medraut. The warrior's name, uttered by a soft voice of a nameless god, whispered through Myrddin's mind.

The warrior rode away from the battle. He vanished, and the image of the plain melted away.

Now Myrddin saw Caerleon again. The capital of Britannia stood half-empty. Most of the soldiers were gone, and a good number of the citizens had packed up their goods and belongings and fled to the countryside. In the absence of the High King, Caerleon was once again reverting to a city of ghosts, haunted by the memory of the Roman legionaries who once tramped its cobbled streets.

The palace was still occupied. Another dark young man, remarkably similar to the warrior in the coat of iron leaves, strode purposefully through its halls. He might have been a king, yet wore no crown.

Llacheu.

Myrddin's eyes snapped open. The water in the helmet

was starting to boil. He ignored it.

"The white and the black," he mumbled, lifting his hand from the stones.

He pondered the meaning of the vision. The knowledge came unbidden into his mind. Medraut and Llacheu were two of the three sons of Artorius, the High King.

The gods had sent Myrddin to help the beleaguered High King. Even though Artorius was responsible for the death of Morgana, the last Seer of Britannia, he was still the shield and protector of the land. The king stag needed to live on, at least for a few more years.

"The red stone stands for war," Myrddin whispered, "white for good, black for evil."

The meaning was clear enough. One of Artorius' sons was a force for good, the other for evil. Myrddin had looked into their souls. Both were equally ambitious, talented and unscrupulous.

If only he could think clearly. Myrddin's wits were still clouded by the horror of Arfderydd. He found it difficult to concentrate for any length of time. He blinked, and once again saw his dear lord, Gwendolau, go down into the dirt with a pagan axe buried in his neck.

Myrddin started to weep. "Men went to Arfderydd," he moaned, "the lone man was broken..."

He scattered the stones with a flick of his hand, and instantly forgot their meaning.

23.

Marcus of Kernow was a wizened, dried-up shadow of the man Artorius remembered. The usual privations of a long siege had weakened the king, but there was something else eating him from inside.

At first Artorius thought the man was ill with some wasting fever or disease. After an evening in his company, when the Companions were feasted in the mead-hall at Caer

Y Brenin, he realised Marcus was sick in mind rather than body.

No stranger to the lust for revenge on his enemies, Artorius had never encountered a man so devoured by hatred. Gaunt, stooped and hollow-eyed, Marcus sat at high table and picked irritably at his hard rye bread and salted meat. He had little else to offer his guests, since the stores of Caer Y Brenin were much depleted after the siege.

"Our enemies caught us by surprise, lord king," he said through a mouthful of beef, "another month of siege, and we would have been reduced to eating my wolfhounds. Or each other."

Marcus glared at the table as though he meant to take a bite out of it. "Kernow had been at peace with Amorica for years," he hissed, "I never thought King Budic would betray me. *Never.*"

His hands curled into fists. "As for Erbin of Dumnonia, that cowardly little snake, I have vowed to throttle him with my bare hands."

He turned to look at Artorius with genuine anxiety in his damp, red-rimmed eyes. "You will allow me to kill him, won't you, lord king?" he pleaded. "Erbin betrayed you as well, but it is my kingdom he helped to lay waste. My people he slaughtered. My cattle he stole. I have the right to kill him myself. Not a right - a duty!"

Artorius took a sip of mead. He winced at the bland taste. There was little mead or ale left after the siege, and Marcus' slaves had been obliged to eke out the remainder by watering it down.

"Budic and Erbin shall be punished in due course," he replied in a tone almost as bland as the mead, "first, your son must be brought to account. He is our chief enemy. My Companions want his head, and soon, in exchange for the slaughter of their comrades."

Marcus bared his yellow teeth. Artorius, who disliked the man, had meant to sting him with the reminder that

Drystan was his son. Judging from Marcus' reaction, the barb had struck home.

"This war has been a great lesson to me," growled the King of Kernow, "in future, I shall drown all my bastards at birth. Or else take them onto the cliffs and drop the little turds into the sea. Yes. Let the sea have them. Let them drown. Let their bones drift for eternity in the deep."

Artorius shifted uncomfortably in his seat. Knowingly or not - and it was difficult to read his companion's twisted mind - Marcus had just reminded him of the death of Ganhumara, his old concubine.

"The sea cannot have Drystan," Marcus added in a low voice, his eyes narrowed to slits, "I have a different fate in mind for him."

His claw-like hand gripped Artorius' wrist. "Let me burn Drystan, lord king," he pleaded, his eyes yearning up at the High King, wide as saucers, brimful of the madness of obsession, "let me put his flesh to the flames."

Artorius also hated Drystan, and wished to see him dead, but this was too much. "Your flesh, Marcus," he said quietly, pushing the other man's hand away, "you made the boy. Fathered him. Don't you wish to grant him a quick death?"

Marcus grinned, and gave a little shake of his head. "No. He must die slowly, and in full view of my subjects. The faithless bitch Esyllt will die with him. Side by side. I will send her bones to her father in a box. None shall dare to lift a hand against me after that."

"After all," he sniggered, with a hideous wink at Artorius, "if we cannot inspire love, our only hope is fear. Is that not so, lord king?"

Artorius preferred not to acknowledge the truth of this, though he had long realised it. He preferred not to endure the company of King Marcus any longer either, but courtesy forbade otherwise.

For the rest of the evening he sat and listened to the

sub-king spout his hatreds and prejudices. In the early hours of the morning, by which time Artorius had gulped down enough watered mead to get himself drunk, Marcus' well of spite finally ran dry. The King of Kernow's head slumped forward and he started to snore with his face stuck to a pool of wine spillage. Artorius rose and looked for a space to sleep on the floor.

Shortly after the siege was lifted, Marcus had sent troops of horsemen out from Caer Y Brenin to chase down his enemies. One of these bands returned shortly after daybreak, bloodstained and exultant.

Their captain laid a pile of seven reeking heads at the feet of the king, who sprawled in his chair, nursing a headache. .

"These are the heads of seven Amorican traitors from the army of King Budic," said the captain of horse, "we caught and slew them last night, while Budic and his army were in flight to their ships."

Marcus glanced down at the trophies. Seven pairs of glassy eyes stared back at him. "You did well, Tegyr," he said, stifling a yawn, "though I wish the head of Budic was among them."

"This is not all, lord king," said Tegyr, "after killing these stragglers, we turned west in pursuit of eight horsemen. We chased them until they took refuge inside an old fortress. I left half my men to watch the fort."

Marcus looked puzzled. "Why should I care for a handful of fugitives?" he demanded, "burn them out, if you like, and bring me their heads as well."

Tegyr's scarred face creased into a smile. "One of them has fair hair, and wears a coat of silver mail. I believe he is Drystan. We have your enemy trapped, lord king."

There was a murmur of excited voices in the hall. Artorius placed a hand on Marcus' shoulder. The King of Kernow had turned a livid shade of red and started to breathe heavily through his nose.

"I will run Drystan to earth," said the High King, "stay here and tend to your wounded."

Marcus glared savagely at Artorius. Twin fires of rage and madness danced in the sub-king's eyes.

Artorius calmly met his glare. "This is my command," he said firmly.

Angry voices were raised among Marcus' warriors. Several officers of the Companions stepped forward, Cei and Bedwyr among them, and laid hands on their swords.

Artorius stepped to the edge of the dais. "This is my command!" he roared.

His voice rang like a trumpet in the rafters of the hall. The voices were quelled, and not a man dared to meet his eye.

Silence fell. Artorius fought to control his temper. During the years of peace he had learned to control himself, and keep the beast within on a short chain. His recent trials, and the loss of so many comrades, stretched the chain to breaking point.

"You," he said, turning to Tegyr, "lead me to this fortress."

Tegyr gave a frightened little duck of his head. "Yes, lord king," he replied.

Artorius chose to ride out with his Companions and two hundred cavalry from Gwent, while the remainder of his army camped near Caer Y Brenin. He neither liked nor trusted King Marcus, and wanted to leave him with a forceful reminder of where the real power lay in Britannia.

Tegyr led him west, through a landscape of quiet woods and hills. Artorius, who found it difficult to trust any native of Kernow, kept a careful eye on the man. At the first sign of treachery, he would slay Tegyr and ride back to Caer Y Brenin, to burn down the stronghold and hang Marcus from the rafters of his own hall. From now on, the sub-kings of Britannia would learn what it meant to betray the High King.

He took comfort from the presence of Cei and Bedwyr. It was many years since these three men had campaigned together, and Artorius' heart swelled as the Companions rode further into the west. This was all he had ever desired: loyal men at his back, a good horse under him, and an enemy to fight.

We are young again, he thought, looking affectionately at his friends, *in mind and intent, if not in body.*

The years had been cruel to Cei and Bedwyr, though the former had at least shed some of his excess weight. Apparently this was down to Llacheu, who had upbraided him at Caerleon for his lethargy and drunkenness.

Still, the advancing years lay heavy on him. He was now almost totally blind in one eye, and his sloped shoulders and thin grey hair suggested a man growing old before his time.

Bedwyr, on the other hand, had coarsened with age. The graceful young warrior was quite gone, replaced by a sour, one-handed cripple who yet carried some traces of his old fighting spirit. He wore a shield strapped to the stump of his left arm, and was driven by an inner fire, a desire to constantly prove himself in front of the younger warriors.

He had also grown cold, and the advice he gave Artorius was both cynical and heartless. For his part, the High King was now ready to listen to such advice, and act upon it. Until order was restored, mercy would be overruled by justice. Harsh, swift justice, delivered on the point of a spear.

After half a day's ride the Companions arrived at a valley, dominated by a large, round hill to the north-west. Far to the south, the sea was just visible beyond a rocky shoreline.

"There, lord king," said Tegyr, jabbing his spear at the hill, "the old fort is inside those trees."

Artorius shaded his eyes to examine the hillside. It was neatly circular, and clearly man-made. He could see the outline of an ancient ditch surrounding the base, now partially filled in by loose earth and stones. The double wall of timber ramparts on the summit was long since rotted away, partially obscured by an overgrown thicket of weeds and other vegetation.

Scattered clumps of trees had grown up inside the perimeter of the fort. They stood like rows of sentinels, and their outspread branches put Artorius in mind of dead fingers, ready to seize and crush to death any who dared to enter the long-abandoned fortress.

A few men had dared. Artorius picked out the glint of sunlight on an iron helmet. Someone peered over the ruin of the outer wall.

The twenty spearmen Tegyr had left behind were camped on the eastern flank of the valley. Artorius dismounted and led the Companions down to join them. While the soldiers exchanged greetings and drank one another's health, he walked down to the foot of the valley.

Cei lumbered after him. "What are you doing?" the steward growled, "the men on the hill might have bows."

"If Drystan is in there," said Artorius, "I want him to see me, and know his time has come."

He halted just out of bow-shot of the fort. Then he curled his fingers around the ivory hilt of Caledfwlch and slowly drew the famous blade from its leather sheath. His golden mail and dragon helm were lost, but he wore the white cloak of the High King, fringed with a purple border.

A gleam of autumn sunlight caught the blade and rippled down its length. For a moment it seemed as though Caesar's sword had burst into flame.

"Drystan of Kernow," cried Artorius, "show your face, if you are any kind of a man. Hide from me, and everyone will know your true worth. Drystan the coward. Drystan the turncoat. Drystan the oath-breaker. Drystan the cringing, bastard-born whelp, who betrayed his king and made war on his own father. You ran from me once. There is nowhere left to run now."

His words were echoed by a cheer from the Companions, followed by a barrage of jeers and insults hurled at the broken walls above. Artorius slid Caledfwlch back into its sheath, folded his arms and waited.

The outer wall of the fort, or what remained of it, was defended by a gatehouse. Most of the timber ramparts were gone, but the post-holes of the gate itself were still visible, flanked by buttresses made of heaped earth and loose stones. Two figures appeared in the gateway. They wore long robes of dark blue wool, and their faces were hidden under peaked hoods.

The hooded figures made their way down the rough track carved into the eastern flank of the hillside.

"What's this?" growled Cei, "does Drystan send monks to treat with us?"

Artorius said nothing. For one so young, Drystan was both devious and cunning, as the High King knew to his cost. He could only guess at this latest ruse.

The jeers of his men died away as the envoys from the fort reached the foot of the hill and pushed back their hoods.

Artorius almost laughed. Before him stood a couple of slender young girls, neither much older than sixteen. They might have been twins, with the same lustrous golden hair and sweet, heart-shaped faces.

One was slightly taller, and had a look of calm authority in her mild grey eyes. "I am Princess Esyllt of Hibernia," she announced, "this is my slave, Golwg. We are sent by my husband, Prince Drystan of Kernow, to discuss terms with the High King."

Cei snorted in derision, though Artorius admired the way she faced down several hundred warriors. Her slave Golwg showed an equal lack of fear, and met the stares of his men with a mocking smile.

"Your husband, as you call him, is no prince," Artorius said quietly, "he is a bastard-born traitor, who has done his best to destroy a happy and peaceful land."

"Best look for another mate, my lady," said Cei, "before the day is out, I will have Drystan's head and privy parts impaled on my spear."

The Companions greeted this with a shout of approval. Artorius raised his hand for silence. Esyllt, he noticed, was unmoved by the threat. She gave Cei a look of withering contempt, and then turned her attention back to the High King.

"In return for his life, lord king," she said, "he offers us both as sureties for his behaviour. Let Drystan and his men depart, and go into exile. They will never set foot on British soil again."

Artorius pondered this unlikely offer. "You called Drystan your husband," he said, "that is impossible. You are already betrothed to King Marcus. Marcus is my ally. I am honour-bound to take you back to him."

Esyllt smiled, and in that moment Artorius understood why Drystan had risked all for her.

"Drystan is my husband," with a careless defiance that took his breath away, "no doubt his father wishes to kill me. Let him."

Her simple courage filled Artorius and his warriors with a kind of awe.

All save one. "It's a trick," said Bedwyr, "any fool can see that. You are under no obligation to accept these sluts as hostages, lord king. Take them prisoner, and let us storm the fort and kill everyone inside."

His harsh, nasally voice cut through the silence. Artorius was repelled by Bedwyr's tone, but understood the cold logic of his advice.

"The men in the fort will not surrender," said Esyllt, "for them, it is exile or death."

Artorius gazed up at the hill. Six men couldn't hope to hold out for long against three hundred. Even so, the slope was steep, and the broken, overgrown defences were strong enough to impede a direct assault.

If he hurled his men up the slope, they would quickly overwhelm the few defenders. However, a few would die, or suffer crippling injuries. Artorius was reluctant to spill any more British blood.

There was no help for it. His attempt at shaming Drystan into surrender had failed, so he could only resort to brute force.

Artorius was about to give the order to attack, when Cei's powerful hand closed on his wrist.

"Look!" the steward said urgently, "the fox has left his earth!"

He jabbed his finger southwards. Artorius looked, and saw a lone rider urging his pony headlong down the crest of the hill. He was a superb horseman, and somehow managed to avoid the rocks and pot-holes that littered the uneven slope.

There was little doubt of the rider's identity. His hair shone like gold.

"I told you it was a trick," said Bedwyr, matter-of-factly. "Drystan sent his women to distract us while he fled."

"He flees alone," said Artorius, "his men must be ready to die for him."

As mine were for me, he thought. Now their situations were reversed: Artorius held the advantage, while Drystan was forced to abandon his followers and escape into the wild.

"We should give chase," Cei said urgently, "send riders after him!"

Drystan had gained the flat. His pony sped across the grassy plain towards a line of trees.

Artorius saw little point in sending men to blunder about hopelessly in unfamiliar woods until nightfall. Drystan could wait, he decided. The boy's power was broken. A lone fugitive with no friends or allies offered little threat.

"Let him be," said Artorius, "we'll put a price on his head. He won't last long."

There remained the men in the hill-fort to deal with. Bedwyr volunteered to lead the Companions up the slope, and after some hesitation Artorius agreed.

He expected Drystan's men to make a fight of it. Instead all but one surrendered. The exception was Hyfaidd, one of the young Companions who had betrayed Artorius and chosen to follow Llwch Llemineawg.

Two Companions carried his body down from the fort and dumped it at the High King's feet. Bedwyr's sword had cut open a fatal wound in his breast.

"We offered him a chance to surrender," said Bedwyr, "but he said we would only hang him as a traitor and an oath-breaker. He put his back to a tree and fought to the end."

"Lived like a rat," grunted Cei, "died like a man. At least that's something."

Artorius was grief-stricken as he looked down at the corpse. Hyfaidd had been one of his most promising young warriors, and looked set to become a future officer. Artorius' son, Llacheu, would have need of such able men when he inherited the crown.

Instead Hyfaidd chose to throw in his lot with rebels. He was not alone. Cei had identified seventeen other young Companions among the enemy casualties on the beach, where Artorius smashed the Swine of Kernow.

Why were the old loyalties breaking up? Perhaps Llwch was right. God had chosen the wrong man as High King. Or perhaps the long peace had made the people of Britannia complacent. A new generation of young men was growing to manhood who knew nothing of real warfare, and played no part in the fight against the Saxons.

Young warriors needed action. An external enemy to fight. Otherwise they would turn on each other, and civil strife was the result. It had started already. Unless Artorius acted quickly, his fragile realm would fall to pieces.

If I have the strength to do it. I grow old.

He shook away the twinge of self-doubt. Even at forty-one, he was still a warlord without peer. He still commanded the loyalty of his veterans. Best of all, he still had Caledfwlch.

"Leave this one to rot," he said, "let the carrion-eaters have him. No man who breaks his oath deserves the honour and security of a grave."

The Companions rode east with their prisoners. Artorius meant to hand them over to King Marcus for judgement. He knew the terrible fate that awaited them, but Marcus was his ally, and Artorius was no longer in a position where he could afford to offend his allies.

Esyllt continued to earn his admiration. She rode cheerfully beside him, as though it was a holiday, and asked him questions: the health of his queen, life at court, the likelihood of good harvest in the summer.

You have seen your last summer, my lady, he thought sadly as they talked. The girl would soon be put to the fire.

He noticed her slave, Golwg, talked much with Cei. The graceless old warrior had always been uncomfortable in the presence of women, and shed few tears when his previous two wives died. Artorius suspected that death was something of a release for any woman forced to live with him.

Even Cei's natural boorishness melted a little. Golwg was young, and beautiful, and twittered away constantly in his ear. At first he ignored her, but the girl's persistence was impressive. The mismatched pair were deep in conversation by the time the Companions reached Caer Y Brenin.

Artorius could scarcely believe it. At one point he feared for Golwg's safety when she rested her delicate hand on Cei's brawny shoulder. To his amazement Cei didn't shake her off, and even barked with laughter at one of her jests.

Esyllt grew silent as they neared Caer Y Brenin. Artorius was not hypocrite enough to try and comfort her.

Not for the first time, he wished he could resign his filthy office and retire to a monastery, tucked away in some quiet corner of Britannia. To spend his last years in prayer and reflection, like the Emperor Diocletian when he too grew weary of power. It was a dream Artorius often entertained.

Not yet. Not while I am still needed. Another five years, perhaps. Llacheu will be ready then.

King Marcus awaited them at the outer gates of his stronghold. He rubbed his hands in obscene glee at the sight of Esyllt, and signalled at his bodyguard to drag the girl from her horse.

"Welcome to Caer Y Brenin, my lady," he cried, "your arrival was somewhat delayed, but here you are at last."

Esyllt slid down before his warriors could seize her, and walked with calm dignity towards the king.

"My lord," she said with a graceful bow.

Marcus' hands twitched. A fleck of spittle appeared at the corner of his mouth. Artorius feared he would kill Esyllt on the spot.

The king mastered himself. "Take her inside," he hissed between gritted teeth, "and lock her up. See she is fed and watered. I want her in prime condition on the day of judgement."

Two spearmen advanced on Esyllt, who smiled and walked before them towards the gate. The ranks of Marcus' bodyguard parted to let her through.

The sound of weeping distracted Artorius from the scene. He turned to see Golwg draped over Cei's shoulder, clinging to his neck as she wept, presumably for her mistress.

Cei was not often caught at a disadvantage. He gave Artorius a helpless look. The High King rolled his eyes and turned back to Marcus.

"You cannot have the slave," he said, "she stays with us."

"As you wish, lord king," Marcus replied indifferently. "I already have more than enough useless mouths to feed."

"Where is Drystan?" he demanded, his voice choked with sudden anxiety.

"He escaped us," said Artorius, and smiled inwardly when Marcus turned white. A streak of angry blood flared on the side of his neck.

If God is kind, this vicious oaf will fall dead of a seizure, and I can place a better man on the throne of Kernow.

"Escaped?" Marcus squealed. He took a step towards Artorius, his hands raised like claws. Cei and Bedwyr moved forward, and the front rank of the Companions lowered their spears. At the same time Marcus' guards shuffled closer together. The threat of violence hung heavy in the air.

"You failed me!" shouted the King of Kernow, "what good is the bitch without the dog? I must have them both! They must burn on twin pyres, before the eyes of my subjects. Burn, burn, burn..."

All the passion drained out of him. He rubbed his brow and chewed his lower lip until it bled. His men watched pensively, clearly baffled as to what their unstable master might do next.

"Drystan is alone," said Artorius, "a hunted fugitive, without friends, in a land he has done his best to destroy. Every honest man's hand will be turned against him. Offer a reward for his capture, and you will soon have him in your grasp."

Marcus came to his senses. "Yes...yes," he muttered, "you are right, of course. There is nowhere in Kernow he can hide. I shall offer gold for his capture. Much gold."

He bared his teeth in a ghastly smile. "Forgive my harsh words, lord king. I was overwrought. Will you dine here tonight?"

Artorius had had quite enough of Marcus' hospitality. "Thank you, but no," he replied hurriedly, "I have unsettled business in Dumnonia. King Erbin must be brought to account."

He ignored the flicker of relief on the other man's face. With Artorius gone, Marcus could practice unrestrained horrors on those who had betrayed him.

There was nothing to be done. Marcus might be unpleasant and half-mad, but his kingdom lay in ashes as the result of a war that had been forced on him. He was entitled to his revenge.

Nightmarish images of burning bodies flickered through the High King's mind as he turned away from Caer Y Brenin, and led his men east.

24.

The campaign in Dumnonia was brief and virtually bloodless. An envoy met the Companions and their allies on the Roman road, shortly after they crossed the border, a few miles north-east of the old provincial capital of Isca Dumnoniorum.

"Hail, king of kings," said the envoy, a tall, elderly man with a long, clean-shaven face. "Erbin of Dumnonia sends his greetings, and begs for your mercy."

He and the two slaves who served him for an escort knelt on the frosted road before Artorius.

The High King glared down at them. "Why is your master not here, then?" he demanded harshly, "is he too much of a coward to face me?"

The envoy visibly shook. He screwed his eyes shut, and his teeth chattered when he spoke. "My...my lord wishes for a fair hearing. A trial before his peers, in the Round Hall at Caerleon. He is willing to present himself before you, lord king, if...if his safety can be guaranteed."

Cei urged his horse forward. "That worm you call

master is guaranteed nothing," he snarled, "save a knife in his heart and spittle on his grave. Let Erbin offer such terms as he pleases. Let him hide where he will. Whatever rat-hole he chooses to take refuge in, we shall follow, and drag him out by his beard."

Artorius usually made an effort to curb his steward's vicious tongue. This time he said nothing.

He was angry, that much was plain. His heavy lantern jaw was clenched, and there was a smouldering fire in his eyes Cei had not seen since Mount Badon.

"Erbin taunts me," Artorius said in a low voice, "it *pleases* him to distract me with false envoys, while he readies for war. Is that not so?"

The elderly man kneeling before him gave a sudden start. "No...no, lord king," he pleaded, "my master only desires peace."

"Then where is he now?" the High King demanded, "speak quickly."

"At...at Isca Dumnonorium," the other man whined. He turned green with fear as Artorius spat out a curse.

"Isca! The strongest town in the south-west, where the Roman walls are still intact, and a garrison with enough supplies can hold out against a besieging army for months. Erbin has holed up in there, has he? Doubtless with all the spears he can muster. A strange sort of peace, this. You have lied to me, little man."

The envoy threw himself onto his face. "No...no," he moaned, "I speak only the truth, dread king...only the words King Erbin placed in my mouth, and bade me repeat. Please - I am an envoy! I cannot be harmed!"

Artorius brushed aside his pleas. "You think to teach me the rules of war? Blood of Christ! I have suffered more insults and losses in recent days than any reasonable man can be expected to endure. How many more knives must I pluck from my back? How many more liars and traitors must I listen to?"

He bared his teeth at the envoy. "You ask for mercy. Very well, you shall have it. Are you left or right-handed?"

The other man, his eyes wet with tears, glanced fearfully up at him. "Lord...lord king?" he stuttered.

"You heard me! Left or right-handed?"

"R...right, lord king."

Artorius twisted in the saddle and stabbed his finger at two of the youngest Companions.

"Gareth, Menw," he barked, "this is your first campaign. Now you will learn what it means to serve a king, and a High King at that. Cut off this driveller's right hand."

Cei watched in astonishment as the deed was carried out, there on the road. The envoy's slaves made no effort to defend their master, who wailed like a frightened child as Gareth and Menw dismounted and advanced on him with drawn swords.

Golwg rested her head on Cei's shoulder and watched impassively as the mutilation was carried out. Menw, the larger of the two young Companions, seized the envoy by the neck and threw him onto his back. Gareth trod on the helpless man's forearm, raised his sword in both hands and brought it down in one clean, powerful blow.

Cei winced at the envoy's shrill scream. He was vulnerable to high-pitched noises, and it passed through his head like a knife.

At least Gareth struck true. His blade neatly parted the envoy's white hand from his wrist. The hand lay on the grass beside the road, twitching horribly.

"Bind up the wound," Artorius commanded. Gareth tore a strip from the envoy's cloak and wrapped it tightly around the bleeding stump.

To Cei's surprise, Golwg did not shudder or flinch from the grisly sight. The same could not be said for Bedwyr. His face had turned grey, and he looked ready to vomit.

Cei understood his old friend's reaction. Bedwyr had survived the loss of his left hand at Mount Badon, but the mental scars never healed.

The envoy's slaves helped their crippled master to his feet, and held him upright while he tottered and gasped in agony. Blood leeched through the crude bandage tied over the stump of his wrist.

Gareth, himself a trifle pale, picked up the severed hand and gave it to one of the slaves.

"Now," said Artorius, "hang it around your master's neck, and conduct him back to Isca. Tell King Erbin this is only a beginning. Tell him I will cut off the sword-hand of every man in his army, and blind and castrate them into the bargain, unless he comes to me in person and offers his surrender before sunrise tomorrow."

Somehow the slaves got their master onto his horse. They rode away, the envoy bent double in pain. Artorius watched them go.

"On," he shouted after they had vanished around a bend in the road. His mare trotted forward, and the long lines of horsemen and infantry advanced in silence.

Cei usually rode to the left of Artorius. This time he lagged behind, so he could stay close to Golwg. Artorius' brutality had shaken him.

He was surprised at his own weakness. The mutilation of the envoy was cruel, but Cei had seen (and done) much worse in his time.

I've grown soft, he thought, *too many years sat idle in Caerleon. All I did for twelve years is stuff my belly, pore over manuscripts and drink myself stupid. I forgot the reality of war.*

Golwg rode close to him, just enough for their knees to touch. Cei was no fool. He knew exactly what the girl was doing. She hoped to play on an old man's folly, flatter him with her attentions, make him fall in love (or lust) with her. Golwg's ultimate goal was to become his wife. Marriage to a wealthy and powerful man offered the slave her only realistic chance of freedom.

Cei didn't blame the girl for wanting to escape a life of enforced servitude. Nor was he averse to the idea of marrying a beautiful young girl, or at least making her his concubine. He was lonely since the death of his last wife, and needed someone to take care of him. Every year he grew weaker, though he would rather die than admit it. The sight in his left eye was almost gone, and the shadow of rheumatism crept remorselessly through his bones.

Once, in the days of his youth and strength, men had feared Cei. Now they mocked him, even to his face. Artorius' own son, Llacheu, even had the gall to march into his private chambers at Caerleon and lecture him on his dissolute habits.

"Enough of this poison," the young man had said, snatching a wine-flask from the table, "it is high time you and Bacchus parted ways. Are you Cei the steward, or shall we call you Biberius Caldus Mero?"

If any other man had spoken to him in such a brazenly insolent manner, Cei would have flown into a violent rage. But this was Llacheu, his old friend's favourite son, and lord regent of Britannia. Cei had always been fond of the lad, and in return Llacheu had never shown him anything but careful respect.

'Biberius Caldus Mero' - meaning 'drinker of wine with no water' - was a mocking nickname given to the Emperor Tiberius, after his habit of drinking strong undiluted wine. Cei wallowed in the same vice, partly to dull the pain of his bad eye, partly to ease the crushing burden of work. To serve as both steward and spymaster to the High King was no easy task, and required mental effort he was no longer capable of.

Cei sat in astonished silence, gaping at the doorway long after Llacheu had swaggered out. Since that humiliation, he took pains to appear sober for at least half the day. Hurt in his pride, Cei was determined to prove the kingdom could not function without him.

Shortly after midday the town of Isca Dumnonorium came in sight. It lay on a wide plain near the coast, next to a river that flowed into an estuary to the south-east.

Cei had never seen the town before, but knew something of its history. Originally a legionary fortress, built to house part of the Legio II Augusta, it had grown over the centuries of Roman occupation into a thriving town and important trading centre.

Artorius ordered a halt when his vanguard reached the crest of a rise, which dropped sharply down to the plain and offered a superb view of the town.

Isca Dumnoniorum lay spread out below. Even from this distance, it was possible to see the town was much decayed. Most of the shops and houses, laid out in a typically neat Roman grid pattern, were in ruins. Cei saw tiled roofs fallen in and open to the elements. Only the grandest public buildings, including the tribune's palace in the centre of the town, showed signs of occupation. Wisps of smoke rose from the flues of the palace bakehouse, and the streets were full of tents and campfires.

"King Erbin is in residence," remarked Artorius, "let us hope he received our message. If not, or if he refuses to heed it, we storm the town."

"Tomorrow at dawn," repeated Cei, with an affectionate smile at his master. "The old ways, eh?"

"They haven't failed us yet," replied Artorius.

The army moved down off the ridge onto the flat ground north of the town. There was room enough to pitch camp here, since King Erbin's troops had razed the suburbs and stripped the land of people and livestock. Artorius and his officers and sub-kings lodged in the cottages of a deserted village, while lines of white tents sprang up all over the plain like neat rows of mushrooms after rain.

No envoy rode to meet them. The gates of Isca remained firmly shut, and the ramparts crammed with spearmen and archers. Despite Artorius' threats, and the mutilation of the envoy, it seemed King Erbin meant to put up a fight.

"I can't understand the little runt," Artorius remarked at a council of war held inside the largest of the cottages, just after dusk. "He's always been so meek in the past. That's why I made him King of Dumnonia. I wanted someone who would obey orders and never question my authority. It seems I misjudged him."

The cottage had just one room, and he and his chief officers and advisers sat on stools on the hard earthen floor. Otherwise there was barely a stick of furniture save for a couple of low benches and a small table, stacked in an untidy pile in the corner.

The inhabitants had clearly left in a hurry: three wooden bowls, some cooking utensils and bits of half-eaten food were scattered across the floor. Cei suspected the people had been forcibly evacuated by King Erbin's troops, herded inside the walls of Isca Dumnoniorum like so many cattle.

Bedwyr was also present, as well as Cadwallon Lawhir, King of Gwynedd, and Caradog Freichfras, King of Gwent. Cadwallon was well into middle age now, his distinctive mane of red hair streaked with grey, while Caradog was nearing seventy. There was something indestructible about the wiry, white-haired old man, one of the last survivors of Vortigern's disastrous reign as High King.

"I have known Erbin all his life," grunted Caradog, scratching at a louse in his beard, "and he was ever a gutless brute. I find it difficult to believe he has found his manhood, now, so late in life. Either he has run mad, or else his officers have overruled him."

There was a hint of implied criticism in his voice. Artorius' decision to cut off the envoy's hand would either frighten the enemy into surrender, or fill them with a desperate resolve to fight to the death. It seemed they had chosen the latter course.

Artorius is making too many mistakes, thought Cei, *like*

me, he grows old. His judgement has started to slip.

"If the fools wish to die, then we shall not disappoint them," said the High King, "if we have received no word from Erbin by tomorrow, an hour after sunrise, then we attack."

His voice had taken on the same harsh quality as earlier, when he confronted Erbin's luckless envoy. "Not a spear shall be left in reserve," he went on, "the army is to be be divided into three squadrons. One, led by myself, shall storm the northern gate. The other two will attack the walls flanking the gatehouse. Caradog, Cadwallon, you each have command of a squadron. We have rams and scaling ladders in abundance, and more than enough men to overrun Erbin's garrison. Any questions?"

Cei nodded in approval. It was the kind of brutally simple plan he appreciated. "Once we have forced the walls..." ventured Caradog.

"The town is to be sacked," Artorius replied abruptly, "no mercy, no quarter. I want the buildings fired, and every living thing inside put to the sword. This rebellion has gone on long enough. It ends here, one way or another."

Cei coughed. "There may be hundreds of innocents inside the town," he said softly, "peasants, slaves and freemen. Women and children. Why should they pay for Erbin's crimes?"

"Their lives are on his conscience," Artorius replied, "not mine. He knows our terms. If he surrenders, all those people will live. If not, he shall answer to God for the consequences."

Cei stayed behind when the others were dismissed. "You have something else to say?" asked Artorius, raising an eyebrow at him.

There was an edge to the High King's voice. Cei suspected Artorius would rather be alone with his thoughts, but ploughed on regardless.

"A minor request," he said gruffly, "the slave, Golwg. I

want her for myself. Can I have her?"

Artorius heaved a sigh, and pinched the bridge of his nose. "You old dolt," he murmured, "got her claws into you, has she? I would have credited you with more sense."

Cei bridled at the insult. "May I take her, or not?" he demanded.

"Why in God's name should it matter to you?" he cried when Artorius didn't reply, "she's only a slave. What else would you do with the girl? Put her in the kitchens?"

Artorius leaned his broad back against the wall. "Only a slave," he said with a weary little shake of the head. "God help us. And you are my chief of spies."

"What do you mean?" shouted Cei, "explain yourself!"

He could feel the angry blood seething in his veins. Pride, the foolish, stubborn pride that had always been Cei's downfall, threatened to overwhelm his love and respect for Artorius.

"Have you not divined Golwg's true nature?" asked Artorius, "she is a weapon. Drystan and Esyllt's last weapon. They have sent her among us, to sow discord and drip poison into the ears of my friends."

He stabbed a finger at Cei. "*Your* ears, you great oaf. Be honest with yourself. Why would a beautiful young girl of barely sixteen summers show such marked interest in a man like you? A man three times her age and five times her weight, ugly and one-eyed and foul-tempered, who stinks of horses and can't keep a civil tongue in his head?"

Artorius smiled as he spoke. Cei refused to hear the affection in his voice.

"The High Kingship has soured you," he said, breathing hard as he fought to keep a grip on his temper, "now I understand why you were so reluctant to take Constantine's crown at Mount Badon. You trust no-one, and see conspiracies everywhere. Daggers glinting in the dark. Is this how it ends, Artorius? A man sitting alone, waiting for his enemies to come and finish him off?"

Artorius' smile faded. "I'm always alone, Cei," he replied quietly, "when the daggers come, I might welcome them."

"As for the girl," he added, "if you're determined to make a fool of yourself, I won't stop you. Nor will I tolerate her presence at court. Golwg is not welcome at Caerleon."

"Now I understand," said Cei, "you won't have her at court because she reminds you of Drystan. Of the defeat you suffered at his hands. The Companions he slew, and the defection of Llwch Llemineawg. Men say I am proud, Artorius, but my pride is nothing compared to yours."

"You may be right," the High King answered after a pause. "Drystan humiliated me on the field. A High King is a man like any other, and feels his defeats just as keenly."

Cei rose to his feet. He was suddenly tired, and wanted to be anywhere else. "I beg leave to go," he asked, all formality now.

Artorius looked surprised. "Go?" he asked, "go where?"

"Away. I don't want to be here. I'm sick of this war. Any war. Let me depart."

Cei had never made such a request before. For over thirty years he had served Artorius loyally and well, and fought alongside him in almost every campaign. Now his anger had given way to exhaustion.

"Go, then, if you wish," said Artorius, "take your slave girl and run away. I think I can defeat Erbin without the aid of one infatuated old man."

Cei was stunned by his old friend's indifference. He had expected Artorius to order him to stay. Instead he was turned loose, like some ancient wolfhound or veteran spearman, too weighed down with years and old wounds to be of any further use.

He stalked out of the cottage and left the High King in shadow.

25.

Kernow

Esyllt was kept chained in darkness, like a dog, with an iron collar around her neck. The collar was heavy, and after a week of confinement the iron had rubbed a livid red weal on her neck. She bore the pain, as she bore the fear and cold and loneliness, with quiet fortitude.

Her prison was one of the timber sheds inside the inner wall of Caer Y Brenin. It had been used as a prison before, judging from the manacles fastened to the walls and the lingering stench of human deprivation.

There were no windows. Esyllt was kept in absolute darkness for much of the day, save for meal-times, when her guard came in with a bowl of stew and a flagon of water. He was a leering, wall-eyed brute, and shoved the bowl towards her with his foot.

"Eat up, my lady," he would snigger, "eat up your nourishing stew. It's good stuff. Beans, pulse, and a drop or two of my spittle. Perhaps tomorrow I'll piss in it."

Esyllt was hard put not to vomit as she forced the food down. She suspected King Marcus had chosen the worst man he could find to guard her. It was a crude effort to break her spirit.

She could read Marcus' mind. He wanted to make an example of her. The mob would see the wretched, half-starved, pitiful creature that had once been Princess Esyllt, and think twice before defying their king.

They will see me burn...

Of all the horrors Marcus might inflict on her, this was the one she truly feared. All her life, Esyllt had been terrified of fire. One of her earliest memories was the bakehouse next to her father's hall burning down, thanks to a careless slave who neglected to tend one of the bread-ovens.

The fire had raged out of control and spread to the

thatched roof of the hall. She remembered being carried outside by one of King Niall's warriors, while the king himself and the rest of his household worked frantically to douse the flames.

Two of his slaves, including the one who started the fire, failed to get out of the bakehouse in time. They survived, but their faces and hands were hideously burned. Afterwards, whenever she saw them, Esyllt screamed in terror and would not be comforted until they were ushered away. Eventually, tired of his daughter's hysterics, her father sold them to a neighbouring chieftain in exchange for four cows.

As she sat alone in the dark, Esyllt was frequently reminded of the scarred and blistered faces of those luckless slaves. They had been handsome men, once, yet the pitilesss fire stripped away their good looks. Their noses and lips were melted away by the searing heat. One lost an eye.

Esyllt had always been vain of her beauty. Not only for its own sake. She had realised at an early age the power it gave her. A measure of influence over men. It was one of her few weapons.

The fire will destroy my beauty before I die, and leave me exposed...the people will see me exposed...

She wanted to weep, but if she did the guard would hear it, and report to Marcus. The king would know he had broken her then. Esyllt refused to give him the satisfaction. She wondered if it would be possible to bear the pain, when the fire was lit under her. Would she be able to prevent herself from crying out? Esyllt pressed her hands together and prayed, prayed fervently to the God she had never really believed in, to give her the strength.

The prison-house was made for despair. Esyllt fought stubbornly against it. She clung to her one sliver of hope, and repeated the same words to herself, over and over, as she rocked gently back and forth in the darkness.

"Drystan will come. Drystan promised. I made him

promise. He will not fail me. He cannot."

Esyllt tried to persuade herself that she was only here because she wanted to be. At the ruined hill-fort, she had persuaded Drystan to let her and Golwg surrender to Artorius. Their plan was to distract the High King long enough for Drystan to make his escape.

At first he protested. They had been man and wife for barely two days. It was no valid form of marriage in the eyes of the church, but Esyllt cared little for that.

She overrode her husband's tearful protests. Esyllt was stronger than Drystan in every way except the physical, and found him easy to manipulate.

"Let me go," she said, gently brushing away his tears, "let them carry me away as a prisoner, and promise you will come and rescue me."

"My promises are worth nothing," he cried, "I promised to make you a queen, and lay the head of Artorius at your feet. I failed."

"Then redeem yourself," she replied lightly.

Despite his flaws, Esyllt still saw potential in Drystan. She owed him a chance of redemption. To deliver herself into the hands of their enemies, and let him go free, was the only way to save them both.

Her hope lay in the fact that Drystan loved her, adored her with fierce passion, and would never abandon her to die.

After three days and nights of imprisonment, doubts started to creep in. How much was his love truly worth? He lusted after her, certainly, and had proved it on their wedding night, on the damp ground inside the remains of one of the roundhouses where they lay together for the first (and possibly the last) time.

Yet Drystan was alone. The Swine of Kernow were destroyed, and his allies scattered. Artorius and Marcus would be remorseless in their vengeance. Even now bands of men with dogs were probably hunting for her husband in the hills and forests of Kernow. How could Drystan possibly save her? It would be a miracle if he saved himself.

"He will find a way," she said aloud, "he must."

Esyllt's words were swallowed up inside the tomb-like blackness of her prison. She closed her eyes. Once again she saw the flames, and heard the faint echo of her own dying screams.

On the morning of the fourth day, King Marcus came to see her. Esyllt shrank at the sight of his pallid, sneering face, and the other man he brought with him.

At first she thought his companion was a priest, come to mumble the last rites over her. Clad in a tattered grey robe, face hidden under a cowl, the newcomer's back was crooked, and he shuffled painfully along on sandalled feet with the toes pointed inwards.

Marcus dismissed the guard, who vanished outside with a last wink at Esyllt. When he was gone, the king turned to study his prisoner.

"You might have been a queen," he said, "why, Esyllt? Why did you snub me? Was my kingdom not enough for you?"

She had expected him to gloat, and was surprised at the sadness in his voice.

"I wanted to be free," she replied, looking him in the eye, "to live on my own terms. You would have made me your slave. Whipped me, insulted me, forced me to bear your children until I was too weak to bear any more. The meanest beggar enjoys more freedom than a king's wife."

"Drystan offered me that freedom. He would have also made me a queen, but a queen in my own right, with the power to do as I pleased. To live as I willed."

Marcus sniffed. Seen at close quarters, he was a surprisingly small man, with bloodshot, deep-set eyes, a hooked nose and an untidy grey beard. He dressed shabbily for a king, and his crimson tunic was marked with spots of grease and food stains. Esyllt noticed the nails of his long white fingers were bitten down to the quick.

"You were a fool to believe in the promises of a traitor," he spat, "you think my son wanted you? Any pretty girl with royal blood in her veins would have done. He wanted my kingdom, and a queen to prop up his stolen throne. Drystan would have used you in the same way any man of wealth and power uses his wife."

Marcus bared his yellow teeth in a grin. "He is my son, after all. I know him better than anyone."

"You know him not at all," she retorted with a flash of her old courage, "he is twice the man you are, and he loves me."

Her eyes flickered to the hooded stranger. All the while he remained silent, head bowed, hands concealed inside their long grey sleeves. He gave off a slightly rank odour, akin to rotting meat.

"Drystan may be the better man," said Marcus, "yet I am still master here. What is he? A hunted animal. Soon to be a dead one."

He sighed, and ran both hands down his bearded cheeks. "I had hoped to burn you together. Side by side, on a cliff overlooking the sea, before my subjects. There was a certain poetry in that. However, I grow impatient."

Esyllt struggled to hide her terror. "If you wish to put me to the flames," she said defiantly, "then do it, and have done."

"Too easy, my dear," he replied, "the fire would purify your soul, and I can't have you going to God with a stainless conscience. Treachery such as yours deserves a lifetime of punishment."

He nodded at his companion. "My friend here has suggested something far more appropriate. Panawr, remove your hood."

The hooded man's arms slowly came up, and the long sleeves fell away to reveal bandaged hands and painfully thin forearms: little more than grey, liver-spotted skin stretched across brittle bones.

He pushed back his hood a little way, enough to show his face. Esyllt stifled a moan and pressed her back against the wall.

Panawr was a leper. The disease was well advanced. His once-handsome face was a sickly grey hue, and the disease had rotted away most of his top lip, exposing black gums and the brownish stumps of his teeth. A few straggling hairs clung to his scalp. Otherwise he was entirely bald.

His large green eyes still burned with vitality. There was life in him yet, a stark refusal to surrender.

"Tell her, Panawr," said Marcus, "tell my former betrothed what you have in mind."

The leper blinked, and made a harsh crackling noise in his throat before he spoke.

"Seven miles from here," he hissed, "there is a village on the coast. It is a fair place. I live there with my brothers. Alas, there are no women left. The sickness kills them first, you see. Will you come and live with us, dear lady, and sweeten our lives?"

Esyllt's blood ran cold. "You will make me live with lepers?" she asked Marcus, who chuckled and rubbed his hands together.

"Yes, indeed," he said happily. "Panawr is the headman of a leper colony on the coast. It was founded by a Christian priest from Hibernia, who shortly afterwards caught the disease himself and died. Pious fool. I allow the lepers to live there. It prevents them wandering over my kingdom, spreading fear and infecting healthy bodies."

"You will go with Panawr to the colony," he continued, "and live among the lepers until you die. Such a death, my lady. It will be slow, and lingering, and extremely painful. Is that not so, my friend?"

Panawr's rotted lips twisted in a grimace. "I cannot describe it, lord king," he muttered, "to be a leper is to pay for the sins of the world."

"Good," said Marcus, "Esyllt has much to pay for. The humiliation of her father, a war between two kingdoms, the needless deaths of hundreds of men in battle, burned villages and ruined crops...yes, a lifetime of slow disease is an entirely fitting punishment."

Esyllt was almost sick with horror. She crouched, dumb and lifeless, as Marcus called in two of his guards to remove the iron collar from her neck. They were clumsy, and hurt her as they struggled to pull out the bolts.

She barely heeded the pain. Far worse was in store. Her mind reeled. For a time Esyllt thought she might go mad. Rough hands gripped her arms and forced her to stand. She took little notice. Sunlight burst in painful waves over her eyes as she was dragged outside. She blinked away the agony.

They piled her aboard a horse and tied her ankles with a length of rope passed under the beast's belly. The effort was unnecessary. Esyllt harboured no thoughts of escape. There was no escape for her now. The gates were slammed shut forever.

Ever cautious, Marcus sent her to the leper colony with a dozed mounted spearmen for an escort. Unable to ride, Panawr sat inside a litter drawn by two horses. He said nothing, though Esyllt was occasionally aware of his green eyes staring at her with intense fascination.

Perhaps he admires my beauty, she thought listlessly, *he is still a man, after all. Of a sort.*

After a while she grew used to sunlight again. A single tear fell from the corner of her left eye and trickled down her cheek. Esyllt lacked the will to wipe it away.

What does it matter now? Let them see me weep. Let them laugh.

More than the pain, Esyllt had feared the loss of her beauty in the flames. Somehow King Marcus had divined her secret fear. There was no limit to his cruel invention. Forced to live among lepers, she would inevitably contract their disease, and be condemned to rot while still alive.

The road to the coast led through miles of quiet woodland, interspersed with the occasional clearing, occupied by small villages and a patchwork of fields.

It was late spring, almost Whitsun, and the land was healing. Some of the cottages were still deserted, others reduced to little more than ash and cinders, but people were slowly returning to their homes. Drystan's attempt to terrorise Kernow into surrender had failed.

Esyllt's thoughts dwelled on him. Was he somewhere nearby? She pictured him hiding in the woods, dirty and bearded and painfully thin, watching helplessly as his wife was taken to her doom.

Drystan was an outlaw now, hated and despised. How long could he survive in the wild? King Marcus' men were out in force, searching for him. He would soon be caught, unless he starved to death first, or fell victim to other predators. Bands of wolves stalked the forests of Kernow, ravenous and desperate after the harsh winter.

Esyllt wept again as she imagined him pulled down and devoured. Hairy grey shapes fighting over his body, muffled growls and barks, yellow teeth tearing at strips of his flesh...

She was faint by the time they reached the leper colony. The road had dwindled to a track, and the forest petered out before the track ended abruptly at the edge of a cliff.

It was a bright, chill spring day. Warm spring sunshine beat down on crystal-blue seas. This was Esyllt's favourite season, and at any other time her heart would have lifted at the sight the ocean. Now she turned away from it.

Fresh tears coursed down her face. The dam was broken, and the flow unstoppable.

Salt tears, she thought, *the sea shall be brimful of them before I am done.*

The officer in charge of Esyllt's guards trotted over to the litter. "Well?" he asked gruffly, "where is this foul village of yours?"

Panawr jabbed one of his bandaged hands at the cliff-edge. "Down," he mumbled, "there is a path cut into the side of the cliff. It is both steep and narrow. You will have to lead your horses down. The village is at the bottom."

The officer paled. "Here is close enough," he said, "take her with you."

His men looked grateful at being spared the ordeal. One cut the rope that bound Esyllt's ankles together, and she climbed stiffly from her horse.

"Come, my lady," said Panawr, with a painful attempt at a bow. He started to limp towards the cliff.

"Princess Esyllt is your responsibility now," the officer called after him. "King Marcus will send regular patrols to check on her. If she escapes, your village will burn, and every stinking leper inside it."

Panawr didn't seem to hear. He continued to limp on down the track with his awkward, pigeon-toed gait. Esyllt reluctantly followed, wrinkling her nose at the stench of his putrid flesh.

The path hacked out of the cliff-face was both steep and narrow, as Panawr warned, and slippery from recent rains. Esyllt clung to the rocks. In places she was forced to slide down on her backside.

Panawr's breath rasped in his chest as he laboured down the slope. She feared the leper would slip and tumble, but he always managed to save himself at the last moment. There was strength in Panawr still, despite his illness. She wondered what kind of man he had been before the curse of leprosy fell upon him.

Below them was a little cove, bound on three sides by sheer brown cliffs. Puffs of strange-smelling smoke rose from a miserable little hut with a straw roof, erected near the middle of the sandy beach. A few lepers, clad in the same tattered grey robes as Panawr, sat outside the hut, spooning broth into themselves from wooden bowls.

Esyllt saw no other dwellings. Then she noticed the base of the cliff was honeycombed with caves. More pungent smoke rose into the air from fires made of dried seaweed burning outside a few of the cave-mouths. More of the sad grey figures huddled beside the flames, singly or in little groups. They looked like so many seals, washed up and abandoned on this desolate beach.

"These are my brothers," whispered Panawr when they finally reached the bottom of the treacherous path, "in time, you shall come to know their names, and a little of their histories. As much as they choose to reveal. We find it difficult to trust, you see. God has betrayed us, so why should we put any faith in God's creatures?"

He paused to catch his breath. Esyllt pitied him and his brothers, wretched invalids, forced to live out their days on the edge of the world, shunned by their fellow men.

Sad ghosts, she thought, *half-dead already, waiting for the corrupted shells of their bodies to crumble away.*

"Come," gasped Panawr, "come and see your new home."

He limped away. For a moment Esyllt was tempted to turn and scramble back up the path. None of the lepers would be able to catch her. Freedom, the precious freedom she spent her life striving for, was again within reach.

She peered up at the cliff. Sunlight flashed off a dozen spear-heads at the top. The officer in charge of her escort was no fool, and had waited to see if she tried to escape.

Hope flickered and died inside her. The path was the only way out of the bay. Except for the sea, of course. Esyllt wondered if she was strong enough to swim for it.

I will break out of this cage. King Marcus' cruelty and lust for revenge has got the better of him. He cannot hold me here long, among these feeble, broken-down creatures. One dark, moonless night, I will scale the cliff or plunge into the sea. if I fall or drown, so be it. Either is preferable to the slow death of leprosy.

She waved at the spearmen, and turned to trip lightly after Panawr.

He led her towards one of the caves. It was unoccupied, though there were scattered traces of habitation outside the narrow fissure of the entrance: a discarded bowl, some ancient bandages, spotted with bloodstains, a few bits of dry kindling and seaweed.

Esyllt didn't want to know who had lived here, and Panawr didn't say. "There are blankets inside," he croaked. "I'll bring you some food and water later. We have to beg from the local villages. None of us is strong enough to hunt."

Esyllt stepped inside the cave, ducking her head to avoid cracking it against the low ceiling. It was dark, and cold, and narrowed towards the rear. The far wall was lost in shadow.

At least the sand underfoot was dry. Esyllt sat down on the relatively clean pile of blankets and rested her head against the wall.

She was tired. So tired it was difficult to keep her eyes open. Esyllt surrendered to the abyss, though not before Panawr's voice swirled around her head.

"I know what it is to love, my lady. And be loved. I was a warrior once, with a place of honour in my lord's war-band. Those were good days. I had the respect of my comrades, and a young wife who adored me. We had three children. The youngest was not long born when the sickness took me. It started in my feet, and spread slowly, like a grey shadow. My wife was horrified. Her love for me was replaced by fear. She ran away, I know not where, and took the children with her. I have not seen them for nine years."

He recited his tale in a dull monotone, like a bored priest reading out a sermon. Esyllt would have spoken some kind words, but sleep took her.

"I know what it is to love...and be loved..."

This line echoed in her dreams. Otherwise they were

shadowy and formless, full of hidden terrors Esyllt dared not examine too closely. The sound of the waves mingled with Panawr's voice.

She woke. The night outside was midnight-black, partially lit by a sliver of moon. All was quiet, save for the crash and rustle of the sea.

"Esyllt."

Startled by the unexpected voice, Esyllt reached instinctively for the dagger at her hip.

Her fingers closed on thin air. The dagger had been taken when she surrendered to Artorius.

A shadow blotted out the moonlight. A cold hand reached out and gently brushed her hair.

"Esyllt, my wife."

Relief swept through her. She caught the hand and pressed it against her lips.

"Drystan," she breathed.

26.

Londinium, the old Roman capital of Britannia, lay spread out before them in all its desolate magnificence.

It had been abandoned by the Britons for years, shortly after Constantine, Artorius' predecessor as High King, had marched out on his final, doomed campaign against the Saxons. Londinium's crumbling walls and ruined streets were symbolic of Britannia's lost imperial glory.

The future had taken root in the decay of the past. Within the shell of the old Roman city, a thriving town had sprung up. Crude timber huts and longhouses occupied the plazas where Romano-British citizens had once walked. The harbour, once filled with Roman warships and merchant galleys from all over the Empire, was now home to keels and longboats with dragon-headed prows.

Londinium was the home of Cerdic, Bretwalda of the Saxon tribes that now occupied almost half of the British mainland. From here, he had spent years enforcing his authority over the lesser Saxon chieftains with a potent mixture of force and cunning. Now the ruined city he had made his own rivalled Caerleon as the beating heart of Britannia.

Drystan knew of Cerdic, but had never set eyes on Londinium. All his short life, save for brief excursions to Hibernia and Amorica, had been spent in the south-west.

Our last refuge, he thought.

He and Esyllt rode together on a single horse, along the paved Roman highway leading to the western gate. The highway was cracked and broken in many places. Weeds sprouted from fault lines in the roadbed.

They rode in silence as the weary horse clopped along the final stretch of road. The journey had taken over a fortnight, from the leper colony on the western tip of Kernow to the east of Saxon-held Britannia. Drystan and Esyllt had spent most nights in the open, curled up together under trees and thickets, their lean bellies aching with hunger. Along the way they had stolen a horse, robbed lonely cottages of food, slit the throat of a shepherd who caught them trying to steal one of his lambs.

Somehow they had endured, though the effort used up every last drop of their strength. Esyllt had suffered the most. She rode behind Drystan, arms clasped loosely about his waist, head resting against his shoulder.

Drystan knew she had lost a dangerous amount of weight. He was consumed by anxiety for her well-being, and cared little for himself. She had slept since dawn, only waking to force down the last of their water and a few crumbs of bread. Barely a word had passed between them for two days. Both lacked the will to speak.

Her joy at being rescued from the leper colony had long since dissipated. Drystan still thought it his greatest achievement. After wandering alone in the forest for a time, he had gone to the lepers to beg for food, and there met with

Panawr. The headman of the colony had heard of Drystan, and approved of the fight against King Marcus. Panawr hated the king, who had slain his old lord in battle. He also hated him for forcing the lepers to live as virtual prisoners in their miserable caves by the sea.

It was Panawr who suggested how Esyllt might be plucked from under the king's nose at Caer Y Brenin. Drystan, who could think of no other way of saving his wife, agreed to the plan and waited among the lepers until Marcus' spearman had brought Esyllt to the village. The joyful disbelief on her face when he found her in the cave would live in his memory forever.

A growing sense of pride filled Drystan as they neared the city. They had won. Despite all their trials and privations, the hunger and cold and exposure, the terror of being caught by King Marcus' huntsmen. God had seen them safe.

"Just a little while longer, my love," he whispered, "we're almost there."

He clasped Esyllt's limp hands. Her fingers felt like brittle twigs, ready to snap if he placed too much pressure on them. She needed rest, proper rest, food and shelter and warmth. Without them, he doubted his wife would live another day.

As he expected, there were sentries on the gate. Two burly spearmen in boar-crested helmets lounged either side of the massive stone arch. They set down their wineskins and marched forward to block the road.

"Who are you?" one asked, "what is your business here?"

To Drystan's surprise, and no small relief, he spoke the British tongue, though with a heavy guttural accent.

"We are refugees," Drystan replied, "enemies of Artorius. We seek refuge in Londinium."

The Saxon scratched his dirty, copper-coloured beard and exchanged dubious glances with his comrade. Both wore leather tunics, and carried the long Saxon knife called the seax at their belts.

"Enemies?" he grunted, "you look like children. Why should Artorius fear a couple of striplings?"

Drystan curled his fingers around his sword-hilt. He was in no condition to fight, but could not afford to lose face.

"I am no child," he said quietly, "as you will find, unless you show me more respect. I am Drystan, the scourge of Kernow. I could send you both to the long house with my eyes shut."

The dirty, bearded faces before him split into wide grins. Drystan breathed an inward sigh of relief. He had heard that Saxon warriors were fond of boasts, and respected no man who failed to crow of his prowess, real or imagined.

"The scourge of Kernow, is it?" said the one who spoke the British tongue, with a mock bow, "we're honoured to have such a mighty champion among us. I am Eadric. Have you come to offer your services to King Cerdic?"

"Yes," answered Drystan, "if he will lend me his axes in return. Take me to him."

Eadric raised a tufted eyebrow at Drystan's boldness. He and his comrade spoke briefly in their own harsh tongue.

"Very well," he said, turning back to Drystan, "hand over your sword first. What about the girl? She looks fit to drop."

Drystan hesitated. "My wife is tired," he replied, "we haven't slept or eaten properly for days. Is there somewhere she can sleep in peace, while I speak with Cerdic?"

Eadric shrugged. "I daresay we can find her lodgings," he said, "our women shall take care of her."

Drystan was wary, and reluctant to let Esyllt out of his sight. He had little choice. She was too weak to stand, let alone appear before the Bretwalda.

He drew his sword and handed it over to Eadric. Esyllt's dead weight pressed against his back as he rode through the gate.

Four more Saxon warriors emerged from a gatehouse beside the arch. They glared at Drystan with hostile eyes until Eadric explained matters to them.

"These men will take you to the Bretwalda's mead-hall," said the Saxon, switching back to the British tongue. Then he turned about and ambled back to his post.

Wincing at his saddle-sores, Drystan climbed off his horse and led the beast on foot down the street. Two of the Saxons went before him, while the other marched behind the horse. Esyllt slumped until she was stretched full-length in the saddle, her head buried in the horse's mane, fair hair trailing loose and unbound until the strands almost touched the cobbles.

The street was awash with mud. Drystan studied the rows of shops and houses they passed with interest and not a little awe. He had never been inside a Roman town before, let alone one the size of Londinium. Most of the buildings were derelict and in a poor state of repair, though a few of the houses had been taken over by families of Saxon ceorls. Dogs, pigs and geese wandered the streets. There were children everywhere, sturdy Saxon infants crawling and fighting and making the place foul with their noise.

The air stank of human and animal waste, the reek of cooking fires. Drystan gagged at the stench, though his guards didn't seem to notice it. His spirits rose a little as he studied their squat, well-nourished frames, and the double-headed axes strapped to their broad backs.

These are the men I need, he thought, *give me a thousand Saxon warriors, and I shall yet drive Artorius and Marcus into the sea.*

At last, after tramping through a maze of streets, they reached a broad central plaza. The ground was paved over here, and the middle of the plaza was occupied by a large timber hall, almost as large as King Marcus' hall at Caer Y Brenin. The hall was built on stone foundations, probably scavenged from Roman buildings. Smoke rose from the hole in the thatched roof, and a troop of gesiths in polished ring-mail stood guard by the double doors.

The officer in charge of Drystan's escort lumbered forward and exchanged words with the gesiths. Two of them advanced on Drystan and seized the reins of his horse.

"If any of you savages lay a finger on my wife," he said, though he knew they couldn't understand a word, "I'll draw out your entrails on a stick and burn them before your eyes."

The Saxons evidently knew a threat when they heard one, even in a foreign tongue, and laughed. One led the horse away, while the other held Esyllt, still fast asleep, steady in the saddle.

Light-headed with hunger and fatigue, Drystan waited patiently as the doors were pushed inwards. They opened onto a vast single chamber, illuminated by an enormous fire inside a central hearth made of square-cut blocks of white stone. A double row of pillars supported the roof. The pillars formed a long avenue, at the end of which was a raised platform.

The platform was occupied by a massive wooden chair, large enough to accommodate two men. A figure in a red cloak was seated on it. The leaping flames of the fire reflected off the band of gold that adorned his brow.

One of the gesiths gave Drystan a hard shove in the small of his back. He lurched forward into the hall.

More bearded axemen in shining mail and boar-crest helmets lined the spaces between the pillars. They were all huge, clearly the pick of Cerdic's warriors, and every one looked capable of snapping Drystan's neck between finger and thumb.

He walked slowly down the avenue towards the platform, past the hearth, marvelling at the complex patterns and symbols carved into the pillars. They displayed scenes of boar and wolf-hunts and bloody battles, heathen gods with gaping mouths and twisted ram's horns sprouting from their heads, longboats cresting the waves of storm-tossed seas, worm-like dragons belching fire, mighty kings and princes sat in gold-roofed halls. Crude imagery, perhaps, but full of life and energy. The skill of the craftsmen was undeniable. Drystan, who had always thought of the Saxons and their kin as savage barbarians, with no knowledge or appreciation of art, was impressed.

His eye was drawn to the figure on the wooden throne. This could only be Cerdic - Cerdic the halfbreed, last of the sons of Hengist, Bretwalda of Saxon-held Britannia.

The Bretwalda was a large, fleshy man in his forties with thinning red hair and a neatly trimmed red beard. He sat at ease in his oversized chair, secure in his power, big hands resting in his lap. Little blue eyes, full of cold cunning, gazed down at Drystan from a flat, smooth-skinned face. Thick gold rings flashed on his fingers. A gold amulet, forged in the shape of a horned god, decorated his muscled throat.

His chair was draped with a wolfskin. Two banner poles were set up behind his chair, crowned with a pair of wolf-skulls. Scented smoke rose from smouldering braziers either side of the platform.

Another man in a shabby black robe stood beside the throne. He looked like some kind of priest, bent with age, his wispy beard long since faded to grey. The priest's sunken eyes regarded Drystan with thinly veiled malice.

The gesith to Drystan's left bowed, placed his hand against his mailed chest, and grunted a flow of Saxon. Cerdic appeared to listen intently, though his eyes never broke from their intense study of his guest.

Drystan received his second shock of the day when Cerdic cleared his throat and began to speak in perfect British.

"So this," said the Bretwalda, "is Drystan of Kernow, of whom we have heard so much."

Unlike Eadric, there was no guttural accent to his voice, which was soft and insinuating, with the hint of a lisp. Drystan remembered that Cerdic was half-British, the son of a native slave-woman. Perhaps he had learned the language from his mother.

"He doesn't look much," added Cerdic, resting his chin on his fist, "can this stringy boy really be the same Drystan who struck down Morholt the Reaver, stole a princess from under her father's nose, and ravaged Kernow with fire and sword? The same Drystan who slew Gwalchmei? Broke the Companions? Sent Artorius himself fleeing for his life?"

Drystan was shaken by how much Cerdic knew of his exploits. The Bretwalda was said to have spies and double agents all over Britannia, even in the far west. Here was the proof.

"I must give you the same answer I gave your sentry on the gate, lord king," said Drystan, mustering the shreds of his pride and dignity. "I am a boy only in appearance. Give me my sword, and I will prove as much on the body of any champion you care to name."

Cerdic smiled indulgently. "Hark to the wolf-pup," he said, "snapping at the old wolf."

There was a ripple of laughter from his warriors. "Brave little pup," he added, "but pups should know their place."

Drystan went down on one knee before the dais. "Your pardon, lord king," he said humbly. "I meant no offence."

The Bretwalda's face was impassive. "I have watched the recent wars in the west with great interest," he said, "you Britons seem intent on destroying each other, which saves me a deal of trouble. I understand you have brought Princess Esyllt with you."

"Yes, lord king," replied Drystan, "she is my wife now. Where she goes, I go."

"Indeed. Why you have you come to Londinium, Drystan of Kernow? Merely to seek refuge, or to beg a favour?"

Drystan worked up his courage. "I came to ask your assistance, lord king. My allies have failed me, but you are forged of different metal. Together we can defeat Artorius. I have seen your warriors. There is nothing to match them in Britannia. Not even the Companions."

Cerdic leaned back and rested his hands on the arms of his chair. After a long pause he beckoned the priest to his side. They spoke quietly in their own tongue, their heads close together. Then the priest hobbled down the steps of the dais and made his way along the avenue of pillars towards the entrance. He shot Drystan an evil look that made the young man's blood run cold.

"I am grateful to you, Drystan," said Cerdic when the priest had vanished through the double doors, "it might have taken me years to achieve what you have in a few short months. Thanks to you, Artorius has suffered many wounds. Llwch Llemineawg is dead. Gwalchmei is dead. Cei has deserted him."

Drystan was unaware of Cei's desertion. He smiled to himself. It seemed Golwg had fulfilled her last instruction, and sown chaos among the High King's war-band.

"Artorius is wounded," Cerdic went on, "and the whole world can see him bleed."

Drystan thought he saw his opportunity. "Let us finish him off," he said eagerly. "Muster your axes, dread king. If we marched west, there would be little to stop us. Artorius has stripped his garrisons along the border of the Debated Lands. Most of his men are in Dumnonia. Caerleon itself is defended by a rabble of civilian militia."

Cerdic toyed with the amulet at his neck. "Artorius is wounded, yes," he said, "but a wounded animal is always dangerous. You are less than honest. Despite their recent losses, the Companions are still formidable. Only a fool would underestimate Artorius. I swore never to fight him again until the odds were stacked in my favour. *Heavily* stacked."

Drystan changed tactics. "Then give me your warriors," he urged, "a thousand men, lord king, and a few hundred auxiliaries. I am the only man who has defeated Artorius in the field. I can do it again. I promise."

Cerdic slowly shook his head. "Not good enough, lad. I don't deal in promises."

In the face of the Bretwalda's indifference, Drystan lost his composure. "Your father, whatever else men say about him, was a great warrior. He crossed the sea with just a few spears at his back and carved out a kingdom. What would he say to your cowardice?"

Cerdic let the insult fly past. "I imagine he would call it good policy, and congratulate me for not blundering into the dragon's jaws."

He held up a hand to forestall Drystan's next words. "It has taken my people twelve years to recover from Mount Badon. We lost six thousand warriors that day. Six thousand! An entire generation, massacred in a single day."

"Only now are our numbers replenished, but my gesiths are still young. Raw, and untried. They will gain battle-experience gradually, and according to my plan. I will not throw them away against the Companions."

His face took on an almost kindly look. "Don't be dismayed, young firebrand," he said as Drystan's shoulders sagged, "you are still welcome as a guest in my city. In time, perhaps, we shall come to an understanding."

Cerdic snapped his fingers and barked an order in Saxon. Two of his gesiths stepped forward.

"These men shall take you to your lodgings," he said. "When Princess Esyllt is recovered, you are both free to explore Londinium. I may ask you to dine with me. Soon."

Drystan took that as the signal to leave. Discouraged, he turned and walked away, followed by the heavy tramp of the gesiths.

Outside he was greeted by the sight of twelve axemen. They stood in single file at the western end of the plaza, blocking the entrance to the street.

The old priest was also there. He rubbed his yellow hands together when Drystan appeared, and croaked something at the gesiths. The men in the centre shuffled aside to open a wide gap in their line.

They revealed Esyllt. She lay face-down on the cobbles. Two Saxon women stood either side of her. The women were young and ugly, with lank yellow hair trailing to their waists.

Both were splattered with blood. Their hair was smeared with the stuff, and their faces, and the long blades of the seaxes they held. Blood dripped from the weapons onto Esyllt's back.

More blood seeped onto the cobbles where she lay. While Drystan watched, horror-struck, one of the girls reached down, grasped a handful of Esyllt's hair, and lifted her head.

They had slashed her throat. Blood oozed from the ragged gash in her pale flesh. Her grey eyes stared through Drystan into eternity.

Drystan stumbled towards her. His heart skipped and thudded in his breast. His mouth was dry. His eyes misted with tears.

"Where she goes, you go," said the voice of Cerdic.

Something thumped into Drystan's back. And again. A hot wellspring of pain opened inside him. He looked down, and saw the bloodied iron tips of two spears protruding from his belly.

His legs gave way as he tried to turn. He collapsed onto his side like a felled tree.

The Bretwalda stood in the great doorway of his hall, a naked sword in his hand, flanked by six gesiths. He gazed with mild interest at the youth bleeding to death on the cobbles.

"Did you really think I would destroy Artorius," he said, "only to set you up in his place? You have been useful to me, Drystan of Kernow. But now it is over."

He advanced on his victim, who tried and failed to crawl away. Drystan's strength flowed out of him in a crimson gush. All he could do was twist onto his back, so he might look at Esyllt one last time before he died.

The breath rattled in his throat as he tried to form words. "I...I'm sorry..." he gasped, and reached out to touch her white fingers.

"Too late," said Cerdic, "far too late."

He stood over Drystan, sword raised in both hands. Drystan saw a brief vision of his father, King Marcus, weeping over his body.

The sword slammed into Drystan's heart and put an end to all his dreams.

27.

Caerleon

Artorius made his way home with a full heart and a heavy conscience. Britannia was at peace again, but the personal cost outweighed any joy.

The High King was a different man. His defeat in Kernow, and the loss of so many old friends, hardened him. The years of peace, he realised, had been an illusion. After Mount Badon he had allowed himself to believe his enemies were defeated. In reality they were merely pushed back into the shadows.

He would not delude himself any longer. Peace was fragile and temporary, a brief calm before the next storm. It was in the nature of man to fight, to betray his brother, to destroy anything good that he built. There was a seed of destruction in his nature. Artorius could only hold back the shadows for a little while, in the hope that one day, long after he was dust, mankind would learn to tame its own worst instincts.

To maintain peace, for as long as possible, required sacrifice. Artorius' first sacrifice was himself. His belief in justice and fairness, the nobler instincts Ambrosius had instilled in him.

He had tried to follow those instincts, and rule by law. The effort failed. Another delusion. His true power had always rested on brute strength, the fearsome reputation of his Companions. For all he pretended to despise tyrants like Vortigern, Artorius was no better. He was a hypocrite, clinging to half-understood notions of Roman law and Roman government. Llwch Llemineawg taught him that lesson. He would never forget it.

There would be no more comfortable lies. From now on Artorius meant to rule by the sword. The next rebellion would meet with savage reprisal, and the next, until he was finally overcome in his turn.

He had already begun. At Isca Dumnoniorum, King Erbin tried to surrender rather than fight. He came at dawn on the second day of the siege, just as Artorius had demanded. By rights he should have been allowed to depart in peace.

Erbin got his peace, of a sort. Artorius cast aside the terms of surrender and had the King of Dumnonia beheaded. Erbin begged and wept and pissed himself as Gareth and two other Companions forced him to his knees. Artorius watched as they hacked off his head. It was a messy business. Seven chops were required before his head finally came off.

The barbaric ploy worked. Erbin's subordinates opened the gates and begged for mercy. They would have done better to fight. Artorius had every one killed in turn, and their heads stuck on spears.

He also punished the common soldiers, who were ordered to form up in ranks on the plain before the main gate. There he revived the ancient Roman practice of decimation. Every tenth man was dragged out of line to be clubbed and beaten to death by their comrades. Artorius spared the civilians, who had played no active part in Erbin's rebellion.

Even Bedwyr was surprised by his master's ferocity. The dead men were left to rot on the field, food for wolves and eagles, and a stark warning to future rebels.

"Let the stench remind them," said Artorius as he turned away from the slaughter, "the stench, and the sorrow, and the bloody bones. We shall have peace on these terms."

It was a long and gloomy ride back to Caerleon. The spring sunshine, and the bursting into leaf of the countryside all around him, failed to warm his soul. Even the cheers of the people, as he rode through the gates of his city, were a hollow and meaningless noise.

They would have cheered Drystan, he thought, *if he had ridden through these gates with my head dangling from his saddle. They cheer any strong leader. Anyone who makes them feel safe.*

His mood lifted a little when he met his sons. They waited to greet him at the steps of the palace, along with the rest of the court. Artorius climbed wearily off his horse to embrace them. Llacheu, he was glad to see, had matured since he last saw him. Cydfan, for his part, had grown even plumper, though there was hard muscle under the deceptive layers of smooth fat. He was growing into a formidable churchman, as hard and ruthless as any temporal warlord.

Gwenhwyfar was there also, no longer the raw girl Artorius had fetched out of Powys but a tall, severe, almost imperial figure, cold and inscrutable, magnificent in her self-imposed isolation. She offered Artorius her thin hand, flashing with silver rings, and a chilly smile.

"My lord," she said in a voice bereft of emotion. "Welcome home."

Artorius spent much time alone in the following days, and left the business of disbanding the army to Bedwyr. He resorted to the bath-house, attended by a few slaves, where the waters soothed the pain of his ageing body.

He knew it was wrong to shut himself away. The people expected to see their king when he returned from a victorious campaign, and the gulf between Artorius and his wife had grown ever wider in his absence. She was a stranger to him now, as distant and unreachable as the fabled mountains of Annwn.

If Artorius stayed hidden inside the depths of his palace for too long, rumours would begin to swirl through the streets and alleys of Caerleon. The High King was ill, they would say. He had suffered a terrible wound in the recent wars, and unlikely to recover. A Saxon agent had poisoned him at meat, or stuck a knife into his flesh.

Rumour would pile on rumour, fear on fear. Artorius could only put a stop to the dangerous cycle by showing his face in public.

Cei would say as much, he thought as he floated gently in his steam-bath, staring at the ceiling, *Cei would not allow me to linger like this. I would never heard the end of his sour, needling voice.*

Artorius sighed with pleasure as the almost unbearably hot water melted away the stress in his muscles. Sometimes he had thought Cei was the true High King, the power behind his throne, constantly chafing and protesting and challenging his master's decisions.

When he had recovered his strength, Artorius's first act would be to send men in search of his steward. Cei was last seen riding north-west with his young concubine.

Artorius had a good idea of where they had gone. In the Kingdom of Gwynedd, near the southern end of the lake known as Llyn Tegid, was a small hill-fort. Unoccupied since the early days of Vortigern's reign, Artorius had gifted the place to Cei, who previously held no lands in his own right.

The fort was called Caer Gai. Cei had never been there, since his duties kept him at court all year round. He did, however, send a party of slaves and workmen to restore the fort and make it habitable again.

"For my retirement," he used to jest, "where I intend to drink myself blind in the other eye."

Artorius was convinced he had taken Golwg to Caer Gai. None of the sub-kings or chieftains of Britannia were likely to offer them refuge. Cei had few friends, and those few were all at Caerleon.

At last, after a week of virtual seclusion, Bedwyr came to Artorius' private quarters. He found the High King sitting alone in his garden in the central courtyard, where Roman governors and tribunes had once sat at leisure with their families.

"It won't do," said Bedwyr, when the slave had announced him, "you must show yourself in public again. There are all kinds of rumours in the town. Two days ago some decayed old soothsayer got up in the fish-market and declared you would die on Friday morning. I had him whipped out of the gates, but there were plenty who listened to him."

Artorius smiled bleakly. "It is now Friday afternoon," he said, "and I feel tolerably well. Perhaps he miscalculated by a few hours."

"This is no jest, Artorius," replied Bedwyr. "A few more days of this, and there will be outright disorder. Our civilian militia outnumber the Companions. If it came to the worst, I don't know whose side they would choose. We can hardly expect them to fight against their own kin."

A ghostly knife stabbed at Artorius' heart. It had been Gwalchmei's task to drill the militia. For a split second the broad, handsome face of his oldest friend flickered before his eyes.

"Gwalchmei," he whispered. Gwalchmei, who had rarely taken anything seriously in his life save drink and women. Gwalchmei, who had cheerfully sacrificed himself so Artorius could live. He, along with scores of brave

Companions, lay dead on a blasted hillside in Kernow, their bones picked clean by carrion-eaters. When the land was settled, Artorius would send men to recover their remains and bring them back to Caerleon for honourable burial.

The weight of guilt was almost too much to bear. Artorius reached out to grasp Bedwyr's remaining hand.

"My burden is very heavy now, Bedwyr," he murmured, "if I go back into the world, it will grow heavier until I am utterly crushed."

Bedwyr returned the pressure on his hand. "Let me share it, lord king."

Artorius drew on the one-handed warrior's strength. Bedwyr, at least, would never play him false.

In the end, overwhelmed by the sense of duty that had driven him for so many years, Artorius resumed his kingship. He staged a grand feast in the Round Hall at Caerleon. The doors were thrown open for everyone, from the highest citizen to the lowest beggar, to eat and drink their fill. Any man, Artorius decreed, was permitted to carry away as much roast meat as he could impale on the end of his dagger.

One glorious evening on the edge of summer, knife went into meat and drink into horn, and there was a thronging in the High King's hall. Gareth, one of the youngest and most promising of the Companions, served in Cei's stead as gatekeeper.

"Welcome," he cried as the guests flowed through the doors, "here you shall find food for your dogs and corn for your horses, and hot peppered chops for yourselves, and wine and mead and ale brimming over, and songs to entertain you."

Artorius sat in his old place at the Round Table, in the midst of all the light and music and merriment. He forced himself to laugh, drink the health of his guests, make customary gifts of gold and silver rings to those bards that pleased him best.

After a time Gareth came to him from the gate. "There is a man outside who wishes to speak with you, lord king," he whispered into Artorius' ear, "he refuses to give up his weapons."

Artorius frowned. It was a rule that none could enter the Round Hall armed, save the High King and his senior officers.

"Did you recognise him?" he asked.

"No, lord king," replied Gareth, "the stranger gave no name, and speaks our tongue with a strange accent."

"Let him in," said Artorius, "under guard."

Gareth bowed and hurried away. Moments later he returned at the head of six Companions.

The music and chatter inside the Round Hall died away. In the midst of the Companions was a man none recognised, tall and sinewy and with a thin, somewhat cruel face, striking rather than handsome, burned brown by distant suns. His long black hair, oiled and combed, shone in the firelight. He wore a gold-hilted sword in a dark red leather sheath at his thigh, a long coat of glistening iron scales, and a round shield with an ivory rim strapped to his back.

This man stepped confidently into the hall, one hand resting on the pommel of his sword, the other placed flat against his armoured breast. His long fingers tap-tapped against the scales as his eyes, dark and glittering, fastened on Artorius.

"Welcome, chieftain," said the High King, impressed by the newcomer's appearance, "you have a noble look about you. Tell us your name, so all may drink your health."

"My thanks," the other man answered in a clear, ringing voice that echoed through the hall. "I am Prince Medraut, third and last son of Artorius and Ganhumara."

He smiled coldly at the High King's stricken expression.

"Hello, father."

***

AUTHOR'S NOTE

The character of Sir Tristan (or Drystan as I call him) occupies a strange place in Arthurian lore. The oldest Cornish and Breton stories of Tristan are lost, though there are echoes of them in the later Anglo-Norman romances. The original tales may have been entirely separate from the Arthurian cycle, but the *Tristan en prose* or Prose Tristan of the thirteenth century, one of the most popular romances of its time, made him into one of King Arthur's most distinguished knights and a member of the Round Table.

There may be historical roots to the story. Near the road leading to Fowey in Cornwall, an ancient stone, seven feet high and set in a modern concrete base, can still be seen. On one side of the stone is a worn Latin inscription, which reads:

DRUSTANUS HIC IACIT
CUNUMORI FILIS
(Drustanus lies here, son of Cunomorus)

In 1540 the antiquarian John Leland claimed to have seen a third line on the stone, now missing, that read:

CUM DOMINA OUSILLA
(With the Lady Ousilla)

It has been suggested that the people described on the stone were the historical Tristan and his lover 'Ousilla' or Esyllt (called Iseult or Isolde in the French and German romances), while Cunomorus is said to be King Mark, Tristan's father: 'Cunomorus' translates as 'Hound of the Sea', which in some versions of the legend was Mark's nickname, acquired due to his skill at piracy. Cunomorus is also the Latinised version of the British/Welsh name Cynfawr, identified by the ninth-century chronicler Nennius as the real name of King Mark.

As usual with Arthurian scholarship, little is certain. Arguments continue to rage over the veracity of the inscription on the stone, and the historical existence (or not) of Tristan, his doomed lover and his treacherous father. I chose to try and incorporate some of the oldest known aspects of Tristan's story into my tale, and present him as an ambitious Dark Age princeling, greedy for power and fame. His mate Esyllt is no different, and rather more intelligent.

My version of the story of Drystan and Esyllt is now ended, but Artorius marches on, painfully aware of the darkness closing around him. How much further he will march remains to be seen...

CPSIA information can be obtained
at www.ICGtesting.com
Printed in the USA
LVOW04s2102280916

506577LV00022B/897/P